Praise for **HILLBILLY HUSTLE**

"Wesley Browne writes like the smart-talking, card-shuffling, bullet-dodging, bourbon-soaked love child of Ron Rash, Elmore Leonard, and the Coen brothers. He's clever as hell, a swift plotter with a heart-bruised sense of character and a brilliant ear for dialogue. I loved *Hillbilly Hustle*, and I'd gamble you will too."

—Benjamin Percy, author of *Suicide Woods*

"Hilarious, exhilarating, utterly gripping. I loved every minute of this book. *Hillbilly Hustle* is required reading."

—Kayla Rae Whitaker, author of *The Animators*

"This tour de force deftly walks the tightrope of being both a page-turner and a language-driven debut that firmly establishes a solid new voice. Cinematic, lyrical, and often very funny, *Hillbilly Hustle* is ripe with memorable characters and a vivid sense of place that sheds light on a whole new kind of Appalachia that's never been seen before."

—Silas House, author of *Southernmost*

"A narrative rolled as expertly as Willie Nelson's nightcap. It takes shape between breakneck page turns and well-timed punch lines."

—David Joy, author of *The Line That Held Us*

"Witty, savvy storytelling at the crossroads of pizza, pot, and noir. *Hillbilly Hustle* is the impish spawn of that lost camping trip *Rounders*, *Pineapple Express*, and *Breaking Bad* took to the Kentucky outback last summer. Step aside, Avon Barksdale and Tony Montana. Burl Spoon is my new favorite drug lord. With *Hillbilly Hustle*, Wes Browne dishes up a smart, tasty debut delivered in an assured voice, one that is sure to create a buzz among readers who like their comedy dry and the pace of their tales brisk."

—Robert Gipe, author of *Trampoline*

Hillbilly Hustle

A novel

WESLEY BROWNE

WEST VIRGINIA UNIVERSITY PRESS

MORGANTOWN

Copyright © 2020 by Wesley Browne
All rights reserved
First edition published 2020 by West Virginia University Press
Printed in the United States of America

ISBN
Paper 978-1-949199-28-4
Ebook 978-1-949199-29-1

Library of Congress Cataloging-in-Publication Data
Names: Browne, Wesley, 1974– author.
Title: Hillbilly hustle / Wesley Browne.
Description: First edition. | Morgantown : West Virginia University Press, 2020.
    | The first chapter appeared in different form in The Pikeville Review.
Identifiers: LCCN 2019038435 | ISBN 9781949199284 (paperback) | ISBN
    9781949199291 (pdf) | ISBN 9781949199291 (epub)
Subjects: LCSH: Kentucky—Fiction | GSAFD: Suspense fiction.
Classification: LCC PS3602.R7373 H55 2020 | DDC 813/.6—dc23
LC record available at https://lccn.loc.gov/2019038435

Book and cover design by Than Saffel / WVU Press
The first chapter appeared in different form in *The Pikeville Review*.

For Valetta, Barrett, and Grady

*K*NOX THOMPSON first crossed paths with the man who would ruin him at a poker game above the arcade in downtown McKee, a forsaken place he had made it a point to avoid. After finding out about the game from one of his Porthos regulars, Knox couldn't resist. It was said to be frequented by a herd of donkeys spilling money, and that proved to be true, but making money and keeping it aren't the same thing. Especially not in Jackson County.

He knew better than to go to that sketchy-ass game, but by mid-2011 the poker boom of the aughts had cooled, online poker was illegal in the United States, and most of the good live games had dried up. At the apex, he had his choice of games in Richmond and Berea, but when poker waned, so did his options. The worst part about it was the shittiest, most casual players were the first to give it up. They say poker lessons are expensive, and it's true. Knox tried to teach at least two nights a week if he could. He had come to rely on poker winnings to keep his pizza shop and his parents afloat.

The worsening drought made him reckless. It drove him up the narrow stairwell with puckered, peeling paint into the dense smoke of the apartment over the arcade in McKee. He had told Darla,

1

his girlfriend, and himself that if the game wasn't on the level or if things went bad, he'd just bail out.

Making his way up, Knox didn't recognize the country music that played. The steps were shallow and about every third one sagged like it was held up by wet sponges. The apartment at the top was a studio with a table and ten chairs in the middle. Off to the side was a kitchen with appliances as old as he was and a sink full of dirty dishes. A feeble folding table teetered under the weight of two Cherry Master video–slot machines. The poker table, which appeared to be from an old dining-room suite, had green felt over the top and stapled tight to the undersides. It was ringed by men, sitting in mismatched chairs that looked to have come from ten different grannies' kitchens. They wore dull flannel or black t-shirts, jeans, and boots or high-top shoes, and most were stoking cigarette cherries or had tobacco spit cups or bottles alongside. The smoke in the room was thick as white gravy but the smell of damp still pierced through. Only one person was vaping. It hadn't fully grabbed hold in Jackson County just yet.

There was one woman at the table, heavyset, wearing glasses and a faded denim shirt. She appeared to be neither smoking nor dipping. She had a half-full twenty-ounce bottle of electric-blue Mountain Dew Game Fuel and an open bag of Funyuns on the table beside her.

Once Knox cleared the landing, all eyes lighted on him, like a strange car passing down a country road. They had no way of knowing what he was: a guy who had built his game reading and rereading dozens of poker books, and playing countless hands live and online. He had worn his white Adidas slides with white socks—one with a Nike logo and the other without—loose mesh shorts, and a threadbare, powder-blue "Trampled by Turtles" t-shirt. He had one tattoo, a full-sleeve of fighting robots in grayscale. The most he'd done all day to his receding, curly black hair and sloppy beard was run his fingers through them. If he had any tells at all, he made sure his appearance wasn't one of them.

The table went back to the hand playing out. It ended with a bet followed by folds and a burr-headed fat kid with a chinstrap beard and diamond-looking stud earrings raking a small pile of chips and adding them to his stack all while dragging from a stubby fag. He couldn't have been more than twenty-five.

A little fellow with painstakingly combed slick dark hair who sat at the head of the table opposite the stairwell raised his chin and looked over the others. "What can we do for you?"

If Knox were smart, and listened to his better inclinations and laboring lungs, he would've said, "Nothing," and walked right back out. Being obstinate—as was his way—he said, "Sidney Fulks told me there's a hold 'em game I could play here."

"He told you right. Games 2/4 cash and they's a fifty-dollar minimum buy-in. You can buy back for less. Grab you a chair." The man pointed at the two open seats opposite each other about midtable. Behind the little fellow stood a hulking man with his arms crossed. He had pale hair, eyebrows, and mutton chops, and a dip the size of a mouse tucked behind his lip. His veiny, thick arms were tattooed in countless flying bats. Wherever the gym was in McKee, he had put in his time plus someone else's.

Knox read the little guy as the table boss in more ways than one, so he took the open seat three to his left so he could play behind him. The chip stacks on the table ranged from around twenty dollars to somewhere around five hundred. The little guy lorded over one of the tall stacks. Knox's rule of thumb was always to buy in for fifty times the big blind, so he peeled off two hundred in loose twenties, laid them on the table to get changed for chips, and was off.

The deal made its way around the table, each player dealing in turn. If Knox had caught any kind of hand he would've played it, but was content to fold his two hole cards and watch the action for a couple table rotations. He quickly found out the game's reputation was accurate, and his instincts were, too. The play was loose as hell and the little guy bullied and stole every stray pot nobody seemed too attached to. One time the chubby boy with the chinstrap bowed up in a small pot in which Knox strongly suspected he had a real hand, and the little fellow must have suspected it too, because after a long deliberation, he laid down what Knox felt certain was a pair of rags.

Like every new poker game Knox had ever played, he eventually got asked who he was and where he'd come from. He was an interloper amongst a lot of regulars, that was clear. He told them he owned Porthos Pizza, which led one player at the table to recollect going there while he was on a bender in Richmond.

The first pot Knox raised to twelve dollars preflop someone piped up. "What do you know. The carpetbagger's playing him a hand. Look out." He was right. Knox had been dealt jacks, which he always hated to play because they got vulnerable quick, but it was still a good hand. He wasn't the only one at the table who was judicious in his hand selection, but there were damn few. Several of the players would at least call the big blind to get a look at the initial flop if given the chance, which suited Knox. Pot sweetener in a cash game was hardly ever a bad thing.

With jacks, so long as no ace, king, or queen came on the flop, and no flush or straight seemed likely, Knox was in good shape if he didn't have too many callers. Jacks were a hand he generally preferred to play without much competition. At twelve bucks he got three calls, including one from the little fellow, which was two more than he wanted. The flop rolled off 10, 8, 9 of different suits, good for Knox's hand. No over-cards and he picked up an open-ended straight draw. A flush hitting wasn't too likely for anyone. If nobody sat on pocket 8s, 9s, or 10s, or jack/queen, Knox was healthy. Still, he decided to push a nice size continuation bet and end the thing right there. The little guy acted first. He checked, followed by the next two. Knox counted the pot at thirty-eight dollars, so he bet thirty-five and got ready to rake it all back in.

The little fellow drew from his smoke. Then he pointed at Knox with it scissored between his fingers. "That's an awful big bet. You hit this flop? Cause I sure as hell did." Knox looked at him and smiled. He'd been to card games where he ran his mouth. In fact, he did at most, but this wasn't one to do it. Even Knox knew that.

The little guy used a small swirly slice of agate as a card protector. He slid it off, bent back his hole cards for a peek, and put it back. He spun a single chip on the felt a couple times before he stacked a full hundred in chips in front of him and pushed them to the center. After it was already out there, he said, "I raise." His check-raise was a perfectly legitimate, perfectly nasty play.

The other two players folded before he'd got the words out. Knox went back over what he thought he might have, and there was a lot that scared him. Sometimes, though, he got a tickle that said, "He ain't got it." Knox's Spidey card-sense tingled like crazy. The little guy's raise and talk seemed tailored to push him out. He called it.

When the dealer peeled the next card, the turn card, off the deck, Knox watched it right until the last. Then he sneaked a look at the little guy, who watched the card hit the table and stared it down. He didn't look at his chips, and he didn't look at Knox, just the cards in the middle. Usually, if a card was real good for a player, they didn't look at it long. They didn't want to seem too interested. It was a red seven. The second heart on the board. Knox had made a straight. The little fellow eventually glanced at his own two cards like he forgot they were there before taking Knox in again. With one more card to go, Knox was pretty sure the guy didn't have much. That was until he said, "I'm all in." The instant he said it, everything Knox was so sure of ran off with its tail tucked.

The only hand the little guy could hold that beat Knox's now was queen/jack. It was possible he could work his way to a heart flush, a full house, or even four of a kind on the last card—the river card—but at that moment, queen/jack was the only hand that bested Knox. Knox's Spidey senses now started pinging with doubt, but whenever anything like that happened, when his thoughts scattered and he lost his nerve, he went to his safe place: the math. He had learned the formulas in his poker books. He didn't have to make a hard decision, just do the math. Knox wasn't even all that good at math, but he didn't have to be perfect, just close.

While everyone watched, he peered at the chips in the middle and pointed at them as he counted. Then he counted what was left of his stack. He had only eighty-four more dollars in chips. He realized he should've pushed it all in earlier rather than just call the previous raise, but he hadn't done it. Now there was three hundred and twenty-two dollars in the pot and Knox only had to call eighty-four to win it. It was possible he was throwing good money after bad, or the little guy had flubbed it and forced him to call a bluff, but either way the math dictated Knox try to quadruple his money.

Even as he pushed in his chips and said, "The math says I call," Knox wondered if he should bother buying back in if he lost, or just go home and lick his wounds from the beating and stay the hell out of McKee in the future.

The little fellow drew his eyes tight and said, "Turn 'em up then," as he flipped his cards, showing 7/10 offsuit. He had two pair. His only hope of winning was to make a full boat on the final card, the river card. He could tie Knox's hand and chop the pot if another jack fell, but that was it. He only had four cards to win and two cards to tie. Statistically unlikely, but by no means uncommon. Knox had been fucked that way enough times to wince at the prospect.

Knox exhaled as he turned his jacks. The little fellow shrugged, looked at the dealer, and said, "Burn and turn, Rockhead. Maybe I'll catch me one." The man had been reckless, but showed no sign of regret. The dealer tossed a card into the muck in the middle. Then he turned a hapless 6 of diamonds onto the pilled green felt. "Well, shit," the little dandy said. "I made my straight." And he had, though lower than Knox's. He directed a single nod Knox's way. "Good call."

There's equity in sitting on a big stack won honest that can't be had by buying in high. Earned money is stronger money. Knox had run his initial two hundred to well over four hundred and that was worth something. Stack-size alone could win certain hands from certain players. Short stacks were liable to push in at any time, but most medium stacks didn't much want to tangle with a big stack if they could avoid it, unless of course they had a real solid hand to double on.

The big stack at the table had grown to a shade over five hundred. After that, there was Knox. The slick little guy had rallied back up to over three bills playing his same hell-bent style. He seemed to cow most everyone at the table, and more than just in cards. The paste sculpture behind him, who they called "Greek," behaved like a dog on a leash. The few instances when someone took a pot from the little guy, they wouldn't look at him. Like they were apologetic, but nothing was ever said out loud. The other players called him "Burl."

The table stayed juicy and loose. Knox's stack climbed mostly slow, and on the way up hit a couple snags. The lady whipped him with a full house after he had flopped trips, but she didn't have a real deep stack. He also traded chips with Burl here and again, but still, Knox climbed. He never got too deep if he didn't have a made hand, because Burl almost always showed down. Burl seemed fixated on getting his chips back from Knox specifically. That was the way of a lot of players. They held little grudges.

Once Knox had earned back his lost chips and then some, Burl scrutinized his near five-hundred-dollar stack. "I'd like to break into Fort Knox over there. That's what I'd like to do." Burl smiled then, but not friendly. "Boys, what do you all think of a man comes to a game the first time and makes hisself a bad guest?" Everyone else looked Knox's way and grunted softly.

Knox measured his words. In most other instances he would have told Burl what to fuck and where he could do it, but he knew better than to say it there. "I've caught some cards tonight, that's for sure."

"That you have." Two fresh cards went out and Burl took a look, measured out a preflop raise, and the subject dropped.

The game ground on until the small hours of the morning. A couple players busted and slunk on down the stairs. Knox yawned again and again, and the yawns grew larger and larger until other people at the table couldn't help but take notice.

The chinstrap kid said, "You might oughta hurry up, Burl. Fort Knox looks like it's fixing to close."

"That so?"

Knox tapped the screen on his phone, which was on the felt, and checked the clock. Then he looked at his stack. He'd made his way over eight hundred and was the big stack by a third. "I probably ought to head to the house before too much longer."

"Hell, I ain't even broke in yet. Surely to god you ain't gonna leave with all my money and not give me no chance to get it back."

Knox pointed at Burl's chips, which were substantial. "You've had a fair night yourself, chief."

"Sure," he said, "but some chips is more special than others."

Knox picked up two of his own, flipped them between fingers one over the other. He looked up like he'd just thought of something. "Who is this we're listening to, anyway?"

Burl tilted his head a touch to one side. "You like that? That's Wayne Hancock. Still plays it like it was meant to be played."

"Is this an album?"

"This one playing's *Thunderstorms and Neon Signs*. It's a goodun'."

"How many songs left?"

"Five or six."

"I'll stay till it's over. After that I got to go."

Burl checked some fresh hole cards. Then he tossed chips in underhand. "Come on in this water then. It's real nice."

Knox wasn't too eager to put his chips in harm's way. He tried the best he could to fold his way out the door, but didn't have much choice but to play when he caught ace/2 of diamonds in the big blind when nobody had raised and the small blind folded. The big blind was a forced minimum bet, so folding without a raise didn't make any sense. Burl and the lady in the denim shirt had called, so there were only three limping into the hand, a rarity at that table. When Knox tapped the felt, signaling his check, Burl said, "Fort Knox ain't closed just yet."

The flop came: king, ace, deuce—the king and deuce both spades. If Knox was beat at that point, both of the other two would have had to be slow-playing a big hand. The only way to find out was to throw in a little bet. There was fourteen in the pot, so he matched it. The woman said, "Well, I missed," and tossed her cards in disconcertedly.

Burl let his eyeballs run all over Knox while riffling his chips. "You make you a hand or you chasing that flush?"

Knox met his gaze. "One way to find out."

"Reckon." Burl flipped fourteen into the center as if he were sowing grass seed.

Neither watched the turn card come off. Their sights stayed on each other. The turn brought a queen of clubs. Burl glanced at it for no more than a wink. Then he scratched his nose, examined his fingers, and scratched it some more. "What do you think about that purty girl?"

There was plenty that could beat Knox's aces and deuces. All strong hands. Aces, kings, queens, ace/king, ace/queen. If Burl was sitting on two spades, he could still hit his flush on the river, too. Knox ran back the night trying to recall if Burl had slow-played any big hands. He couldn't remember one time.

Knox wanted to lead out with another bet and see if Burl would go away, but feared Burl might go up over-the-top. If he did, Knox would have to think about dumping the hand, which pained him.

9

There were forty-two dollars in the pot, but since pot-sized bets seemed to beckon Burl to call, Knox dialed down to thirty, thinking that might spook him if he thought Knox was betting for value.

Burl ground his jaw like he was working a piece of gum, though he wasn't. He didn't say one word, didn't do anything, just looked at the chips in the middle and caressed that agate cross section he used to protect his cards. He said, "I call," then sat there a bit longer before extracting his chips and flipping them into the middle.

The river card was on the felt right on the heels of Burl's chips going in. Almost as if the card had silenced it, the country album timing Knox's play ended. Nobody stirred, nobody made a sound. For the first time, the drips from the kitchen faucet that had been pelting the dirty dishes in the sink all night were audible. The card was the ace of spades. A card worthy of such quiet. A card that made Motörhead play in Knox's mind, and made him study the other haggard faces at the table and wonder if any of them heard the same tune. It was a card that brought answers, but not all Knox needed. Not nearly.

He had a full house. Aces full of twos. Burl couldn't have two aces in the hole because Knox held one, so quad aces were out. Burl could have been playing for a flush and made it, but Knox had that beat. Knox also knew that the ace of spades hitting made the flush play less likely, as fewer players chased any but the ace high "nut flush," but with the hands Burl played, there was no telling. There were two hands Knox feared: ace/king and ace/queen. As wily as he already reckoned Burl to be, he could conceive of him doing that. If he had, Knox was beat by a bigger full house.

The simple fact was, Knox didn't know what Burl had. He'd bet into Burl twice already and figured out nothing. Knox decided to try another tack. He reached out slowly and tickled the felt with his middle finger, signaling a check, secretly hoping Burl would do the same behind. They'd show it down and, win or lose, Knox would get out with a decent profit on the night.

10

Burl started talking. "You make your flush there, Fort Knox? Is that what you done?"

Knox shrugged.

"You slow-play aces? You do that? You wouldn't do that to me would you, hippie-pizza-man? Just when we was getting to be friends."

Knox shrugged again.

"Kings? Queens? You make you a big healthy hand?" Burl nodded. "I know you ain't got two queens cause that's what I got. I got queens full. You done let me lay around too long." He took a peek at his cards, whistled, and smiled. "Ain't they purty. You wanna see 'em?"

Burl slid his cards out and peeled at the corner like he was going to show, shook his head, and brought them back. He leaned back in his chair, took a cigarette from a pack of Marlboro Reds he had sitting on the table, flicked a matte-black Zippo from his front pocket that flamed just as quickly as he opened it, drew hard on the cowboy killer, and blew out the smoke swift and long. "I'm all in."

Knox pushed his lower lip into his upper, and his upper into his nose so his mustache hairs tickled his nostrils. "That's a bold move."

"No it ain't. It ain't bold at all when you got what I got."

Here's where Knox went into circuital psychology. In poker, strong is weak. Everybody knows that. Because everyone knows, there are people who act strong who are strong, thus giving reverse-reverse signals. But if Burl knew this, and he knew Knox knew, he could have been doing reverse-reverse-reverse psychology. So Knox was in limbo. He was pretty sure Burl didn't have the queens he said, but then again he might. Knox had seen it done. In that particular hand, Burl would be better off with only one queen and an ace. In a matchup of full houses, the higher top three cards determine the winner. Knox had aces full of twos: three aces and two twos. If Burl really did have two queens in the hole, he had queens full of aces, and it lost. That hand may have looked prettier, seemed bigger, but it was a loser.

To buy a little time, Knox asked a relevant question. "How much you got left in your stack?"

Without the slightest pause Burl said, "Four hundred thirty-five," puffing on his cigarette without touching it. Pasteurized milk–skinned Greek was peering in, trying to get a look at what all was out on the table, the whole time never uncrossing his bowling-pin forearms.

If Burl won the hand, Knox's big night was lost. He'd give back all he made and then some. It was supposed to be his last hand. He didn't have the best possible cards. He didn't have the nuts. He also didn't have a feel for whether Burl had him beat or not, but Burl gave off like he thought he did. The question that struck Knox was, if Burl wanted to take a chunk, why push him out of the hand? Burl had played the hand slow, and now at the end he was shoving it all in. Was that to extract the maximum, or to get what he could without showing down the hand? Knox wished for the answer, but didn't have it. Lacking the answer, and without too terribly much in the pot, the smart move was to fold and take home the hefty winnings he would have left. He needed that money. His parents needed it. Math didn't compel Knox to stay in the hand. He was lost in it, so he should've just gotten out. That was smart the thing to do.

The faucet continued to *drip drip drip*. Knox said, "I call."

$\mathcal{B}$URL TRIED to get Knox to turn his cards first, but being as he'd called him, Knox balked. "Hold on now, chief. I called your bet."

The pale-headed muscle truck behind Burl took half a step, but Burl signaled him to stop.

Knox waved his hand. "You know what, never mind. It makes no difference. I'll show."

"Now, no. You want to see my cards you can see my cards."

"Same time, then."

Burl turned over a pair of kings, but was more intent on what Knox was rolling over. Once Knox had showed, the boy with the chinstrap huffed out, "You got him, Burl."

Burl studied what was before him. "No, I ain't."

Disbelieving, Chinstrap said, "He's got aces and twos, you got aces and kings."

Knox was mum.

Burl stood up and pointed his open hand at the cards on the table. "Yeah, and he's got more aces'n me, you dumb bastard, so quit running your yap, Daniel." Burl glared the boy down. Then he turned his eyes back to the table and stared as if he were standing over his own dead dog. He shook his head and pushed his chips to the middle.

Knox stood halfway and with both hands dragged all Burl's chips, plus what was already in the middle, to him, and started stacking. He had about as many chips as were left between all the rest of the players. It's usually bad form to leave a game right after winning a big hand like that, but having said he was going after the album, Knox didn't hesitate. "I think I'm going to cash out. It's past time."

When Knox looked up, all the faces were solemn. It wasn't until then he started to worry in a way he probably should have much sooner. The echoes of Darla's warnings suddenly got loud. It was well after three in the morning and he was in downtown McKee, surrounded by a bunch of boys he didn't know. Even not knowing them, he absolutely *did* know—due to all logic, reason, and probability—that at least some, if not most, had seen the inside of the jailhouse that stood not a hundred yards across the street, appended to the old courthouse. That was to say nothing of who might lurk outside. This was a regular game. If Knox found out about it in Richmond, surely to god every outlaw in Jackson County knew about it. Jackson County lacked a lot, but one thing it had in abundance was outlaws.

Knox's oxidized blue Volvo was around the corner and down the block from the door at the bottom of the stairwell where he'd come up. When he had parked his heap against the curb just after nine that night, there wasn't another soul about in the darkened streets. Knox wasn't the gun-carrying sort, but just for a moment he wished for one, and if he had asked if anyone at the table had one close at hand to sell, he might've struck a deal.

He flinched and raised his elbow to block the bat-laden arm of Greek as he suddenly came from behind him and reached for Knox's chips. Greek's sinewy arm felt like a dense packed sandbag and was about as big around. His other hand fell on Knox's shoulder and grabbed it so hard Knox slid down in his chair like he was filled with liquid.

Burl said, "If you want to get paid, you best let Greek count your chips. What do you *think*, he's going to jack you right here in front of God and everybody?"

Knox twisted his shoulder away with Greek still squeezing. "Sorry. I just didn't know what he was doing. Kind of startled me."

"If you'll get on out of his way, we'll get you paid out and get you on the road back to Richmond."

Knox scooted his chair a bit to the side as the monolithic man started sorting and stacking chips with his enormous hands. Knox rubbed his right shoulder where it'd been grabbed.

Knox was wary of Greek doing the counting, but what could he do? He watched his every move and never saw him out of line one time, and the final count—one thousand three hundred and twenty-eight dollars—jibed with what Knox thought he had. Greek first laid six hundreds on the table, twenties after he ran out of hundreds, and finished with a five and three ones. It was a fat fucking stack and there wasn't a one in the room who didn't watch it being doled out. What spooked Knox the most was the guys who had already left and the ones still in the room who had their phones in their hands, texting. God only knew what he was walking into outside. He thought of calling the police for an escort, because the game wasn't illegal or anything, but damn if he trusted the law in McKee either. As he stuffed the money in his front pocket he had no idea what he should do next. Under his breath, he said, "Well, here's another nice mess I've gotten me into."

That was when Burl said to the rest of the table, "Deal me out, boys and girl, I'm going to go see our new friend off." He came to Knox and put a hand on his arm. Burl smelled strongly of smoke, cologne, and talcum powder. "You don't want to go out there by your lonesome. You're liable to get robbed before you make it five feet down the sidewalk."

"I appreciate it."

Burl sucked on the stub of his cigarette as he walked Knox toward the stairs with Greek following behind. "I kindly thought you would."

At the base of the stairs, Burl opened the door, letting the night air in. It was still as frozen water in a bucket. There were a few vehicles parked here and there, but nobody was about. A speckly cat sauntered across the street and sat at the lip of a storm drain, watching the men with its incandescent eyes.

Before Knox could get a foot away, Burl flicked his butt down the sidewalk, where it spun and glowed, and took Knox by the back of his tattooed upper arm. "Here's the thing, pizza king. If you ain't packing you probably shouldn't be walking to your car by your lonesome. There's known to be some rough folks about this time of night. You carrying?"

Knox shook his head.

"I didn't reckon. You don't look the type. Now, I can have Greek go with you and see you off safe, but I only offer that service to my business associates."

Greek had the same flat expression he wore all night. "Associates?" Knox said.

"Sure. Was you thinking a man could earn a living in Jackson County on an arcade and a poker game?"

"I hadn't really thought about it, to tell you the truth."

"No, sir, no. They ain't no coal here worth digging, so a Jackson County man's got to be diversified. What you seen here, these are just my hobbies. They ain't my real businesses. Those are a little bit different. One of them's getting your ass safe on back home, and that brings me to the other. You said you got you a pizza shop?"

"Yeah."

"How's it doing?"

"We're doing all right."

Burl closed one eye and scrutinized Knox with the other. "That so?"

"I mean, pretty good."

"I don't know. I'd say you could be doing better. A man's prospering in the pizza business don't come creeping up my stairs to this game all by his lonesome. Naw, I don't think so. It just ain't smart." Burl picked at the corner of his pinky nail and shifted his gaze to the tangerine street lights. "You've cleaned up pretty good here tonight. About as good as I seen in the whole time we been doing this. You may think you cleaned me out, but I'll be just fine. Like I say, it's just a hobby for me. Some of them other boys might be smarting a bit."

Knox glanced at Greek, who was unwavering. He turned back to Burl.

"What I'm getting at is, if you got yourself a pizza shop, and it ain't doing too good—as I suspect it ain't—what you need to do is to get yourself diversified. That's where I can help you."

"How's that?"

"By making you my business associate. You do that, hell, you won twice tonight." Burl shot a weak punch into Knox's bicep. "And—and this is the best part—you get Greek's services seeing you off safe and sound. You bought in for two hundred, am I right?"

"Yeah."

"That means you got at least eleven hundred to spend. I got business opportunities starting at an even thousand. That would get you a full pound of OG Kush. Now, if you aim to get fancy, I can put you in some Sour Diesel at a good price, but that'd put you out twelve-fifty."

"You want me to buy a pound of pot?"

"Sure. Why not?"

"What am I gonna do with a pound of pot?"

"By hell, sell it. You think I was gonna sell it to you for your own personal use?"

"I'm not a fucking drug dealer."

"We ain't talking about drugs, Knox, we're talking about weed. You sell goddamn pizzas. Don't get all high and mighty on me. Weed ain't no worse for a man than pizza. Hell, it's probably healthier."

Knox gazed skyward and curled his lip. What could he say?

"Now, I ain't offering you no pills or no poison like that. But pot. You seem like a man whose seen him some good times, and seen him a good lot of weed. When was the last time you smoked?"

It was the day before. "Hell, I don't know."

"Yeah, I bet you don't. Look, I'd like to get back to my game, so I'm going to need a yes or a no."

"Can I think about it?"

Burl sighed. "Let's go on in, Greek. Knox don't see reason."

"Hold on," Knox said. "Are you asking me to do a drug deal right here on the sidewalk?"

"There ain't nothing to be afraid of." Burl pointed across the way. "You see that."

Knox squinted into the shadows beside the courthouse. Burl held up one finger and twirled it. Right after he did, blue lights on top of a car spun a single rotation.

"Now, don't be thinking they'll be of any help to you should you decline my proposition. They was sound asleep before I rousted them, and they'll go right on back to it."

"So, if I buy a pound, nobody's going to bother me getting out of here, but if I don't . . ."

"If you don't, me and Greek go on up these stairs and you can take your chances. Maybe you'll just go on your merry way. You never know."

"That's not what's going to happen, is it?"

Burl laughed like a car trying to start but missing. "I can't predict the future, but I know how I'd bet it."

Knox put a hand in his right front pocket and grasped the wad he'd stuck in there not five minutes ago. His fingertips rested on the car keys below it. He looked out at the police car in the darkness, and the other cars, and the corner he had to reach before he even made it to the street where he was parked. He had on those slides. Not the best equipment for a footrace, let alone one involving his fat ass. The old Volvo didn't even have working remote door locks. Burl was now chewing his pinkie's cuticle. Greek still looked on as if he didn't care what happened one way or the other.

Knox deflated. "I'll just take the fucking Kush."

Burl took his finger from his mouth. "You see that, Greek? I knowed he was a smart man."

While Knox counted back a thousand to Burl, Greek clicked a key fob and popped the trunk of a white Malibu not thirty feet away. He reached in and came back with two bundles of marijuana wrapped in clear plastic, bound together with copious amounts of silver duct tape.

Once Knox had placed the last bill in Burl's hand, Burl raised one thumb real high. Two heads popped up from a darkened car parked in front of the courthouse. The engine fired, the headlights came on, and it pulled away.

Burl reached in his pocket and produced a white business card. "Burl Spoon," he said. "Thank you for your business."

Knox took it and held it in the orange light. It read "Spoon Convenience, LLC" in black letters at the top. It had a PO box and phone number under that.

"You should know, can't nobody touch me here in Jackson County. Not nobody. Let me know if ever I can do anything else for you." Then Burl turned, opened the apartment door, and went back up the rotting stairs.

*P*ORTHOS PIZZA sat on a dilapidated block a hundred yards north of the Eastern Kentucky University campus. It was embedded in a row of buildings at the bottom of a hill a block and a half off Main Street on the edge of downtown Richmond where the city and the college blended. There was a rundown apartment building with a hardware-store "For Sale" sign hanging from the balcony on one side, a vacant storefront with Sunday comics masking-taped to the windows on the other. There were no gaps between the buildings. If any one of them burned, it most likely would've taken the whole South Second Street block. Knox lived in a one-bedroom apartment over Porthos that could be entered from inside the pizza shop and from down an alley.

When Knox got back from McKee after the poker game packing that first pound of Kush, he left it in his trunk out back. He was scared of it. The most he had ever bought at one time before was an ounce, which was a small fine if he got caught, and even that made him anxious. Anxious like at the pool when he was a kid and had to take off his shirt. Now he had sixteen times that much, which the law assumed was trafficking in Kentucky.

Trafficking carried one to five years in prison. Knox wasn't cut out for prison.

Knox slept into the late afternoon. When he finally woke up and thought about going to get the pot, he pictured Richmond police cars descending as soon as he opened the trunk: drug dogs, SWAT gear, all that shit. He crept down the alley with an empty suitcase to the parking lot behind the shop where his car sat. He opened the trunk and there it was, lying on top of a pizza delivery bag, exactly where he had watched Greek put it during the early morning hours the same calendar day. Somehow, seeing it there reminded him of Christmas morning as a kid. He knew there'd be toys under the tree, but it didn't seem real until he got up and saw. The unmistakable pine/citrus smell reached his nose, and there was no denying it.

Knox got the adrenaline shakes as he set the suitcase in the trunk. He opened it, put the weed in, and zipped it back up. The only people around were a handful of Indian international students in the parking lot across the way playing cricket. They definitely weren't paying attention to what Knox was doing. He swiveled around one last time, and seeing nobody other than the cricket players, he took the suitcase out, closed the trunk, and did his best to seem nonchalant walking away.

The shortest path to his apartment was through Porthos's back door, into the kitchen, across the dining room, and up the interior stairs. The less time he spent outside, the better. He punched 3332 into the keypad and the door unlocked. As soon as he crossed the threshold, the tension loosed.

Rob was in back chopping green peppers on a stainless-steel table as Knox came in hefting the suitcase. He was Knox's right hand. Gabe, a shift leader, was on the line saucing a pizza.

Rob looked up from his work. "You going on a trip?"

"No, long story. Anyone in the dining room?"

"Nope." Rob squinted. "What's wrong with you, man? You're all jittery."

Knox looked past him to the front of the shop. He raised the case. "I have a fucking pound of pot in here."

Rob stopped chopping and set the knife down on the table. "Do what?"

"I have a fucking pound of OG Kush in this suitcase."

Rob tilted his head and his mouth came open and stayed that way.

Knox giggled like it was health class. "Yeah."

"But . . . whose is it?"

"It's mine."

Rob shook his head so fast his lips flapped. "A pound? Of pot? How'd you get a fucking pound of pot?"

"I had to buy it."

"What the hell are you talking about?"

"I had to buy it. I'll explain later, but right now I just want to get it up to my apartment and fucking hide it until I figure out what to do with it."

"You bought a pound of pot and you don't know what to do with it? Why didn't you just buy a pound of enriched uranium?"

Gabe laid the pizza he'd been making on the oven conveyor and came toward the back of the shop. "What're you all whispering about? Why do you have a suitcase?"

"Oh." Knox looked at it like he forgot he was holding it. "It was in my trunk."

"It's full of weed." Rob smirked. "Knox bought a pound of weed."

Knox cut his eyes Rob's way.

Gabe pointed at Rob. "Is he for real?"

Knox huffed before he spoke. "Yeah, but you don't understand. I didn't want this." He shook the case.

Rob come-hithered with both hands. "Bring it my way, then. I'll take it. I mean, if you don't want it."

Knox started for the swinging door between the kitchen and the dining room. "I'm not giving it away. I just have to figure out what to do with it."

"Hey, man," Rob said at his back, "why don't you sell me some then."

Knox only said, "I'll think about it."

Behind him Gabe said, "What the hell's going on?" but Knox didn't break stride. He had gotten the package from his car to the building. The first step was out of the way. The next was telling Darla.

$\mathcal{W}$**HEN SINFUL SKIN** Tattoo Studio opened on Main Street in Richmond in 2008, the city already had something like five tattoo shops, so it didn't make much of a ripple for Knox. Except for a couple longstanding stalwarts, the other places came and went.

Sinful started burning Porthos up for deliveries pretty soon after going into business. The owner complained about the two-dollar delivery fee every time one of the drivers went up there. She finally went off on a server over the phone, so Knox got on the line thinking he could talk her down. That's not really what happened.

She came out of the gate hot as a soldering iron. "It's like a block to my place. You really have to charge me an extra two dollars to bring a small pizza a fucking block? It's not like I don't tip."

"You could always come get it," Knox said. "Like you say, it's only a block."

"No, I couldn't. I'm the only one here. I just opened. I can't be leaving all the time. I'd think if anyone would understand that, you would. I'm trying to support a local place, and I feel like you don't even appreciate it. I could just as easily order from Domino's, but I don't want to do that. This is over two fucking dollars."

"Yeah, the thing is, most of that money goes to my drivers. How am I supposed to decide who has to pay and who doesn't when it's not my money? It's for their gas and their car maintenance."

"For one thing, they shouldn't have to *drive* up here. You want to talk about environmentally irresponsible. It's idiotic, not to mention lazy as fuck. For another thing, I'm a small business owner, too. Why wouldn't you make an exception?"

"I don't know."

"I don't fucking know either."

He had never met the woman. All he knew was her name— Darla—and that she was pissed. Maybe he could smooth it over. Maybe he couldn't. Either way, he decided to take it head on. "I'll tell you what I'm going to do. I'm going to bring this order up there myself, and we can talk about it."

Darla ticked her tongue a few times while he listened. She said, "Make sure to bring me some red pepper flakes? I always ask, but about half the time your drivers forget."

Knox's head was kind of all over the place on his way up to Sinful. Darla was hateful on the phone, but he could kind of see her point. It *was* a really short walk to her place. There was also something about the way she cut loose on him that intrigued him.

Her shop was truly a hole-in-the-wall. A small sign hung over the doorway. It opened into a stairwell that went up to a little space over an IT outfit. From the moment he stepped in off the street, Knox could smell fresh paint.

When he reached the top of the stairs, Darla was on the opposite side of the room behind a half wall near the front window that looked out on Main Street. She was at a table leaned over a sketchpad working away. He couldn't really make her out except that she had auburn hair and was wearing a dress. She had to have heard him come up, but she stayed on her sketch with him standing there holding the hot bag. Neither of them said anything.

Her studio didn't look like the other places in Richmond. Knox had run countless deliveries to all those places. Each of them had scads of tattoo designs on the walls in the waiting area. Darla's was different. Her walls were deep red, and on each there were black silhouettes of curvaceous women, and nothing else.

Near where Knox stood was a round table with a photo album on it, a couple flimsy chairs, a small black loveseat, and a narrow table against the wall with another stack of photo albums. There was also a red door with "Water Closet" hand-painted on it, and a hallway with a little "Staff Only" sign over it.

Darla finally laid down her pencil, rose, and came Knox's way. She was ample and not shy about it. Her print dress hugged her curves up top but flowed out below her chest. Her wrists were visible below the ends of her sleeves, and both were tatted in orchids. The feature that sent Knox reeling was her pinup-girl hair, a dead ringer for the original Silk Spectre. Her curled bangs and spirals framed shining brown eyes. The hairs on the back of Knox's neck rose.

"So, you're Knox?"

"That's me."

She went into a little satin handbag for money. "Darla."

He slid her pizza out of the hot bag. "Nah. This one's on me."

"I want to pay for it." She held out a twenty.

"No way, Darla. It's my welcome gift to you."

She shook the money. "Please take it."

"No way." He laid her pizza on the round table, then went into the bag and dug out an absurd number of red-pepper flake packets. "Brought you these, too."

She put her hands on her hips and looked it all over. "Are you mocking me?"

"No. Why?"

"Because that's like a year's supply."

"Yeah, but when my guys fuck up again—and we both know they will—you won't have to worry about it." Knox picked up a photo album and sat on the loveseat. "How's business so far?"

Darla bobbled her head side to side. "Pretty okay. It's kind of hard to get the word out, but I keep thinking my work will get noticed." Darla stepped one foot into the staff room and came back with a bottle of green tea and uncapped it. "There's some fucking hacks in this town, that's for sure."

Knox had always thought most of the local tattoo places were pretty good. "Tell me about it. That's why I've never pulled the trigger."

"You not inked?"

"Nope."

"Not at all? That's kind of shocking." Darla sat in one of the chairs at the table and opened the pizza box.

"Why do you say that?"

She tore open three pepper flake packets at once and poured them on the pizza. "Because look at you. You seem like a guy that'd have at least one tattoo. I'd have guessed more."

"Really?"

"Yeah. There are types. Some people are tattoo types, and some aren't. Some people who aren't get one anyway, and some people who are the type don't have any. I guess you're the latter."

"Maybe, but I've never been under the gun."

She creased her nose. "There's no gun. No decent artist calls their tattoo machine a gun." She took a bite of her pizza.

"Really? I've always heard it called that." Knox turned a few pages of the photo album and looked up. "Did you do all these?"

Darla held up one finger and finished chewing before she said, "Of course. Why would I display someone else's work?"

Knox suddenly knew why Darla thought the other local artists were hacks. Her tattoos looked like photographs, like charcoal sketches, like comic-book art. Every last one was exceptional. Still staring at the album, he said, "You're a fucking maestro."

"A maestro, huh? That's a new one."

"Virtuoso, whatever. Your shit is good."

"I like to think so. Maybe it's time we got you tatted up."

Knox stared at a tattoo Darla had done of a woman's face in black-and-white surrounded by hundreds of tiny ornate flowers in what seemed like a thousand different colors. "Fuck. I don't know. Maybe so."

"Let me know." Darla took a sip from her bottle of tea.

Knox kept looking at the photos, marveling. Every now and then he stole a glance at Darla. The more he absorbed the aspects of Darla, the more intrigued he became.

Knox soon passed two new rules at Porthos. The first was, no delivery fees for Sinful Skin. Second, if Darla ordered anything while he was in the building, he took the delivery. Whenever he delivered, the food got comped. Darla argued with him, which gave him an excuse to loiter and transition to other subjects.

The third time Knox took a pizza up and wouldn't let her pay, Darla refused to take it. "Once was cool. Twice was unnecessary. Now I'm just starting to feel guilty. If you don't let me pay, I'm going to have to start ordering from someplace else."

"Don't do that. I'm just trying to make up for those delivery fees. I've also been thinking about what you said the first time I was in here. That I'm a tattoo guy who doesn't have one. Since you like my product, and seeing as I'm tattoo deficient, why don't we just trade out? You do some work for me, and I give you pizza. All you want." He extended the box again.

"Are you being serious about that?"

"Absolutely."

Darla took the pizza and laid it on her table. "So, as far as art, and location, do you have anything in mind?"

Knox raised his arm, looked at it, and rubbed it up and down. "I've been thinking about it, and I want, like, fighting robots all over my arm. You know, like mechas. Not ones that actually exist."

"You mean originals?"

"Yep."

"Are you talking about a full sleeve?"

"Fuck yeah."

He was afraid he lost her when she said, "That's a lot of fucking pizza."

"We can figure something out. It doesn't have to be all pizza. I can pay, too."

"What are you thinking in terms of color?"

"Black."

She creased her nose. "Grayscale would work better."

"Yeah, that."

"All right, Knox," Darla held out her hand. "Let me work up some sketches and see what you think. We can decide on price once we settle on something."

They shook on it. Knox looked at his hand immediately after he let hers go, and it was weird. He knew it as soon as he did it. She looked at him funny. He said, "My hands are cold," even though they weren't.

Once Knox was out on the sidewalk going back to his shop, he jumped and clicked his heels together. When he did, one of his slides fell halfway off and he tripped over it.

$\mathcal{E}$ACH TIME Darla had a new sketch to show Knox, she texted him. He brought her a pizza when he went up to see it. She did sketches of each individual mecha—five total—and finally one of the entire sleeve. He initially chose a big tattoo for one reason and one reason only: he wanted to drag it out as long as possible. It wound up working even better than he thought because Darla was so meticulous.

Whenever he went to Darla's studio, he hung out and they talked. In this way, he gradually got to know her story. She was divorced with no kids. Her ex, she said, left her with a lot of debt and otherwise wasn't worth discussing. She had been a tattoo artist for ten years in Pittsburgh, but she never had her own shop. She moved to Richmond and rented a house with a friend who took a job at the Bluegrass Army Depot destroying chemical weapons. With the low cost of living and cheap rent relative to Pittsburgh, she thought she could make it on her own, but it bled through that she was struggling financially. They agreed that Knox would pay a hundred bucks every time she worked on his tattoo. Darla planned to do it in five sessions, one every other week. Even with pizzas thrown in, that was a steep discount.

Darla wanted to start on Knox's shoulder. That way, if he bitched out and didn't finish, it wouldn't look as stupid. Knox was hurt by how seriously she took the possibility. She shaved, swabbed, and slicked up his shoulder before starting that first day. She was clinical about getting the job done. Her focus only made Knox more smitten.

After his shoulder was prepped, Darla snapped on a fresh pair of black latex gloves, got the ink prepped, and fired her tattoo machine. "I need you to lie back now."

It was sudden. He didn't expect her to dive in so quickly. "You don't use a stencil or anything?"

She laid her left hand on the ball of his shoulder. "I don't. Most artists do. Is that going to be a problem for you?"

He caught her eyes and held them. It calmed him down. "However you do it."

It felt like an electrified knife cutting into his skin, but he forced himself not to flinch. Darla's hands were gentle. She bit her full lower lip as she worked. She rubbed his shoulder again and again between bursts of activity. It all seemed so tender. Knox wondered what it would be like for a guy to do it. Whether it would be homoerotic. For him, he knew it would be. As much as Knox liked to dwell on the smooth apples of Darla's cheeks, he let his head fall back, closed his eyes, took in her sandalwood scent, and savored her touch.

A Tom Waits album played in the studio. A plunger-muted trumpet squawking between grinding refrains blended with the hum of the needle. Knox became so profoundly relaxed, he felt like he was dreaming, and it wouldn't have surprised him if he shuddered awake. That went on for a half hour of what Knox regarded as pure bliss. The mood broke abruptly when Darla took both her hands away and quieted her machine. "What the fuck, dude?"

Knox twisted his neck to look at her. Her eyes rolled vigorously. He was clueless. "What's wrong?"

"You need to get a grip." She didn't look that way, but she raised her machine and pointed in the general direction of Knox's knees.

He craned his head. On the horizon was his adamantium-hard erection, a tent pole hoisting the thin mesh of his shorts like an Arapaho teepee sprouting from the plains. There was nothing he could say. It was undeniable. He tried anyway. He waved his hand above his groin. "Oh shit, I'm sorry. I just do that when I'm relaxed."

"You must be pretty fucking relaxed. Do you need a break or something?"

"I'll do whatever you want. We can stop, or I can keep going."

"Yeah, I bet."

He propped up on an elbow. "I'm sorry, Darla. It's fucking embarrassing." He gestured at his unyielding penis. "It's, like, a bodily function. I don't mean to."

Darla averted her eyes and raised a gloved hand. "I get it. It's just unsettling. I always want to do my best work, and it's distracting as hell."

"Maybe I could get up a minute. Walk around or something. Do some stretches."

She shook her head. "It's up to you. We can keep going. I'll ignore it."

"You sure? Because I could take a minute."

"Let's just keep moving. There's no point in being dramatic about it. This is headed where it's headed."

He shifted and studied her expression. "What are you talking about?"

She pushed him back down to a reclined position and flicked her machine back on. "You're so transparent. I was okay with it, but then you got that ridiculous erection. I just wish you'd be a little less obvious about it."

"About what?"

She flipped her machine off again and jutted her lower jaw. "Jesus. Come on, Knox. Don't be stupid, and especially don't treat me like I am. We won't do it here, but we're going to end up fucking." She squeezed his bicep with a gloved hand. "Don't ruin it."

Knox laid there, eyes wide open, staring at the ceiling, his penis pointing ever more urgently in the same direction. Darla fired her machine again and resumed her outlining. After a minute or so, she started whistling along with the trumpet as she worked.

*D*ARLA AND KNOX started out pretty simple. He brought her pizzas, she worked on his tattoo, they had sex now and again. Eventually, she finished the tattoo, but the pizzas and sex continued. Then, one night at Knox's apartment, Darla was stepping into her dress while Knox was at the sink brushing his teeth. He spit a frothy plop of toothpaste and rinsed it down the drain before rattling his toothbrush into a crusty cup. He leaned against the countertop and considered a moment. "Hey. I wanted to ask you something."

"You don't need a permission slip."

"Okay. So, what would you think about us maybe going out somewhere? Like, together."

"I don't know." Darla came closer, the back of her dress still open. "I could use a break from my studio, that's for sure. What'd you have in mind?"

"I haven't figured that part out yet."

"So, you want us to go somewhere, but you don't know where?"

"Not really. I didn't get that far. I didn't know if this was all you wanted. If it is, that's fine. But if it's not, that'd be okay with me, too."

"Zip me up." Darla turned her back to him and held her hair off the back of her neck. "I'd like to see Lucinda Williams. She's coming to Covington. I asked Karen, but she can't go." Karen was Darla's roommate. "I'd rather not go alone. Last time I checked it wasn't sold out yet. What about that?"

Knox went slow, trying not to let the zipper catch. "Yeah. Okay. I'm in for that. You want me to get tickets?"

"If you want. I'll pay you back."

"What if I just bought yours?"

Darla spun on the balls of her feet to face him. She knit her lips to one side, considering it. "I guess I'd let you."

That got to be the way of things. Knox and Darla still slept together, but they also went places: to shows, to restaurants, to the movies. It went that way for months and neither one examined it too much. That is, until Knox forced the issue. He hadn't given it much thought beforehand—none, in fact—but they were in his bed on a Sunday afternoon, getting after it. He blurted it, "I fucking love you!"

Without easing up at all, grinding her hips back into him, Darla slapped one finger across his lips. "Shut the fuck up." She twisted some unaccountable way, and somehow managed to get that same finger up his ass, and nothing else was said about it.

When it was over, they sat on the couch watching an old videotape of *My So-Called Life*, but Knox was unsettled, quietly obsessing. He said it and she didn't reciprocate. He couldn't abide her silence. "You heard what I said?"

She didn't look at him. "Obviously."

"And?"

Darla picked up the remote, paused the ancient VCR, and set it back down. "It was a throwaway."

"What do you mean it was a throwaway?"

"I mean it was a throwaway. It would have meant more if you said it when we were walking down the street, or waiting in line at the grocery store, or whatever. To say it then, it was a throwaway."

"But I meant it. I love you. You're my fucking heart's delight, goddamn it."

"Okay."

"Doesn't that elicit anything from you?"

Darla turned her eyes to him and jutted her lower lip. "I'm glad, I guess. I don't know."

She unpaused the show and kept sitting there staring at the TV like nothing was happening while Knox huffed and sighed. It made him feel small and stupid. Sure, he blurted it out during sex, but it was genuine. It was like an extreme version of trying to give someone five and having them ignore it. He was actually pissed. He went on like that, blowing in and out, but Darla didn't even glance at him.

He got up, packed a bowl, and paced around hitting it. He was behind the couch starting to calm down a little as a nice head buzz set in.

Darla still didn't move. "I fucking love you too, asshole. Okay? Now sit down here, pass that, and calm the fuck down while I rewind this. We missed the last ten minutes."

He froze and stood staring at the back of her head, not knowing if he wanted to go sit with her, or cash the bowl and go down to the shop. He finally sat beside her and slipped her the pipe. She drew slow, leaned into him, laid her head on his shoulder, and blew the smoke out in a long thin jet.

$\mathscr{T}$HE **POUND** of OG Kush from the card game looked like even more after Knox had cut open the bundles and poured them out into a Trader Joe's grocery bag. In the years since they had first gotten together, Darla and Knox had become such fixtures in each other's lives that although they both kept their own places, they carried keys to the other's. She sat on the edge of the old wingback chair in his apartment and brought the flowers to her nose with both hands. "My god, this smells amazing."

Knox paced behind her. "I know. It's like when I was a kid and I would dream I was in a candy store. Like, I had that dream all the time and it was always so disappointing when I woke up, but there was also no way I could eat all that candy. It's so much fucking weed. A pound is a ridiculous amount of weed."

"Jesus Christ, man. How'd you let this happen? Only you could do something like this. I told you not to go to that fucking game."

"I know."

"And did you listen?"

"Is that a real question?"

"No, it's not. It's a fucking point." Darla raised a single bud in front of her face and examined it. "I in no way condone you selling this, but I honestly don't know what you're supposed to do with it. You should probably just ditch it."

Knox stopped pacing and held his hands palms out. "I have to sell it. I thought, like, maybe I could sell it all at once, to one person, but I'm more afraid of doing that than I am of selling it a little at a time."

"So, you're going to be a drug dealer?"

Knox screwed up his face. "Do you really consider pot a drug?"

"The cops do."

"I guess. Maybe. But all my money's in it. I can't afford not to sell it. I went to that game specifically because my parents' mortgage and my rent are both due next week. If I didn't buy this, I would've gotten cleaned out completely. I hung onto a little of my cash and I got this. It was my only chance."

Darla twisted to look at him. "So, you really think you would've gotten robbed?"

"Are you kidding me? Yes. You're looking at a pound of OG Kush they just casually had in the trunk of their car. They sold it to me right there on the spot. There were literally both cops and robbers sitting there waiting for me. He had fucking hired muscle with him. A goon whose only job as far as I can tell is to be a goon. He looked like a goddamn pro wrestler. I'm not exaggerating. What part of any of that leads you to believe they wouldn't rob me?"

"Which brings me back to the lunacy of you going to that game in the first place."

Knox twined his fingers on the top of his head. "I think we've established pretty conclusively that you were right and I was wrong."

"Give me a second so I can get my phone. I want to record you saying that."

"I was desperate. You know I was. Now I have to sell it. I really don't have a choice."

Darla leaned back and snaked her arm around Knox's waist. "I think that's a terrible idea, but if you're going to anyway, I also feel like we should test the product beforehand. It would be irresponsible not to."

$\mathcal{S}$**ELLING IT** turned out to be easy. Knox sold to Rob. A couple other employees approached him after that. Then it sold itself. Friends tipped friends who tipped other friends. People who smoke pot tend to know other people who smoke pot, and Porthos was a nonthreatening place to buy weed. The only person in the shop who had a problem with it was Gabe.

He cornered Knox in the kitchen a couple days after Knox started selling. "I'm working on my future. I can't be around this. It's one thing to smoke weed, it's a whole 'nother thing to deal."

"I just have to get rid of it. Once it's gone, I'll quit. Nothing'll happen."

"What if you get busted?"

"Then I get busted. It won't affect you."

"Yeah, you know, as the only black person who works here, I find that kind of hard to believe. They'll probably arrest me first, and I don't have anything to do with it."

Knox wasn't even that scared anymore. Once he got started, it felt like no big deal. Most of the people he sold that first pound to were familiar faces, which was fortunate, because he was wholly unprofessional. The only scale in the pizza shop was imprecise, so he mostly guessed weights based on past experience.

He'd say, "Does that look like about an eighth to you?"

Pretty much everyone would go, "A little more."

He didn't even care, he was just trying to get it gone. He and Darla smoked a lot. The thing was, even dipping into it, even using shitty business practices, the money was good. The thousand he put in turned into almost thirty-two hundred. He was able to help his parents with their bills and hardly even feel it. By the time it ran low, he'd gotten accustomed to the extra cash. After it was gone, people kept showing up looking for it.

Rob in particular was crestfallen. "It was like a job perk, man. It's not like I get a 401(k), or dental, or anything, but at least I had a weed plan."

After a couple weeks trying to sell pizza to people looking for pot, and having to spend his proceeds with another dealer, Knox's money started to run thin again. The prospect of trying to find another card game, and the risk involved in it even if he could, all made it seem kind of silly to go that route when he knew a much easier way to make money. Money people were willing to hand over to him.

He dug Burl's card out of his car console and called the number. The lady who answered said Burl wasn't there but took Knox's name and number. Twenty minutes later he answered a 606 area-code call and heard, "Fort Knox."

$\mathcal{T}$HE FIRST TIME he went up to Burl's farm, Knox thought it'd be easy based on the directions. "Turn left at the arcade. When you get to the Four Corners Shell Mart, make another left. I'm in a white farmhouse up a driveway at the end of the road. You'll run right into it."

Even though it was only a county away, it took Knox nearly an hour to get to McKee, the last thirty minutes of it winding through hills. When he finally got to Second Street in downtown and turned left in front of the arcade, he had it in his head he was nearly there. But Second Street in McKee turns into 89, and it was another twenty minutes of serpentine twists between wooded slopes just to reach the Shell Mart, and after the turn off to Burl's house, he weaved for another ten minutes or so. The road ended in a cul-de-sac with a single white mailbox. It had no name on it, only numbers. On the mailbox post was a neatly painted brown on white sign that read "Absolutely No Trespassers." The driveway in looped up from the holler where the road laid. It was a series of gravel switchbacks so severe it felt like treading in place. Knox found himself in the thick of the Daniel Boone National Forest, the driveway a blighted scar in otherwise heavy growth.

He expected the terrain to flatten out for what Burl called his farm, and it did a bit, but the hills never slacked. The pictures in Knox's mind on the way there were of all these wild backwoods scenes. Most incorporated a metal gate, cars on blocks, dogs on chains, trailers, thugs prowling with automatic weapons. Movie shit. What he found was from some other film entirely. Burl's house and yard rested in a level spot, but the landscape on all sides around it tilted vertical. His grass was neatly kept, the mowing lines in a crisscross pattern. The white farmhouse shone bright from within the backdrop of green. It was trimmed with starkly contrasting black shutters. Red flowers flowed from the dozens of hanging baskets that decorated the wide wraparound porch. The porch was also decked with a quantity of rocking chairs Knox had previously only seen out front of Cracker Barrel restaurants.

Knox was greeted at his car door by two black labs, both barking, but with their tails flagging joyously. They were young, lanky dogs, and they jockeyed for position as he tried to push open the door with them in the way. Each dog pressed its muzzle to his groin and dipped its head so he'd pat it, which he did.

He was still engaged with the dogs when Burl shouted, "Waylon! Johnny! Come on now, boys!" He stood on the porch with a tall glass in one hand and a cigarette in the other. He stuck two fingers of the cigarette hand in his lips and let loose a sharp whistle. The dogs tore away across the lawn and up onto the porch. "Y'all lay down now." He pointed to his left and both dogs were soon on their sides flat to the concrete surface, moving only their restless tails.

Knox held up a hand. Burl waved back and called to him like they were old friends. "You done found me, Fort Knox. I was beginning to wonder. Leave your phone in your car. We ain't got no signal anyway. Come on to the porch and let's have us a drink. What can we get you?"

Knox hobbled across the lawn, unseen bugs chittering all around.

He'd stiffened up over the course of the going on two hours he'd spent in his Volvo. As the crow flew he hadn't come far, but as the asphalt ran, it'd been a tedious affair. "I'll take an ice water."

"I got stronger but suit yourself." Burl opened the front door and hollered in, "Colleen, can you bring my friend a tall glass of water with plenty of ice." He drew out the word *ice* in the way mountain people often do, starting with an *ah* sound, and it struck Knox for the thousandth time how a short distance in Kentucky can take you so far culturally.

Burl gestured at one of the rockers. "Have you a seat. Let's chat a bit, shall we."

The night he met Burl at the card game, Knox had guessed him to be in his forties, but in the daylight it was obvious he was older. His dark hair looked to have been dyed, and the lines in his face were deeper and more plentiful than Knox had noticed. He now guessed late fifties.

The day's heat had begun to wane, but it was still near eighty, and the humidity was Kentucky thick. Burl wore deep-blue slim jeans, a black western shirt with silver trim and snaps, and ornate boots with pointed toes. Knox had on mesh shorts, a pocked and punctured t-shirt with Gary Coleman's perturbed face on it, and slides with socks. He poured sweat like a fat kid at a picnic. Meanwhile, Burl's face was dry as hardtack. They looked like one of those mismatched duos they put together to hand out Grammys.

Knox sat deep in his chair and immediately began to sway. Burl perched at the edge of the rocker beside him to his left. His jeans rode up his right ankle exposing a small brown gun holster. Knox didn't have so much as a pocketknife. He said, "This is a beautiful place you have out here, Burl. I had a hell of a time getting here, but it was worth the drive."

"Ain't it though. I can sit here of an evening all by myself and be content as a tick on dog's hind end. I don't gotta do nothing."

The screen door behind them sung open and a soft woman about

44

Burl's age in khaki shorts and a short-sleeved gingham blouse came out with the glass of water he'd called for. The door whipped back and clattered shut behind her. "Colleen," Burl said, "this here's Knox. He come a visiting from Madison County. He's got him a little pizza shop over there. Fort Knox, this is my wife, Colleen."

Knox took the water from her. She had a full face, and it was clear at a glance she'd turned many a head when she was younger, and probably still did turn some. "Well," she said, "we ought to go by there and get us one sometime."

When she turned to go in, Knox said, "Come on by," but she was already nearly inside by the time he'd gotten it out, and she made no acknowledgement.

Burl watched her backside depart. Then he turned to Knox with a hint of a smirk. "She ain't much on small talk." He took a long drink from his glass, which was loaded with ice cubes and brown liquid that could have been about anything. "You know, after we played cards, I told Greek, 'We'll see that boy again.' He was none too convinced, but I knowed once you'd got you a taste of it, you'd not be able to let it lie."

"I guess you were right."

Burl pulled in air, sighed it out loud and slow. "That brings me to an unpleasant something I have to ask you."

Knox was taking a long drink, but stopped and looked at him, a little water dripping down his beard onto Gary Coleman's forehead. "What's that?"

"I'm going to need you to take off that shirt and drop them drawers. I've got to be convinced you ain't wearing no wire or packing no camera before we can commence with any business. You're welcome to turn your pecker away, ain't nobody out here going to see nothing but me."

"Are you serious?"

"As a fucking snake bite." Burl didn't flinch, his eyes never wavered.

Knox sat blinking a moment before he set down his glass and stood. He pulled off his shirt, which was stuck to his back a bit on account of the sweat against his car's seat, and laid it on his chair.

"You ain't got to take your drawers all the way off. To the ankles is fine."

There was no reason for it, other than obstinance, but Knox didn't turn when he dropped his shorts and boxers. He made Burl confront his dangling ding-dong in all its relative glory. He held out both his hands as if to say, Good enough for you? Waylon and Johnny watched with a bit of interest from down the porch.

Burl shook his head. "You ain't shy are you?"

"I've been called a lot. Never shy." Knox bent over and hitched his shorts and underwear back up, took his shirt and rolled it back on. "I have to ask you, why would you sell me a pound of Kush hardly knowing who I was, but strip-search me here?"

Burl pointed his glass. "Easy. You ain't going to wear no wire, or no camera, and play poker for six hours like you did. And you ain't going to go to the law and tell them I sold you a pound of pot you didn't know you was going to buy. Where's your upside? How do they make that case? Today though, today's different. I got no problems here in Jackson County. None at'all. I got me the judges, and I got the law, and I got whoever else I need. Only thing I have to worry about is someone outside the county come poking, and to tell the truth, I ain't even too worried about that."

"You don't do anything outside Jackson County?"

"Do I ever leave Jackson County? Course I do. Do I do business when I leave? I won't say not never, but not too often." He held up one open hand and motioned in all directions. "Everything we sell, we grow right here. I got over eleven hundred acres of hills and hollers. I got me plenty of room. I got me four grow houses to get me through the year. I got me some smart business associates, like yourself. You may look like a damn ragamuffin, but I knowed you was smart from playing poker with you. And I knowed you was a businessman. You should know better than anyone how much you can learn about a man at a card table if you pay good attention. I knowed you was a man who could live outside the law. I know my kind."

"What about KSP? Don't they do marijuana flyovers and all that shit they put on the news?"

Burl took one last draw from his cigarette, then stubbed it out in a brass ashtray with wavy edges that sat between his feet. "It's like this, Fort Knox. Even Kentucky state troopers like to have them a good Christmas. Only worry I got's the feds, but they never give us no trouble. People think the feds is out breaking up criminally orientated businesses like mine, but they ain't. They follow the lead of the local boys. They show up when the pictures is taken, or later. Our local boys sure ain't going to lead them here, or anywhere I operate.

"Only way I get tripped up the triflingest bit is someone outside the county informs on me. I try to avoid them sort of people. I try to do business with folks who won't do such a thing. Take you, for example. You got family in Frankfort, and parts east, who you care about. You also got you a nice girlfriend doing tattoos in Richmond."

Knox's eyes went to the dogs, who lay mostly still, but who peered at him hopefully. He didn't acknowledge one way or the other.

"Sure you do. If you was to inform on me, you don't just got to worry about the harm would come to you, you got to worry about every other person you care about." Burl shifted back in his chair. "Because harm would come. No question. Why would you do that? That's simple. You wouldn't."

Knox studied the holster on Burl's ankle. "I wouldn't."

"You met old Greek. Greek served him three tours with the rangers putting down Muslims in the Middle East. I got him in charge of my security, but I'd say he feels like he's retired after all that. He knows people all over who'll do all sorts of jobs. I'd say he

47

keeps me pretty safe. You'd be amazed what we know about you. Your head'd pop off."

Knox only nodded. "Can I ask you something?"

"Why sure."

"If the police do show up at my place, what do I do?"

"That's a good question. I'm glad you asked it. First off, find you some way to get rid of everything if you can, and I mean everything. It'll be a short-term loss, but long run it'll pay. Some might say you could get charged for tampering with evidence, but if there ain't no evidence, there ain't nothing to be tampered with. If there's evidence left, that's a bigger problem than any old tampering charge. You got to figure this shit out in advance so if the time comes there's nothing but to do it."

Burl reached around the back of his neck, stuck his hand down his shirt collar, and itched with one eye closed. When he was done, he snuffed a bit at his sinuses. "Damned allergies done eat me up. Anyway. If the law asks you questions, you don't say shit. Give your name, that's it. They want to know one more thing, and it ain't about the weather, say you want a lawyer. They'll try to talk you out of it, but it's bullshit. Nobody ever helped hisself out talking to the law. Not nobody. We got us a good little lawyer over here, tough as a pine knot. People think she's a lesbian but she ain't one. I'll get you her number here in a minute. You call her, she'll come see you. She'll get with Greek and we'll help you if we can. Know one thing though, expenses is on you. We can lead you to water, we might even front you some water, but you got to pay for that fucking water your ownself."

"I don't call Greek direct?"

"Hell no. We don't aim to be tied to this shit. You ain't likely to hear from us except through the lawyer. If we *was* to call, you ain't going to know the number. The thing about all this is, if you're smart, the law ain't going to bother you. They ain't interested in no pot dealers anymore unless they're made to be interested. They got harmful shit to worry about. Fucking pills, fucking meth. Shit, they say heroin's coming back. Don't do no stupid shit and they probably leave you alone."

"Seriously?"

"Seriously. You ain't our only boy in Madison County. Ain't none of them had no problems except the ones that's dealing pills. We find out you done some stupid shit like that, Greek'll come calling, or someone else'll come calling, and you got to find yourself a new business associate, and maybe a new something else."

"You don't have to worry about me."

Burl took a pull from his glass and let an ice cube flow into his mouth. He spoke with it still in there. "I didn't figure I did. That's why we're sitting here. You and me both know goddamn well marijuana ain't dangerous. Only thing makes it dangerous is the fact it's illegal, but that's also what makes it lucrative. Hell, I hope they don't never legalize it. The good news is, them boys in Frankfort are too dumb to do it, which is just fine by me. Keeps me in business. Keeps you and Greek and a whole lot of other people working. I'm a job creator, son."

"You the biggest employer in Jackson County?"

"Nah. They's the state, and the school board, then me." Burl ticked off each one on his fingers. "One more thing I got to warn you about now that you're getting in this thing serious. Don't be making no bulk sales. Couple reasons for that. First, I ain't looking for no middle man. Don't want one. If anyone pushes that issue, you let us know. Greek'll handle it some way. The other thing is, small sales is misdemeanors. You shouldn't be selling more than an ounce at a time. Should you get tangled up with the law, that'll plead out easy to probated time. You understand all that?"

"Yeah, I got it. That won't be a problem." Knox twisted side to side, trying to stretch his still road-weary back. "I was wondering something."

"What's that?"

"Where's the name Greek come from? I've tried to figure it out ten ways around, and I can't come up with anything."

"That's easy. I trade in agate. I got me a piece of Greek agate, and it's pearly white, just like Greek himself. I took to calling him that, and everyone else just followed suit. Agate's a pretty good business. All kinds is into agate. You ever heard of our circuit court judge, Gary Wayne Trimble, from Clay County?"

"No."

"Useful sort of fellow, for me anyway. Crooked as a dog's hind leg, but otherwise a good man. He's made news on account of a few peculiar rulings. Judge Trimble also trades in agate. I've helped him in a couple races, and I keep him in agate. Nearly every bit of agate in Kentucky's in Estill County except for one creek over here. That one creek flows from Estill. It's called Middle Fork. Wouldn't you know Middle Fork runs right through my property."

"You know that when you bought it?"

"I bought my land up piecemeal. I sure was aware of it when I bought them tracts. You want to take a tour? I just got me a new RZR I was going to take out if you didn't show up soon. Four-seater. If you want, you, me, Waylon, and Johnny could take us a ride and I could show you Middle Fork." The dogs shifted to their haunches, having heard their names and eager to move.

Knox thought of Gabe back at the shop, already pissed off he was covering the first part of Knox's shift, and he thought of his drive back. "I'd like to, but it's getting late. I gotta get back. Another time."

"All right then. Another time." Burl leaned forward and scratched down inside his boot. "Let's you and me get down to conducting some business."

*P*OT MADE Knox money, but it wound up costing him a lot. Those losses started with Gabe.

The doorway to Knox's apartment sat between the bathrooms at the very back of Porthos's shabby dining room. The carpeted steps going up were a little bit tricky to navigate because there was shit all over them: books, grocery bags, an automotive funnel, a deck of Tarot cards, loose golf clubs, shoes, an equestrian trophy, a stack of unopened ThunderCats action figures, and other miscellanea. The steps were simply the rat's tail of a more extensive collection.

The stairs opened to a living area/kitchen. The entire place was a cornucopia of random bullshit piled on top of itself. It was like a maze in which you could get to Knox's coffee table, his couch, his refrigerator, his bathroom, etc.

When Gabe went up at close on a Sunday night with the cash drawer, Knox was on the couch, shirtless, holding a book, with his socked feet on the coffee table on top of two other books. Where his feet rested was the lowest point in a rabble of even more books, magazines, DVDs, remote controls, dishes, glasses, and ashtrays.

"What up, chief? You got the drawer?"

"Yep." Gabe took it to him.

Knox accepted it and slumped back down like he'd been ladled onto his couch. He set the drawer beside him and cleared some space on the coffee table before extracting the twenties and beginning his count.

Gabe remained in the same place. "So, I was wondering . . . what about selling me a dime bag or something?"

Knox looked up from his count through the tops of his lids. "I thought you didn't approve."

"Aw, man. That was just at first. Maybe I overreacted. I've been having some back pain, you know. It's really been hurting me. I was thinking maybe I could use a little medicinal marijuana and see what that does. You have anything good for that?"

"It's all good for that. I just got this Northern Lights hybrid that's supposed to be great for pain. If you really want some, I could hook you up."

Gabe shook his head slow. He reached to his waist and peeled off his sweaty Porthos Pizza t-shirt and flung it one-handed into Knox's face. "Naw, man. I quit."

Knox knocked the shirt away. "What?"

"You fucking lied to me." Gabe crossed his arms across his bare chest. "You said no more after that first batch."

"Just like that?"

"I don't owe you nothing. You said when what you got was gone, you wouldn't get any more, but I knew it. Why should I stay one day longer after you lied to my face?"

Knox let his head fall back, dropped his hands into his lap, and exhaled. "I guess that's fair. I didn't know I was lying at the time. It's just, my parents are having trouble, and the shop's not exactly killing it. I didn't feel like I had a choice. I needed the money. What can I say? I just needed it."

"We all need money, Knox. And we all make choices. Quitting's my choice." Gabe was not a big guy, but he was cut, especially standing there with his fists clenched, agitated. "I can't be around it. I done told you. If I wanted to mess with weed, I could've stayed in Harlan, but that's not why I'm here, and that's not why I'm in school."

"I'm sorry, G."

"Yeah. Not sorry enough, I guess."

$\mathcal{K}$**NOX'S DAD** was a commercial truck driver for most of his adult life and he made good money. Enough that Knox's mom had never had to work. He ran a local route out of Frankfort, Kentucky, the state capital. Then, in 2009, he failed his CDL physical. That seemed catastrophic enough, but it wasn't the worst of it. He failed because he had Parkinson's. Not only was he out of work, but he had to deal with the disease. That meant medical bills.

First, Knox's mom asked Knox if he could pitch in for an electric bill. Not long after that, he kicked in on their mortgage. Eventually, Knox's dad found a new job as a sales clerk at Ace Hardware, but they weren't okay. The wages weren't close. Poker had helped Knox fill the gap for them, but selling weed helped on a completely different scale.

Before he knew it, Knox was picking up one to two pounds a month at a gas and grocery Burl owned on top of Big Hill at the northern tip of Jackson County. He didn't even get out of his car most of the time. If he was in a hurry, he drove around back, and an employee brought it out in a cardboard box that had had bread, or cereal, or snack cakes, or whatever in it, before it was emptied and repurposed for pot. Knox handed his money out, and they loaded it in his trunk and sent him off with no more than a few lines of small talk. He might as well have been picking up dry cleaning.

It wasn't quite as simple when it started. The first time he went to pick up at the gas station, he parked out front and went inside to the counter. A familiar face was waiting. The chinstrap-beard kid from the poker game stood behind the register alongside what was undoubtedly somebody's granny. She was smoking and had hair that was dyed an unnatural orange/red color but was grimy gray at the roots. The place smelled like cigarettes and a deep fryer. The boy recognized Knox straightaway. He smiled when he walked up. "Fort Knox. Where you been? You never came back to the card game. I wondered what became of you, but Burl said you was coming by today."

"Hey, man," Knox said, shading his eyes as if it would help him see better even though they were inside. "I remember you. Tell me your name again."

"Daniel." The boy had skin tags on the sides of his neck scattered like pills on a polyester shirt and those same fake diamond studs in each ear.

"Yeah, Daniel, that's right. How you been, chief?"

"Not bad. Earning a dollar, running them hollers." Daniel scratched his chest with a thick hand. "You ain't been back to cards since you wiped out ol' Burl."

"I haven't really been playing."

"Well, I'll tell you, nobody ever done him the way you did." He took a drink from a green glass bottle of Ale-8 soda.

"I had a good run of luck."

"That was more than luck," Daniel said, shaking his head. "Took him down a peg. It's good for him. If you ain't playing no cards what're you into, then?"

"Slinging pizza."

"Oh yeah, how's business?"

Knox became mesmerized by a clear plastic case of fried apple pies that sat atop the counter. A white paper sign taped to it said they were "$2.50 each or 2 for $4." The sign had turned light brown everywhere except under the taped part. He could taste those pies looking at them. "Steady." He pointed. "Can I get one of those pies."

"Surely Temple," Daniel said, and took a pair of tongs and got a cloudy white waxed paper sleeve to drop the pie into. Knox tried to pay the old smoking lady with three ragged dollar bills, but Daniel held up his hand. "Naw, this one's on the house."

The lady stubbed out her cigarette vigorously in a little glass ashtray beside the register. "You can't be doing that stuff, Daniel."

"Burl ain't going to miss one pie. He wouldn't miss a hundred."

The woman glared at Daniel through the tops of her lids but said no more. Knox had no sooner gotten his pie than he took a bite of the golden-brown imperfect half circle of cinnamon sugar heaven.

"You park out front?" Daniel asked.

"Yeah," Knox said with his mouth full and crumbs falling into his beard.

"Why don't you pull it on around back and I can get you the rest of your groceries."

Knox looked at him quizzically.

"Ain't you here to get some groceries? Didn't you tell Burl you needed you a pound of cheese?"

Knox opened his mouth wide. "Oh yeah. That. I do need that cheese."

"Thought so."

$\mathcal{H}$**AVING A PLACE** like Porthos was terrifying for someone like Knox. He was never what you'd call organized, and he hadn't had any savings in years. For him, owning Porthos was kind of like being president of a Third World country: some little island nation that made all its money off citrus fruits and fishing. Rob was his vice-president. They held the place together, but it felt like it was on the brink of financial collapse at any second. When shit got complicated, they had to make up something on the fly to deal with the situation.

Knox used to manage to build up at least a little money for a rainy day, but as Porthos's profits got leaner, and his parents relied more on him to supplement their income, his margin for error got thinner, and surviving a crisis got sketchier. If it took a bad enough turn, the shop could go down for good. He didn't have any collateral to put up for a loan or credit line. He really didn't want anyone looking too closely at his books because they'd fucking run. In an old shop like Porthos, equipment went down all the time, and it was only getting worse because Knox couldn't afford to replace anything.

Barry, who owned A+ Refrigeration and Restaurant Services, was good to Knox, cut him slack on bills, and tried to fix anything that broke down even if it wasn't really what he did. When the AutoFry went down and Barry couldn't fix it, Porthos just couldn't sell any fried food for a few weeks until Knox could pay someone else to repair it. He had to build up weed money to get that done.

It was basically just Knox and Rob managing after Gabe left. They tried other people at shift leader, but nobody stuck. There was a five-day stretch where Knox worked open to close every day because Rob took time off after his girlfriend left him. She'd gone to rehab for pills and wound up moving in with one of her male counselors before it was over. Rob wasn't all that upset about her, but she had a four-year-old daughter he was helping raise and she took her away, too. He went into a massive funk. He initially said he was going to take two weeks off. He wound up coming back sooner because he was so miserable sitting at home missing the little girl.

Rob ran mostly days because Knox stayed up late making weed sales and running night shifts. Knox got a text from him one Thursday morning just before opening. He said to get down to the shop, it was an emergency.

"Fucking walk-in's down," Rob said as a greeting when Knox came in the kitchen. "Dough was spilling out of all the trays when I opened it. Hot as shit."

The air in the walk-in was wet and funky. The yeast in the dough had overactivated, causing blobs to expand and spill the stacked dough trays onto the floor. Knox stuck a meat thermometer into a bag of slimy pepperoni and it read sixty-two degrees. Not only did they lose most of the nineteen-hundred-dollar food order they had gotten on Tuesday, but they also lost another three thousand of back stock. A lot of what they lost was cheese. It was a fucking catastrophe. Everything that wasn't in the freezer or the makeline had to be loaded in the trash and taken to the dumpster. Knox was on the verge of tears.

He barely had enough money for the walk-in repair and definitely didn't have the money to replace the lost stock. They could hurry and make warm water dough, which didn't have to proof, but it wasn't as good. Even so, they only had enough cheese in the makeline to stay open a little while. Cheese was everything, and it was also the most expensive ingredient in the house. Once the cheese was gone, they'd have no choice but to close the shop, which meant no money coming in. Knox told Rob, "This could be it. We might be done."

Porthos's primary food supplier was a company called Mangia!. Their regular truck came every Tuesday. Knox could get an expedited reorder from Mangia! but they wouldn't extend him any credit. It was strictly cash on delivery. Darla had a good business, but not that good. He could never ask her for a loan. In fact, he couldn't think of a single person in the world who would loan him the kind of money he needed to get bailed out. Then he thought of one person.

$\mathcal{Y}$OU THINK I'm a fucking bank? A credit union?" Knox had initially spent a few minutes dawdling after arriving at Burl's store, in no hurry to get around to what he wanted. Burl had finally gotten impatient and told him to get to the reason why he'd asked him to meet already. Burl's reaction to Knox's request was exactly the reason he had stalled. "If your business ain't profitable, why the fuck do I want to put my money in it?"

"It is profitable. It's just that it's summertime. The students are gone. If they were here, I'd be fine. It was an act of God. I just need a little boost to get by." Did Knox really believe that? Yes, he did. In his mind, brighter days were always just up ahead.

"God didn't break down your damn cooler. Bad luck ain't what done it either. Once a cooler goes one time, it ain't never right. I know good and goddamn well about that." Burl did know something about it. He owned not one, but three gas-station/convenience stores spread throughout Jackson County. The hubs of his local operation. "I'll fix a cooler exactly one time. If it goes down again, I get rid of the damn thing and get me a new one. How many times has your walk-in been down?"

"This is the first time," Knox said, but thought to himself, *this*

60

year. The walk-in came with the business. There was no telling how old it was. In the past they always caught the problem before Porthos lost any stock, and they moved everything to the makeline, or the freezer, or the refrigerator in Knox's apartment, while they got the walk-in fixed.

Burl spit on the vinyl-tiled floor in his stock room, rubbed it in with the toe of his boot. "Yeah, I bet."

"If the answer's no, tell me and I'll look somewhere else."

Burl fell quiet. Knox waited. "How much you needing?" Burl said, breaking the silence.

"Ten thousand."

Burl drew his head back. "Shit hell. Why not twenty? Why not fifty?"

"You asked me what I need. That's what I need."

"How much product of mine you got?"

"Very little."

"Thought so." Burl clicked his tongue and gazed at the ceiling. "I tell you what. I'll spot you five, and—and I make this offer only because I don't want to lose my foothold—I'll let you sell some Diesel on spec. That ought to move pretty good for you."

"How much will you take back on that?"

"By hell, I ought to keep all of it, but I ain't gonna. You keep ten percent. You do that, I won't charge you no vig on the money the first month. You get me paid back quick, you move all that Diesel, you won't owe me nothing extra. Even make a little scratch for your ownself. After a month, it's three points a week. I ain't too good at math, so it's best you get me paid that first month."

His helter-skelter poker style didn't reflect it, but Burl was incredibly good at math. Knox knew it, but didn't call him on it. "Seems fair," Knox said.

"One more thing."

"What's that?"

"Pizza. If ever I'm in Richmond and I get me a taste for some pizza, it's going to be on the house. You understand?" Burl pointed between Knox's eyes. "I don't want anyone giving me no bill."

"I got it. No problem. When can I get the money?"

"I'll be back at the house in a couple hours. Why don't you go on back and get me a pizza and bring it when you come. Go on and throw everything on it."

"You serious?"

Burl's eyes widened. Then he cracked a smile and punched Knox in the arm. "I oughta be." He walked out with his boot heels clacking on the floor.

*D*ARLA SENT Knox three texts before nine on a Saturday morning trying to get him to meet her for coffee. She got no reply. She eventually gave up, pulled on short-sleeve green coveralls, put a black zip-down hoodie over them, and headed to his apartment. She had tired of her pinup hair a long time back and transitioned to wavy curls, which did better some days than others. So far, this was a pretty good day. The Kentucky heat was on its late-September last legs, and at that time of day it wasn't much above sixty. It would find its way into the seventies eventually.

Darla's roommate, Karen, had moved back to Pennsylvania after her two-year contract at the depot was up in 2010. Darla stayed behind. Her tattoo studio had gotten busy in those two years, and she had built a good reputation that she only hoped to grow.

Knox offered to let her move in with him when Karen moved, but she wasn't interested. She had her pick of reasons why, really. The hovel state of his apartment for starters. His aversions to deodorant and frequent bathing were on the list, too, but she seldom complained unless he got particularly ripe. He considered his hygienic habits European-style virtues. She bought him all-natural deodorant and encouraged him to find the shower just a little more often, but that was about it. She had always liked her men a little on the earthy side.

Darla wound up renting a one-bedroom apartment downtown over an insurance office a couple blocks from her studio. Nothing between them changed right away.

When they'd first gotten together, Darla and Knox went places like Asheville, Cincinnati, and Nashville for concerts. They stayed overnight and came back. She went with him to the pizza show at Belterra Casino in Indiana one time, but she hated it. She got him to go with her to a tattoo expo in Chicago. In their four years together, that was the farthest they ever went from home. They hadn't been anywhere in some time.

Porthos didn't open until eleven, so Darla went to Knox's apartment the back way, down the alley off Water Street, behind the empty apartment building next door. The alley was so narrow it could only be walked. It was the kind of alley people in movies get mugged or murdered in, and it had almost everything you'd expect to go with it: trash, leaking pipes, utility boxes, grates over underground openings, rusty metal stairwells. There really should have been rats, but Darla had never seen any.

She stood on the landing at the top of the stairs while she went into her purse for her key to the ancient metal door. She took in the musty, vaguely sewer smell as she turned the cylinder. The crusty metal hinges creaked open and she entered the rabbit warren of Knox's earthly possessions. His bedroom sat at the opposite end.

It was still dark in there, the light kept out by mismatched bedsheets thumbtacked to the window frames. Knox lay balled up on his side uncovered and naked except for his CPAP mask. He had one arm sticking out with his head on it, his CPAP mask strapped around his skull, the hose extending to the machine on his nightstand. The only sheet on the queen bed was a fitted one that had come loose from the sides, and he lay half on, half off it, the rest of him on the bare blue mattress.

Darla leaned against the doorframe and listened to the quiet hum of the machine. Then she rapped hard on the wooden frame.

Knox startled and struggled with his mask before ripping it off and twisting to look at Darla with bleary eyes. "Jesus, I thought you were the cops." He rubbed around his mouth and nose where the mask had been. His face was still embedded with the shape of it.

"Get dressed. We're going to Purdy's for coffee."

He lay there a bit longer. Then, at once, he sat up and dangled his legs from the side of the bed while he scratched his hairy stomach. "Okay."

Darla enjoyed the roasty smell of Purdy's nearly as much as she liked the coffee. The interior was calming. The owners had exposed a lot of brick and painted the rest of the walls deep earth tones. They had also hung old business signs throughout. Aside from that, the rest of the place was typified by dark wood.

Darla and Knox waited in line behind a bald professor of who-knows-what—there was no doubting his general profession—and ahead of him three pony-tailed sorority girls in gray sweatshirts and black leggings. Though together, the girls were more engaged with their phones than with each other.

Darla stroked Knox's arm. "How late did you stay up last night?"

Knox took in a long slow breath, like he had to gather himself just to talk about it. "Too late. I was almost asleep around one when I got a text from some kid out in Idylwild at a party. I call him, and he wants me to deliver product. I tell him *no*. Like thirty minutes go by and I'm finally almost back asleep and he calls back and wants to know how much for a half ounce if I deliver it. I say two hundred just to get him to go away and he's like, *sold*."

"So, you went out there?"

Knox shrugged. "Two hundred bucks."

"You're getting kind of old for that."

"You're never too old for two hundred bucks."

Darla drew her hand back and looked square at Knox. "What if they were luring you out there to fucking rob you, Knox? You ever think about that stuff?"

"Nah. I know this kid. He's a Saudi. He's got money. Normally he comes by, but they were all too drunk to drive. The only reason they were calling me is all the liquor stores were closed. I get those calls all the time but usually the money's not there. Last night, it was."

Like Gabe, Darla had believed that first pound of pot was all Knox would ever sell. He didn't consult her before reordering. She hadn't signed up to date a pot dealer, it just happened, and she had no say in it. "Bud, you keep this up and you'll be just barely holding your head above water right into broke-ass retirement. That is if you don't go to prison before that."

Knox clamped his lips tight until they made it to the front of the line and gave their order to the little Asian woman working the counter who always worked the counter. She asked where they were going to sit and Darla said upstairs.

They sat in small leather armchairs on either side of a tiny rustic table in the front window looking out on Main Street. The vent near the window blew lightly on the white lace curtain, making it shimmy slightly.

Knox's coffee cup rested on a coaster on the little table. He sat back with his fingers twined across his belly manspreading to his fullest. Darla sat forward, elbows on knees, peering into her cup and at Knox.

"I just have to break out of this cycle. I'm telling you. The economy's on its way back. Porthos will come back with it. Also, my parents are starting to get out from under their bills. Once that happens, I can quit with the other stuff. All I have to do is weather the storm." Knox nodded along with his pontification.

"You really believe that, don't you?"

"Yeah. Why?"

Darla fell quiet. She turned her cup in her hand, trying to get the coffee not to ripple as she did so. A game she played every time she had a cup. Knox looked her over. The answer to his question would never come.

"So, I wanted to let you in on our plans."

Knox creased his brow. "Who's the *our* in this scenario?"

"You and me. We have plans."

"We do?"

"Yep. Now shut the hell up and let me tell you." Darla took a sip. "My little cousin's getting married in Pittsburgh in November. The one I told you about who I used to babysit. It's the first weekend and we're going."

"Isn't he in his thirties?"

"So? He'll always be my little cousin. We can stay with my Aunt Fern. She's got a house in Crafton with an extra bedroom, so we don't have to worry about a hotel. I'd like to go Thursday and come back Monday. I want a little extra time so I don't feel rushed. I didn't figure it'd matter either way since Porthos is closed on Monday anyway."

"I'd miss a lot of fucking work."

"Yep. Me too."

Knox leaned forward, picked up his cup from the saucer, took a long drink, and set it down again. He sat back like he was thinking a moment. "I just don't see how I can do it. That's our busiest time."

"Have Rob cover. Train somebody."

"I mean, that could work for Porthos, but not for the rest."

"I don't give a damn about the rest."

"I don't really have that luxury. I'm under a lot of pressure to sell."

"Having a goddamn life is not a luxury, Knox. I feel like you've forgotten that."

Knox was quiet. His hands were clasped together. "I know what

67

you mean. That's what I'm working for. That's why I can't go out of town like that."

"I understand you think you can't, but you can. You need to. For me. This means something to me. I really don't ask that much."

"Can I think about it? Let me think about."

"I don't see why you should have to think about it, but whatever." Darla clapped her cup onto her saucer and sat examining Knox without speaking.

Knox's slides were off. He shifted his weight and brought one socked foot across his knee. "What do you have today?"

"I'm booked up starting at noon. I probably won't finish until after eight."

"Can you come by late? I'll be done at Porthos by about nine. After that I'll just be minding the shop upstairs. We can watch *So-Called*." Getting stoned and watching episodes of the lone season of *My So-Called Life* was one of the great traditions of Knox and Darla's relationship. Darla held particular affection for the show because it was set in Pittsburgh.

"I can't."

"Why not?"

"Scratch that. It's not that I can't. I don't want to. We'll only get interrupted like fifty times by texts and you getting up to make sales. Then you'll probably get some fucking delivery request you just can't pass up. Sorry. Not into it. Not tonight."

"Are you punishing me?"

"No." Darla polished of her coffee in a long gulp, stood up, and smoothed her clothes. She leaned to Knox and put a peck on his cheek. "But I'm not burning a Saturday night in your apartment watching you deal. Have a good one. I've got to go get ready for my day."

*W*HAT KNOX didn't understand at first, but he later suspected Burl did, was he put Knox in a position to fail. He didn't loan Knox enough to do what he needed to do, and by making Knox deal for him instead of himself, he cut Knox's profit on pot sales way down. Knox also couldn't afford to buy any more of his own supply until he paid Burl. This is the reason there are unions, Knox thought. He had no power to bargain. He was fucked. Porthos was fucked.

The five thousand loan was only enough to replace Porthos's food stock and get a half-assed repair on the walk-in. After that, Knox never could get ahead and never could get Burl paid off. The vig kicked in. Knox was making no more money in pizza than he had before, and he lost most of his side income. He kept selling for Burl just trying to cover the vig, but his percentage was way too low to catch up.

There was no way of paying Burl back. Knox's parents had actually started to right themselves after getting caught up on his dad's medical bills, but Knox couldn't feel it. In fact, he was more broke than ever. He considered going back to poker, but that was a fantasy. The money was already dried up when he quit, which was half the reason he left it, and now that he had to sell Burl's product, he barely ever got away from his apartment or the pizza shop. Knox got Rob to fill in selling for him some, but he couldn't do that too much because he had to pay him something, which was usually weed, and that only put him further behind.

When Knox's finances were at their peak, in the early 2000s, he had managed to get himself to Europe a couple times. He spent ten days in Japan once. He wasn't dating anyone back then, and Porthos was still in good shape. Out of financial necessity, his travel had slowly narrowed. When Darla arrived in town, his reach was pretty short. Now it was nothing. He couldn't even go to Pittsburgh. Even though she was pissed, he held firm. She had no way of knowing just how deep his problems ran.

When Knox accepted the loan from Burl, he didn't tell Darla. If she knew, it would have sent her over the edge, Knox was sure of it. He came within a hair of admitting it when she went to Pittsburgh alone, to try to take the heat off, but he didn't think it would be worth the price he'd pay. If she was mad he didn't go, he could only imagine what she'd say when she found out it was because he borrowed money from Burl without telling her. Plus, it would confirm everything she'd been saying for the last year. It was enough having to reckon with Burl on his ass without amping Darla up too. And Burl was most definitely on his ass.

"You going to have to up your sales there, Fort Knox," Burl kept reminding him. And he did. Not so much in pizza, but in pot. Knox went from picking up two pounds at a time to three. He got more reckless about who he'd do business with and where. Still, each time Burl tabulated what Knox earned and subtracted it from what he owed, all he seemed to do was tread, or go further underwater.

Three points a week didn't sound like a lot, but it was. Burl capitalized every ten weeks. After the very first ten weeks of vig, Knox owed an extra fifteen hundred bucks. And it just kept climbing. He made some dents in it here and there, sure, but he couldn't keep up with the math. Poker math Knox could do, but he used a lot of tricks and shortcuts. Burl didn't seem like he used much math when he played poker—it was almost like he took a break from it—but he sure as hell did in business. Knox mostly had to take his word on the figures. What was Knox going to do? Tell the cops his pot supplier was ripping him off on a usurious loan and giving him a bad cut of weed sales?

Knox became another cog in the works of Burl's operation. He felt like an indentured servant and wondered constantly if Burl had set him up for the situation. Burl managed to get a satellite location in Madison County without having to actually conduct any business there. Although Knox was far from satisfied with the way things stood, he didn't have any significant uneasiness about the arrangement because Burl made no move to call in the debt. Burl was like a redneck credit card Knox couldn't pay that kept sending higher bills.

Knox trudged along, broke and unhappy, but relatively sedate. The change in his anxiety level was sudden and dramatic. Daniel had been absent from the Big Hill store for months. Although he had noticed, Knox didn't make much of it. The new guy just said, "He's quit." Knox didn't see Daniel again until one night when his face turned up on the TV news. Beneath the photo and his name was a tag that said, "Body of Missing Man Found in Jackson County."

Three weeks before Christmas, an Appalachian Wireless employee had stumbled on Daniel, burned to char, on a cell-tower easement near a little hamlet called Egypt in southeast Jackson County. There was a gunshot in the back of his skull. The news crew found the least articulate person in Egypt to interview—like they always did—and that guy said his family had started locking their doors for the first time, and he wanted to know what the world had come to. The local police asked for leads. Knox knew they probably weren't actually looking for any.

Knox could see Daniel on his knees with Greek behind him, a gun in his hand glinting like a hunk of coal. Then Daniel falling forward into the splatter of himself. A can of gas spilling out. A match in the air and a flash. Until his next meeting with Burl, the scene looped through Knox's mind, but it wasn't always Daniel he saw falling and lighting ablaze. He saw himself meeting the same end.

Knox rarely went all the way to Burl's farm anymore. Typically, they met in the room over the arcade where they had played cards. Burl had certain days he conducted business there, and on those days he called Knox in to pay his sales proceeds. After Burl collected his money, he tabulated the current debt. It had climbed to nearly ten thousand in spite of Knox's best efforts. Sometimes Greek was at Burl's side, at other meetings it was another from the revolving cast of surly-eyed heavies who stood second to him. Knox understood that Greek sat atop the hierarchy of Burl's underlings, and he was there with him on the day Knox went in still jittery from the news report.

"What're you thinking, son?" Burl said when Knox crested the stairs in shorts, slides, socks, a winter coat, and a knit cap.

Knox looked from Burl, who was seated at the felt-topped table with an adding machine, ledger book, a stack of what looked like invoices, a blue binder with three-to-a-page checks, and a legal pad covered in writing and numbers, to Greek, who stood nearby with his phone in hand pecking at the screen. Knox braced for another lecture about the importance of paying down the loan he had no hope of paying down. "What?"

"It's twenty goddamn degrees outside. Why in hell are you wearing short pants? Your top half knows it's cold, but your bottom half ain't got no sense at all."

Knox peered at his own legs and feet, knowing just what they looked like but looking anyway. He shrugged. "Keeps me alert."

"Keeps you something," Burl said, now leafing through the legal pad. He settled on a page and tapped his pencil eraser on it. "These numbers don't look too good, Fort Knox. I suspect you know that."

"I know it." Knox's hands were dug deep in the pockets of his heavy coat.

"What're we gonna do with you? You ain't no closer to getting this paid now than you was six months ago, you further."

Knox nodded. Greek looked up from his phone, reached out and tapped Burl on the shoulder, and pointed side to side at Knox.

Burl held up a hand. "I'm sorry, but Greek wants to see them hands. I know it ain't necessary with you, but humor him. He's had a time here lately."

"Seriously?" Knox took them out and immediately began kneading them together.

"What's got into you, Fort Knox? You don't seem yourself? You ain't cutting up or nothing."

"I'm all right." Burl peered at Knox like he was trying to read something written in small print on his forehead. "I was just thinking about something's all."

"What's that?"

"I saw on the news where they found Daniel, and it's got me kind of shaken up."

Burl glanced at Greek so subtly that Knox questioned whether he actually had, but he knew what he'd seen. Burl shifted back in his chair, stuck his legs out, and crossed them at the ankles. "Awful ain't it? Got hisself crossways of somebody. We all tore up about it."

Knox studied Burl. His expression remained unwaveringly serene. Greek held his phone just as he had been, and his head was still down, but his eyes were up looking through his brows. Both seemed to be waiting on Knox.

"Some scary shit," Knox said.

Burl licked his lips. "You can't be too careful. There's some hard people in this world, but even those people do what they do for a reason. I suspect Daniel gave someone a good reason, don't you?"

"I guess so."

"That's the thing about these mountains that's different from

73

cities. Cities is violent. You can get yourself killed in the city any old time, and you ain't even gotta know the person who done it. In the mountains, when someone's killed, it's their kin that done it, or it's someone they know, and it's the knowing that causes it." Burl twisted his lips, like he was trying to free something stuck in his teeth. "Whoever it was done Daniel that way, I suspect Daniel knowed just why. Still, it's damn sad."

Knox wanted to burrow his hands back in his coat but couldn't. With his hands having nowhere to go, he felt off balance. He couldn't tell if he was swaying for real, but it felt like it. He felt like he would fall over.

Burl tapped on his pad again. "About these numbers." He had already moved on. "We got to make some progress. They ain't good. You got any thoughts on how you going to square up on this. I like you, Knox, but I don't aim to carry you forever."

Knox got distracted by that and started to stick his hands back in his pockets. Greek cleared his throat and narrowed his eyes at him. Knox moved them away again, fast as a Catholic girl, and rubbed his palms down the sides of his coat. He started, "I was thinking of something," but lost steam and looked out the window at the brick face of the vacant building across the street. There was a vinyl "For Rent" sign on it so old it'd faded all over and frayed on one end. It shimmied side to side in Knox's vision, although it was still. He drew breath and tried again. "I was thinking, maybe you'd like to own a pizzeria."

Burl shifted his chin and frowned.

"It's just, I've been trying to figure out some way to get this paid down, and the fact is, I can't see how I'm going to. Not the way it's going. I was thinking, I could just sell it to you. Equipment and everything. It's—"

"Naw."

"But it's—"

"Never gonna happen."

"But, I got offered fifty thousand for it all before."

"Maybe you should've took it."

"Maybe I should've."

"Maybe you still should."

"It was this lawyer who buys pizzas from me. I've asked him since, but he says he's moved on. He doesn't have time for it anymore."

Burl shook his head. "Well, I ain't interested neither. Not in a failing pizza shop. Not in Madison County. None of it. You're going to have to come up with something else."

"I wish I could."

"Hell, I wish you would."

DARLA HADN'T seen Knox in her studio in weeks. For years after they got together, he would turn up unannounced and sit and talk with her while she worked. Her regular clients got used to his presence, and so did Darla. He'd come up and burn an hour or two chatting with her and whoever else was there getting ink.

Knox's visits had slacked off. Darla didn't register anything at first, but eventually it was undeniable. Something had changed, and she didn't know what. Him declining to go to Pittsburgh with her only punctuated the shift.

Darla was in the midst of doing an ornate full back for a regular named Janelle. Janelle fascinated Darla because she'd been raised in a Holiness Church, something Darla had never heard of until she moved to Kentucky. Holiness girls wore skirts all the time, didn't cut their hair, couldn't watch TV or go to the movies, and on and on. Janelle rebelled, and when she did, she rebelled hard. She wore her hair in dreads, had gauges, and had spider-bite piercings in her lip and another in her nose. One of the few connections to her past life in the church was that she was a potter, something she learned as a child from a church member.

Like many of the best potters in Kentucky, Janelle lived in Berea. She and her boyfriend were making use of Berea's backyard-chicken ordinance. Janelle lay face down on Darla's tattoo bed, grimacing slightly as she spoke over the buzz of the machine. "No, you don't need a rooster."

"How do the hens lay eggs without a rooster? I thought they had to get laid to lay eggs." Darla never had any trouble talking and working at the same time.

"They don't need to. Hens lay eggs either way, the eggs just aren't fertile if there's no rooster involved. You can still eat them."

"No shit."

"Yeah. They slow down after a few years no matter what, but they keep laying. It's better for us not to have a rooster because the noise would just piss off our neighbors anyway. Plus, who wants to get up that early? I'm good with my girls."

"Do you save a lot on eggs?"

"Hold on," Janelle said and raised her left arm, "I need to shift just a little." Darla withdrew the machine and her hands for a moment while Janelle twisted a bit. "That's better," Janelle said once she had settled again. "Anyway, no, you don't save nothing. At least we don't. We only have four chickens, so we don't buy that much feed at a time, but I don't think we save any money. We just like having chickens is all. It's not like you save money having a dog or a cat. They cost money. It's the same thing for us. The eggs are just a fringe benefit. We can't even eat them all. You want some?"

"You want to trade some eggs for work?"

"Maybe. Or I could just give you some. I don't care."

"I've traded tattoos for food before. I'm not above it."

The door at the base of the stairs below rattled. It was locked because Janelle had her shirt off. After some clicking, it opened and closed. Lumbering footsteps made their way up.

"Speak of the devil," Darla said.

Knox appeared at the top of the stairs. "Oh. Hey, Janelle."

Janelle raised her head and smiled. "Hey, Knox. What are you into?"

"Very little."

Darla sat up. "Well, isn't this a rare occurrence. I thought you lost your key."

Knox held it up. "Nope. Still have it."

"Janelle was just explaining to me the ins and outs of chicken ownership. Did you know they lay eggs even if there's no rooster?"

"Huh. Wow." He took off a winter coat, revealing a black shirt with "Orange Whip?" emblazoned on it.

"You want some eggs, Knox?" Janelle asked. "We've got more eggs than we know what to do with. You're a cook. Maybe you could use some."

Even though Janelle was talking, Knox's eyes were on Darla. There was a little delay before he seemed to register the question. "Maybe."

"You feeling okay?" Darla dabbed a little more ink but was examining Knox.

"I'm fine. Just tired."

Darla leaned into Janelle again to resume her work. "You seem a little touched. Maybe you should get some rest."

Knox slumped into a chair without responding.

"Next time I'm up, I'm going to bring you guys some eggs," Janelle said.

Janelle and Darla carried on their conversation with Knox sitting alongside, rarely interjecting. Janelle didn't seem to make anything of it. Darla stayed engaged in her work, but every now and then she stole a glance at Knox. Normally he wouldn't shut up. She knew something wasn't right.

Once Darla had finished the session with Janelle, she was done for the day. After Janelle left, Knox sat in Darla's studio while she cleaned up. They wound up in the same place they seemed to so often.

"If you don't want to do it, then don't do it."

Knox didn't look at her. His eyes were down. "It's not that simple."

"Why the fuck not? Most people in the world don't deal pot, Knox. It's not complicated. If you're doing it just to keep Porthos open, it's time to let go."

"I have to think about my parents."

"Yeah, because your parents definitely want you dealing. Jesus, Knox, how long are you going to have to prop them up. I thought you told me they were starting to dig out."

"They are. They're doing better."

"Well, maybe it's time for them to get by on their own. I know your dad's getting up there, and he's got the Parkinson's issue, but has your mom *ever* worked?"

Knox shook his head, lips pursed.

"Times is hard, dude. Maybe, just maybe, she could get a part-time job. She could be the 'Welcome to Meijer' lady and hand out sale flyers or something. I know, gasp. Your mom actually *work*. My mom has worked her whole life. She's seventy-three. Your mom's not that old."

He looked at Darla, his eyes wide. "You don't understand. My dad won't let that happen."

"Maybe it's not up to him. You're out here basically wasting your life and risking your freedom selling goddamn weed. You're still barely scraping by. Is that all because your dad doesn't want your mom to work? Not everyone has that luxury."

"It's not just them, though. I couldn't keep Porthos going without it, either."

"Then don't keep Porthos going." Darla threw a waded paper towel across the room into the wall and it fell on the closed trash bin below. She stood with her hands on her hips staring Knox down. "You keep saying it's coming back. It's not coming back. The economy has turned, Knox. If Porthos didn't turn with it, it's not going to. That's the hard truth. You've got fifteen years' experience running a restaurant and you work your ass off. I know you do. Someone will want you."

"There's nowhere around here that'll pay anything."

"Porthos doesn't pay you shit anyway. If there's nothing here, let's go." She pointed her open hand at the steps leading down. "I'm ready. I've had two national magazine spreads. I get offers all the time. I could be working in a lot hotter market than Richmond, Kentucky. I can go anywhere."

"Lucky you."

"It's not luck. I earned it."

Knox's eyes were down again. "Well, have fun. I can't go."

Darla took a step closer. She was right in front of him, shouting now. "Why can't you go? You don't have any good reason!"

Knox stood up fast, and, for the first time, he was shouting, too. "Because I fucking can't, okay! I came up here because everything is shit, and all you do is make it more shit. So, thank you. You want to tell me what I should do but you don't understand anything. I'm fucking stuck, okay. I'm fucking stuck."

Darla shook her clenched fist beside her face. "Why are you stuck? Explain it to me."

Knox's eyes had gotten wild, but they slowly receded back to calm. His body was swollen out like an animal trying to defend itself from a fight it didn't really want. It shrank back, too. He seemed to start to say something again and again, but each time stopped himself. Eventually, he said, "I just am."

Knox and Darla stood looking at each other for the longest time. Knox had his hands at his sides doing nothing, as if he was anticipating what would come next and didn't know how to be. She waited for him. She needed more than he seemed willing to give her, because his path, his choices, his stubbornness, they made no sense.

Darla finally pulled another towel from the roll and went back to cleaning. Knox watched her without moving from his spot. Then he pulled his coat back on and disappeared down the stairs without another word, leaving her alone.

*A*FTER KNOX graduated Franklin County High School, he never looked back. Never wanted to go back to Frankfort at all. He moved to Richmond to take classes at EKU and stayed through the summers. He started working at Grover's Pizza during his sophomore year. By his junior year, he had dropped out of school to help manage the place. He was twenty-six when he bought it and renamed it Porthos. He rented the building and paid three hundred dollars a month for three years to his old boss for the business. He became entrenched in Richmond, but that was okay with him, so long as he wasn't in Frankfort, a place where he never felt like he fit.

Only one thing drew him back to Frankfort: his parents. Being an only child, there was pressure on him to at least stay close. Since Porthos was closed on Mondays, his mother would prod him to come have dinner. The week after his fight with Darla, he went.

Knox's parents' house was out a ways, five miles from the second Frankfort exit off I-64 headed west toward Louisville. It lay on the crest of an acre and a half of countryside, surrounded by low chain-link fence. The red brick ranch was built in the fifties and bought by Knox's parents in the early seventies before he was born. Knox's mother had painted the wood paneling in the dining room white.

It was the same stuff that was there when they moved in. Knox's parents had come from Hazel Green in Wolfe County when his dad took a state job. He lasted a few years with the state before getting his CDL.

Knox loved a nice piece of fish. His mother's salmon patties didn't quite qualify. Made of canned salmon, saltines, onions, salt, and a few other modest ingredients, she pan-fried the blobs in oil on her stovetop so that even after they were gone the scent of them lingered for three-and-a-half days. Knox didn't dislike them, but their appeal was based more on nostalgia than anything. His parents, on the other hand, marked salmon-pattie nights as special occasions.

In spite of the fact it was a salmon-pattie night, Knox's parents were sour and grumbling. "Could we turn off the news while we eat?" Knox asked.

His dad's eyes didn't move but his head shuddered just a bit. "I'm watching it."

"That's kind of the problem. Do you like being pissed off?"

"We like being informed, Knox," his mother said.

Knox pointed at the set. "If you really want to be informed, you should probably try a different channel." He looked from his dad to his mom as they visibly bristled. "They'll still be ranting about this same stuff after I leave. Could you at least turn something else on while I'm here? How about 'Wheel of Fortune'?"

"Pay attention and you might learn something," his dad said.

"Oh, I'm learning something."

His dad squeezed his napkin in his unstable hand and finally looked Knox's way, "What does that mean?"

"All I mean is, I think we'd could have a lot better dinner if we watched 'Wheel of Fortune,' or something like that. You guys love that show."

"Oh, fine." Knox's mom got up, took the remote from the back of the plaid couch, and turned on the game show. Knox's blood pressure immediately dropped at the sound of Pat Sajak's voice. He got the feeling his parents' did too, only they weren't happy about it. He decided quiet was the best balm for the current situation, so he went back to his food and watched the wheel go round.

After dinner was done, and Knox's mom was clearing the dishes, his parents seemed to have forgotten they had been aggrieved by changing the channel. Knox had gently transitioned to probing about their finances, because theirs and his were inextricably linked.

"We've about got flush," his dad said. "I'm hoping we can get by without calling on you for anything this month."

"That would be good," Knox said. "You know I don't mind helping, but I've been a little thin myself, lately."

Knox's dad got a grave look. His mother, who had carried a stack of dishes to the sink, stilled and looked to the table where Knox and his father still sat.

Knox looked from his dad to his mom, and back again. "I mean, I'm okay. We're always a little slow after the holidays. I just need a few weeks for things to rev back up."

"We certainly intend to pay you back everything," his dad said.

"No, no, I don't even care about that. I was just saying, it's good that you guys are getting back on your feet."

"Your father has worked all he can." Knox's mom's brow was knit. "It's been a struggle."

"I know that. It's okay. I'm glad I could help. You all poured a ton of money into me over the years. I haven't done much at all next to that."

"We intend to pay you back," his dad repeated. "Every cent."

"I know you will, Dad." Knox studied his father, who in spite of his best efforts, shook the slightest bit all the time. "But it would be okay if you didn't."

"I'm going to." His father seemed absolutely sincere in his belief that he would someday pay Knox back in full. Maybe in death—they had a house after all—but in life, there was no way. With each passing day, Knox's parents' financial possibilities became slimmer. The longer he looked at his father, the longer he wondered whether he was looking in a sort of generational mirror.

There was a clatter in the sink when Knox's mom finally laid down the stack of dishes she had taken over there. She turned the water on and began scrubbing. Knox used the sound as an excuse to look away from his father for a moment. When he looked back at him, his father's eyes were still on him, and his resolute expression hadn't changed.

*W*HEN DARLA took her last appointment of the day depended largely on the size of the piece and the complexity. She normally aimed to finish her nights by at least eight, even on weekends, which was atypical for a lot of tattoo artists.

Clients ran the gamut, from great to lousy, easy to difficult, generous tippers to irritating hagglers. Tattoo artists' patience with bad behavior varied similarly depending on talent level. Darla had reached a stature where she didn't have to put up with much. Richmond wasn't a particularly lucrative market, but she had all the work she wanted, and turned away clients who had burned her in the past.

She had no reason to turn away a low-voiced man who called her studio in January asking for a late appointment on a Wednesday. He explained with economy that his work schedule required that he come in, "as late as possible, whenever that is." He wanted only a half-inch-by-half-inch one-color tattoo. Darla booked him for a 7:30 appointment and collected a deposit of the full price just in case he stood her up.

It was long dark by 7:30 on the night of his appointment.

Ten minutes went by and he still hadn't shown up. Darla called the number he left but it went to voicemail without ringing. The account wasn't set up, so the call disconnected. After fifteen minutes, she chalked it as a no-show and started down the stairs to lock the door so she could finish closing up.

Halfway down, a man entered. He looked up the stairs at her. His clothes were dark. His head jumped out from that background. His close-cut hair and sideburns were white as a bar of Ivory soap. His skin tone was similarly pale.

Darla stopped with her hand on the rail. "Are you Kyle Staley?"

"That's right."

"You're late."

His expression never changed. "Yeah. I warned you about that."

Darla didn't move. Something in her said to tell the man he was out of luck, but something louder said to give him what he had already paid for. "Come on up, I guess."

The man followed Darla. As she washed her hands, he took off his coat and hung it on the coatrack on the wall. A black chest holster crisscrossed his body which he also removed and hung beside his coat leaving him in a plain charcoal t-shirt. Solid black tattoos began on his hands and were scattered up his pale arms and into his shirtsleeves.

She snapped on a pair of gloves. "You a cop?"

His chin was cocked down so that he seemed to be looking at her through the top half of his eyes. "No."

As it turned out, all the man wanted was a single black bat on his forearm to join the two dozen or so already there. Darla asked for details as he filled out his paperwork. He only responded, "Make it match, but make it different."

Normally painstaking in her work, Darla hurried to prep the man's arm as he sat staring straight ahead, not speaking. She chose a needle she could outline and fill with both. She got a #9 ink cap and added black pigment. She had fired her machine and begun to outline a simple bat with wings fully extended when the door at the base of her stairs opened and closed and footsteps made their way up.

A little man in a red shirt with silver snaps and stitching at the breast wearing dark blue jeans and boots with shiny silver toes reached the top. He removed a black Western hat revealing a somewhat compacted pompadour. "Ain't you done yet, Greek?"

Realization was immediate. Darla drew the machine away from the pale man's arm and her eyes took in the little man more fully. She caught herself and tried to seem casual, but she knew it was too late. He had seen. She resumed her work, but even though she didn't know these men, she *knew* these men, and she kicked herself for not grasping it sooner. Knox, not one for discretion, had told her all about Burl and Greek. They might have just happened into her studio, but from everything she had heard of them, that wasn't the case.

"It ain't nothing but a little bitty bat. I'd have thought you could scribble that goddamn critter in about a minute. How much you charge a square foot anyway? I paid for the damn thing."

"It was fifty."

Burl prodded a tooth with his pinkie as he came in for a closer look. "Well, he earned it." He pointed at Greek's arm with the spit-moistened finger. "You see, most of them fucking things he earned overseas, but that one he got him right here. It's untelling when he'll get him another one."

Darla trained her eyes down at her work, not allowing herself to so much as peek at Burl again until she'd finished filling the little bat with black. Burl prattled on about the tattoo with what seemed to be some purpose that escaped her in the moment. She killed her machine once she was satisfied and let Greek examine it. His nod was subtle but perceptible. She cleaned him and bandaged him and had him ready for the door as quickly as she could.

Greek had returned his holster to his chest and put his jacket on when Burl snapped his fingers, causing Greek to still. "I wish I could tip you, but I can't."

Darla was tidying her work area, throwing away all her disposable items. "No?"

"Naw. That'd be more money moving the wrong direction. You know why that is?"

Darla had stopped and was staring at Burl who stared right back. It became clear he wouldn't go on until she answered him. "I don't."

"Ask that boyfriend of yours. He'll know." Burl replaced his hat on his head and tipped it Darla's way. "It was a pleasure making your acquaintance." He pulled his thumb at the stairwell. "Let's go to the house, Greek."

Darla didn't move again until the door down the stairs had opened and closed. Once it had, she went down, locked the bolt, and turned out the stairwell light. She sat on the third step staring out the glass door at the sidewalk lighted by street lamps. Now and then a person or two would pass by never suspecting Darla was sitting just a few feet away, wringing a paper towel in her hands.

*I*T HAD been a slow night at Porthos for both pizza and weed. Wednesdays were unpredictable like that. Sometimes people started their weekends early and things would be jumping. Other times it was more like Tuesday part two. Knox and Rob speculated about the phases of the moon playing a role, but really, they could never put their finger on why some days were better than others.

The only person who came in the door the whole night was a red-haired mountain kid packing a sticker-laden guitar case. He wanted to know if they'd let him play in there. Once he took stock of the place, he seemed to lose interest and shuffled out. Knox had retreated to his apartment and left Porthos in the hands of Rob and a driver named Anthony. Knox was on standby if things unexpectedly got hairy. He was on his couch with his nose deep in a volume of *Lone Wolf and Cub* he had already read when his phone chirped beside him.

It was a text from Darla. *Where are you?*

Apartment. He watched the screen for a response, but nothing came. He went back to the book. A few minutes later, the lock rattled on his alley door and Darla came in. He found a carry-out menu on his coffee table and stuck it in his book.

He stood up, expecting her to come kiss him. "Hey, baby. You came to see me."

"Yeah, you could say that." Darla didn't approach the couch. She went to his wingback chair, which was under a pile of stuff, per usual. She gathered up everything and flung it.

"Something wrong?"

Darla exhaled hard as she sat. "Guess who was just at my shop?"

"Bob Newhart?"

She glared at him. "Fuck off. This is serious."

"Okay. Sorry. I have no idea."

"Greek the fucking famous albino. And guess who was with him?"

"Aw shit." Knox's forehead dropped into his left hand.

"Burl the goddamn sawed-off cowboy. How you fucking like that?"

"What'd they want?"

"Oh, you know, a fucking bat tattoo, to match his fifty other ones."

"That's it?"

"Burl was talking some shit about how Greek had just earned it. How he got the old ones overseas, but he got this one here. You have any idea what in the fuck that's about?"

Knox did have an idea. Daniel. He stared down at the book in his right hand. Then he raised his eyes and looked directly at Darla. "I have no clue."

"Yeah, well, he also said he couldn't tip me because of some shit that made it sound like you owe him money. That little pygmy fucker was all mysterious about everything. The only thing that wasn't mysterious was that they came in there for the express purpose of fucking with me." Darla jabbed her finger at Knox. "And that's because of you. Do you owe Burl money?"

Knox squeezed the book in his hands. "A couple hundred bucks." He shook his head. "Nothing big."

"So, they came to my shop, Greek wearing a fucking giant gun, and scared the piss out of me because you owe Burl a couple hundred bucks?"

"I mean, I don't know why they did all that—Greek's kind of scary in the first place—but I only owe him a couple hundred bucks. I was a little short the last time I picked up, so I owe him. It's no big deal. Maybe he really just wanted a tattoo."

Darla looked at Knox, not saying anything, blinking a few times. "You know, when I was growing up, if me or my brothers tried to pull some shit, and we wouldn't own up to it, my dad always said the same thing: 'There's a rat in the woodpile somewhere.'" Darla pointed at him again. "There's a rat in this fucking woodpile, Knox." A loud knock came from the door at the base of the stairs. Knox looked at Darla, questioning. She cuffed the air.

He shrugged, but he had seldom been so grateful to hear someone at that door. He shouted, "Come on up!"

Rob reached the top of the stairs pretty quickly with a serious look, but when he saw Darla there, he broke into a smile. "Hey, Darla. Where you been hiding? You haven't been coming around much lately."

"Same old place."

"You should come see us more. We miss you."

"Yeah. I don't know."

"Well, I hate to break up this visit with bad news, but we've got a situation. I don't know what he was doing—if he was texting or what—but Anthony took out a mailbox. Like one of the big ones that belong to the post office. Cops are there. They let him call me. He's got two deliveries with him and I've got one more hanging. Somebody's going to have to go meet him and make those runs."

Knox frowned at Darla, as if saying, What am I supposed to do?

She stood up and turned to go. "Y'all handle your business.

This shit's not going anywhere." There was a stack of board games that didn't really seem like they were in her way, but she kicked them over. A few playing pieces spilled out. She didn't break stride. "Ever."

*I*F KNOX was paying attention at all, he would've realized what it meant when Darla stopped coming around. He chalked it up to her being busy. To her needing space. They had gone through down phases before and it always blew over. He didn't see any difference this time even though the difference should have been plain.

After a stretch of a few weeks with little contact, he went to her shop with a peace offering of some Bubba Kush he'd skimmed. Climbing the stairs, his spirits rose at the smell of green soap. When she told him her plans, it was like he had slipped on a patch of ice: it was sudden and shocking. But it shouldn't have been.

"Austin? Fucking Texas? When were you going to tell me?"

"I'm pretty sure I just did." She was closing her studio for the night, wiping down her counters. She didn't look up from it. She already had her equipment put up.

"But, why? Why so far?"

"I got an offer to come down and share space in a really good shop. I felt like I should take it. I've been pretty fucking unsettled. You had to know that."

"I guess I didn't."

She turned to him, a towel gripped in her right hand pressed against her hip. "How the fuck do you not know that? How's that even possible? Your fucking weed supplier came in here talking all cryptic with some goddamn goon with a gun the size of my arm. You don't think I'm unsettled by that? What the fuck, Knox. Are you really that fucking thick?"

"I don't think they're serious."

"Are you fucking kidding me? That's your whole fucking problem. You wade into this shit, and you don't think it's serious. Smoking weed may not be all that serious, but people who live off it by god are. When someone can go to prison if they get caught, they take it seriously." Darla glanced two fingers off her temple. "Do you even realize you're one of those people now? The people up the chain from you will hurt whoever they have to. Don't you get it? I'm a fucking target, dumbass. That's why they came here. To send you a message."

Knox rustled the bag of Bubba in his front pocket. "I don't know. Greek has a lot of tattoos. Maybe it's coincidence."

"Are you being serious right now? If you're being serious, you're a goddamn idiot. If you're joking, then you're an asshole. Which is it?"

"I guess I'm an idiot, then. Thanks."

"Oh, boo-hoo." Darla balled a fist and put it to the corner of her eye. "I hurt your feelings? Good. Maybe you'll wake up. I know you're lying to me. I don't know exactly what's going on, but those guys weren't here over a couple hundred bucks, and you aren't glued to your apartment over a little bit of money. Something flipped and I don't know what, but I'm not staying to be in the middle of it. I'm gone. It's not like all this was easy."

"You're making it look easy."

"It got easier here at the end. Jesus."

"What if I quit? What if I stopped dealing?"

"That'd be great. That'd probably be the best decision you ever made. I'm still leaving. I already committed. It's done." Her expression was neutral.

95

"What about me? You don't think you committed anything to me?"

"Please. Commitment goes two ways. Part of your commitment was not putting me in fucking danger." She swiveled back to her work. "You were the only thing keeping me here. I can have a studio anywhere. I'm ready for it to be someplace else."

"What am I supposed to do?"

"I don't fucking know. I made it pretty goddamn obvious I was scared and you didn't do anything. Anything. I didn't even see you. You didn't even bother."

"I thought you needed space."

"Ha. Guess what? You were right. And I'm getting it."

He couldn't think of anything to say to that, so he slumped onto her love seat. "This isn't fair."

"It's very fair."

"It's not."

Darla came nearer to him. She pulled a chair her way, sat, and stared at him as he stared back. "Knox, I love you. I do. But it's time for me to go. We had fun. I wish you the best. I hope I'm wrong about some things, but fuck—what am I supposed to say? Neither of us ever said it was forever. It started one day, and now it's ending. That's okay. It was good. It got less good. Let's remember what was good."

"This is bullshit."

"Oh, I agree. Absolutely. I've been saying that for a long time."

She told him she already gave notice at her studio and apartment. She'd be gone within a week. All that was left was to wrap things up, load a U-Haul, and go. She asked for help moving, and he told her "fuck no."

When the day came, Knox and Rob plodded to Third Street to help Darla load her things. She was all packed, so there was nothing to do but move furniture and boxes from the dull hardwood floors to her rented truck. They hefted one load after another down the narrow stairwell, turning couches, tables, and box springs this way and that to make them fit.

Soon, Darla's apartment was all blank tan walls, some toiletries, and a suitcase. After Rob slid the last box into the back of the truck, Darla gave him a long hug out on the sidewalk. He said, "Take care of yourself."

"You do the same. Watch out for this lug, too. Try to keep him out of trouble." She knuckled Knox in the shoulder.

"If only I knew how."

"He fights it."

Darla and Knox wound up alone in her empty apartment. She dipped a finger into her cleavage. "I'm so sweaty. It's not supposed to be eighty in March. Of course that's the day I pick."

"It's global warming telling you not to go to Texas."

"I'm going to have to take a shower."

"You want me to leave?"

"I want you to get in with me."

"You serious?"

She pulled off her skin-tight, damp, baby-doll shirt. "Old times' sake." She stepped out of her shorts and went in her bathroom. Knox felt like he should resist. That he shouldn't give in because of the way she'd handled leaving him. Instead he stripped down and followed her in. They had one last go in her shower, they dried off, and they got dressed. He followed her down to the sidewalk.

"Austin's not that far, love." She laid her hand on Knox's chest. "You ever get away from all this, come see me."

"I don't know how—"

"Shhh." She held up her hand to quiet him. "If you want to come, you'll find a way."

They kissed, and Darla was gone.

$\mathcal{K}$**NOX WAS** a tank. Always had been. He could get drunk, get high, stay up all night, generally mistreat the shit out of his body, but still drag his fat self out of bed, open Porthos, and work all day. He rarely swerved outside his wheelhouse of substances: alcohol and pot. Every now and then, when the conditions were right, Rob jumped the fence around his neighbors' cow pasture in Poosey, and he and Knox would partake of some pilfered mushrooms, but that was about it. Well, except the coke. Knox had a short dalliance with cocaine in his early thirties, but it was a passing fancy. And a few pain pills ingested for sport, but he didn't much enjoy them.

Since he had hit forty, Knox's threads had begun to show a bit. In the days after Darla left, he stayed sober during the day, but when night fell, he descended. He called and texted with her, and at first she indulged him in long talks and text strings, but he was always drunk/high as hell, and at some point there wasn't much more for her to say. She told him if he missed her that much, come to Texas. His calls and texts went unanswered and unreturned more frequently as the days passed. When he couldn't reach her for a stretch, he tried watching *My So-Called Life* to kindle some feeling of closeness, but he got too sad, so he had to turn it off.

Rob still opened Porthos most of the time because Knox was staying up half the night drinking and smoking, then sleeping late. He had taken to having employees and even some bud customers hang out with him just so he wasn't alone. This was during his prime sales hours for pot. Drunk and stoned wasn't a real good state for someone who was also trafficking. It was especially problematic because Burl had just sent him a pound of Girl Scout Cookies, a hybrid strain of weed that had a huge THC content. Knox was hitting it hard. It helped him feel better, but in a business that was best conducted sober, profound impairment was a bit of a problem.

Knox got a late-night text from one of his regulars named Angelo asking if he had a half pound of anything he would sell. Angelo owned a small landscaping company he operated from his place on Red House Road, which was out in the county. He was a former EKU frat boy now in his thirties who made a good living cutting grass. He always had money during mowing season and bought full ounces pretty often. He very seldom bought less than a slice at a time, which was an eighth of an ounce, the name being derived from the fact that most large pizzas have eight slices.

A half pound was something altogether different, and even in an acutely addled state, Knox knew he shouldn't do it. Angelo was normally pretty lighthearted and fun to deal with, but for whatever reason, his texts were short and insistent. Knox had a half pound of the Girl Scout Cookies still wrapped tight, and it crossed his mind that there was no way it would get back to Burl if he sold it all at once because Angelo was always so solid.

If Knox were still able to buy weight from Burl, a pound of Girl Scout Cookies would have been fourteen hundred dollars. If he sold the whole thing in small quantities, it would have brought back about four thousand, so he would've cleared twenty-six hundred. Knox's cut from Burl on that pound was only 10 percent, so he would make four hundred dollars for the same amount of work.

What sucked him in was when Angelo said he would pay three

thousand for a half pound if Knox would bring it to him. When Knox asked why he needed that much, Angelo said he was leaving town to go fishing in the morning. For some reason, that made sense to Knox. Because people need a half pound of pot to fish. Also, when Knox ran the numbers through the calculator on his phone, he realized he would clear an extra thousand on the full pound if he did the deal with Angelo for half of it. That was an extra thousand on top of his four-hundred-dollar commission. So even though the Angelo deal didn't really make sense, the numbers did from Knox's end.

What it really came down to was, even though he was glued to his couch, drunk, stoned, and sweaty, Knox missed Darla terribly. He didn't appreciate her while she was around, but now that she was gone, he couldn't get over it. With an extra thousand bucks in his pocket, he could go to Austin for at least a couple days. He could drive, stay cheap along the way, and Rob would probably be willing to deal with his absence because he was so sick of seeing Knox mope. If he left on a Sunday after day shift, he'd get there by Monday night. He could head back on Wednesday and work the Thursday night shift. He would only miss two days of work. Doable.

Knox rose from his couch on unsteady legs, stuck the bundle of Girl Scout Cookies in a plastic grocery bag, and headed down the alley to the parking lot, zig-zagging in spite of his best efforts to walk in a straight line.

Second Street turned into Red House Road near Madison Central High School. The farther Knox got from downtown Richmond, the darker the night became. The city lights receded altogether not long after he passed the seedy strip mall beyond the school. Once Knox crossed Union City Road, it was black as pitch. The stars were out but the moon was thin. Most of the homes on Red House sat back off the roadway and were visible only if their porchlights were on.

Angelo's place was several miles outside town. Knox felt like he was driving pretty decent. There weren't many cars out and he never saw a cop. He hit the rumble strips on the side of the road only six or eight times all the way there. His vision was hazy, and all the lights he saw were multiplied, but all in all he felt competent driving. Knox had never been to an actual rodeo, but if driving fucked up *was* a rodeo, this wasn't his first.

Angelo's driveway had a metal farm gate at the bottom maybe fifteen yards off the road. His house, not visible from the road, sat up the drive behind some woods. Angelo had said he would meet Knox at the gate. When Knox pulled in, he didn't see anyone. He sat in his car, squinting into the darkness up the drive, looking for movement. He texted Angelo and waited. Angelo texted back that he was on his way down. When nothing happened for a few minutes, Knox finally decided to get out. He left his lights on so he could see up the driveway, his engine running and his door open.

Knox padded up to the gate with the glare of his headlights at his back. Bugs buzzed and chirped at top volume. The rhythmic sound was everywhere around Knox in the crisp air. The atmosphere smelled of clean water and newly green plants. He put his hands on the red metal gate, damp from dew, and peered up the drive. "Hello?" he shouted. "Angelo. Where you at, man?"

All that came back was the incessant drone of the nocturnal bugs. Wind rolled through and ruffled the young leaves. Then, behind him, a sound cut through the rest: creaking. Knox spun and was blinded by his own car lights, but they weren't steady. They sunk a fraction, and there was activity in the car. Knox moved that way, ponderously, lumbering to his open door, his own breathing oddly loud in his ears.

As he came around the car door, a body thrust headfirst out and threw its elbow into Knox's taut, bulbous gut, forcing the wind out of him like he was an untied balloon. He didn't feel himself fall; he was just suddenly on the ground. Feet pounded the pavement away, in what direction, Knox didn't know. He was too disoriented to understand much more than that he was on asphalt and couldn't catch his breath. He looked up at the clusters of stars above him, and it occurred to him that they looked like the lights from small towns on the ground when you were in an airplane at night. Something he hadn't seen in years. Not since he had the money to travel. And he marveled that he thought of this in the moment of his defeat, because he already knew, without having to look, that the half pound of Girl Scout Cookies that were the key to his reunion with Darla were under the man's arm when he hit Knox in his belly.

$\mathcal{A}$NGELO HAD been in jail the whole time. He'd gotten into an argument on a client's front lawn when the guy refused to pay a bill. The client's wife called the cops. Things went bad after the police showed up. Bad enough that they decided to arrest Angelo for disorderly conduct. Then he shoved one of the cops and got himself tased. The police turned up his stash while arresting him, so he got a possession charge. They also tacked on a DUI since he had driven there, because why not? The basic facts were in the online edition of the *Richmond Register*. Knox found out the rest after Angelo got out of jail.

Angelo's mowing crews were made up of sketchy locals, high-school kids, and migrant Mexicans. Angelo's best guess was that a guy named Gerald who mowed for him had used his phone to set Knox up, because he never saw Gerald or his phone after he got out, but Gerald knew where Angelo got his weed. Gerald had a felony rap sheet, but he was a hard worker, not that he would ever work for Angelo again. It really didn't matter to Knox because he couldn't go to the police and he couldn't go to Burl, both for different reasons, but in each case, it boiled down to it would only make it worse. The Girl Scout Cookies were gone and not coming back.

That represented a two-thousand-dollar shortfall. Deep shit had just gotten deeper.

A driver no-showed that week's Thursday opening shift—a frequent occurrence at Porthos. Rob had called Knox down to run deliveries. During a lull between runs, Rob leaned against the pizza makeline while Knox stood at the catch end of the double-stack conveyor oven holding a peel, the giant wooden-handled metal spatula used to get pizzas out of the oven, waiting for a pie to come out.

"Dude, I still can't wrap my head around it. Why would you go out there?"

Knox bit his lip. "Because I'm a fucking idiot. Because I was fucked up. Because both."

"Goddamn. Two grand. How are you going to make up two grand?"

"I'm still trying to figure that out. Suggestions are welcome."

Rob massaged his chin. "What about all that shit you have up in your apartment. Could you sell any of that? Do you have anything up there that's actually valuable you could get rid of?"

Knox shook his head.

"No? Nothing that's valuable? In all that stuff?"

"It's valuable to me. I've got stuff worth twenty or thirty bucks to the right buyer, but nothing where I could hit the whole lick in one sale." Knox grimaced and looked upward.

"What?"

"Forget it."

"Why'd you make that face?"

"There's one thing, but it'd kill me."

"What is it?"

Knox looked down and away. "*Prisoner of Azkaban*. Copyright to Joanne Rowling."

"I thought it was J. K. Rowling."

"It is, and they messed it up. That's why it's valuable. I bought it when I was in England. Mine's not even in good shape, but it's worth at least a couple grand. I can't do it though."

"You have all that shit and the only thing that's worth any real money is that one book?"

"That's the only thing worth more than, like, fifty bucks. I'd have to sell tons of stuff and get top dollar. I don't have time for that."

"Except the book?"

"Except the book."

"What happens if you go to Burl without his money?"

Knox thought of Daniel on that cell-tower site. He must've made a face.

"I get it," Rob said. "When do you meet Burl again?"

"Eight days."

"You've got three days to come up with a better idea, then we're selling your fucking book, so get used to it."

There were no better ideas. There was nothing else. There was never going to be another outcome. Knox handed the book over to Rob on Saturday night. Rob sold it for him online. Knox couldn't bring himself to be involved. *Prisoner of Azkaban* netted a shade over twenty-three hundred dollars. Alone, in his apartment, after Rob brought him the money, Knox sat on his couch with the lights and TV off, and he wept.

*T*ORI BRANCH had no intention of applying for a job when she went in Porthos to pick up a carryout. She usually just got delivery, but by August her loan money was getting thin. Plus, she had time on her hands. She had finished her last few credits for her degree during the summer session. The help-wanted sign on the register snared her interest: "Make Dough Making Dough. Now Hiring, All Positions. Management Opportunities Abound. All Shifts."

After she paid for her pizza, Tori lingered at the counter. On a lark, she asked the girl working, "Hey, do you think I could get an application?"

The girl had her short sleeves rolled up revealing a tattoo on her right bicep of little red riding hood holding a big knife. Riding hood's cloak nearly matched the black-cherry Kool-Aid color of the girl's brightly dyed hair. She stared at Tori momentarily like she didn't understand. Then she looked under the counter for no more than three seconds before she gave up and addressed someone unseen in the kitchen. "Hey, Rob, somebody wants an application," she said with marked vocal fry. She turned her back on Tori, took her phone from the waistband of her black yoga pants, and walked away.

A voice from the kitchen came back, "Hold on."

Tori held her pizza with the box half on, half off the black Formica counter. The air was heavy with the smell of baking dough. It was an intoxicating smell in the moment, but would seem less so after it permeated Tori's clothes and hair and lingered all day. She wore a Nike Dri-FIT t-shirt, athletic shorts, and Saucony running shoes the same color as the Ms. Pac-Man on the side of the game cabinet in the Porthos lobby. Tori had been the tallest person in her fifth-grade class and grew to a rangy five feet eleven, which compelled her to play volleyball in high school at Ballard in Louisville. She wasn't that good at volleyball, but it helped her avoid basketball.

A guy in his mid-to-late twenties came from the kitchen in a royal-blue Porthos Pizza t-shirt with a white fleur-de-lis on it. The shirt looked two-tone because the front was dusted in flour. He hadn't shaved in days. The red bandana on his head was wet with sweat, as was his blond pony-tailed hair, his face, his everything. He was shorter than Tori. He dried his hands on a brown paper towel as he approached. He reached under the counter, came up with a single application, and laid it on Tori's pizza box. "You can fill it out and bring it back during business hours."

"Is there anyone I should give it to?"

He shrugged. "Whoever." Then he squinted one eye. "Probably not Meredith. You give it to her and maybe we see it, maybe we don't. Meredith was just up here."

"You're Rob?"

"You got it."

Tori stuck out her hand and said, "Thanks." Rob looked at it. Then he looked at his own. He took Tori's hand. Tori didn't realize that kitchen workers hesitate to shake because it means they have to wash their hands again.

The application was short and at the bottom it had the website address where it had been downloaded. Tori started to leave with it and her pizza, then turned back to the counter. "You know what, if I can borrow a pen, I'll just fill it out now."

Rob glanced around, found a plastic cup next to the register with pens in it, and laid a black one with no cap on the counter. "Okay, I've got to catch some pizzas real quick." He went back into the kitchen.

Tori put her purse down and sat at one of the tables in the lobby. The dingy floor was a shade of gray that had clearly been lighter when it was laid. Traces of the old shade were visible now only at the corners and along the walls. Old video games dinged and pinged around her. About a third had out-of-order signs taped to their screens.

Tori worked on the application with her brown pizza box beside her. It was a splurge for her to get Porthos, considering her dwindling finances. They were pricey, but they had the best pizza. The shop was a dive, but they had the best pizza. They weren't really all that fast, but they had the best pizza. They didn't always get your order right, but they had the best pizza.

After she finished the application, she took it to the counter. Meredith came back, but when she saw Tori standing there, she said, "Rob," and walked away again.

Rob returned to the counter. "Looks like you're done." He took the paper and reviewed the scratched-in application. Without raising his eyes, he said, "So you've never worked in food service?"

"Not really."

"Not at all?"

Tori shook her head. "Unless you count a lemonade stand."

"You in school?"

"I just graduated."

"EKU?"

"Yep. I'm taking some time to figure out my next move. Probably law school, but I'm not totally sure. If I decide to go, I won't start until next fall, so I'm looking for something to do for at least a year."

Rob said, "Huh." He tightened his eyes at something on the application. Then he looked up. "I'm assuming you can pass a criminal background check." He flopped his hand back and forth in front of him. "Small stuff's okay. Pot, public intox, that kind of thing. Just no stealing, or murder, or whatnot."

"Is it cool if I'm in a street gang?" Tori smirked.

"I guess," Rob deadpanned, "but don't be recruiting in here." He pointed at a line on the application. "You didn't put anything down for available hours?"

"Nah, I'm wide open. Whatever you need."

Rob drooped his lower lip and nodded just a bit. "We need cooks and drivers right now. Server hours will probably open up at some point. Cooks start at minimum. Goes up if you stay thirty days. Drivers make five plus tips and delivery fees. A lot of people train for both."

"Both's good with me."

"You got a car? Does it got insurance?"

"Yep."

"Wait. Yep to which?"

"Yep to both. Car and insurance."

"I'm guessing you don't have a food handler's card?"

"You got me there. I don't know what that is."

"Something that says you're qualified to work in a kitchen. You have to take a test on the health-department website. They charge a fee. It's not hard."

"Okay."

Rob nodded and went back to Tori's application. She watched him a little longer before her eyes wandered. She tried to read the fine print on a big can of Rockstar Energy on the shelf behind the counter. Then she studied a framed black-and-white picture of Bob Dylan that leaned against the wall beside the register.

"This looks all right," Rob said.

"You think I can get an interview?"

"No, we're good."

Tori cocked her head.

Rob spun the pen on the countertop still examining Tori's application. "You just had it. Why don't you come in Saturday morning at ten to train. You need to get that food handler's card first."

Tori blinked about a half dozen times. After a long pause, she said, "Okay."

"Bring a hat. Or some kind of head covering. It can be whatever."

She said "Okay" again.

Rob went back into the kitchen and left her there. Tori stared in at the ovens and metal tables a little longer before she picked up her pizza box and left.

Rob was upstairs counting the day-shift drawer a few hours after he hired Tori. Knox was supposed to relieve him, but he wanted to finish an episode of *Doctor Who* first. Rob sat at Knox's kitchen table thumbing down singles. "I hired someone today who I think could potentially manage."

"Oh yeah."

"I'm training her for everything. Driver, server, and cook."

"Wow. That's ambitious. When's she start?"

"Saturday. She was ready to go. Has to get her food handler's card, but that's it. She seemed pretty put together. Like, I don't know why she wants a job here but I'm not questioning it, put together."

"Sweet. What's her availability?"

"Open." Rob tilted his head and creased his nose. "She's like, mid-twenties, so she's not a kid. Just graduated EKU and I guess wants to go to law school or something. For the time being she just wants to work."

"Sounds like a promising prospect. What's this blue chipper call herself?"

"Tori."

"All right. Cool. Just don't go hiring any Whigs. I don't want 'em to fight."

Rob smacked a stack of singles against the palm of his hand a couple times. "That is absolutely terrible, man."

*T*ORI GOT to Porthos about fifteen minutes early on Saturday. She was out front in a gray tam with a silver purse looped over her left forearm when Rob showed up a couple minutes later. He eyeballed her as he stuck the key in the lock. "I'll be damned."

"What?"

"I can't remember the last time I trained anyone who got here before me."

Tori had to fill out paperwork first thing, then clock in once Rob had her in the point-of-sale computer, which was a touch-screen unit where they entered orders and whatnot. Then she got two blue fleur-de-lis t-shirts. The money for them would come out of her first check. She got it back if she stayed ninety days.

"We didn't used to charge for them, but people would get hired and work a day just to get a free shirt," Rob said. "There was one guy who went out on a smoke break an hour into his first shift and never came back. That was when Knox started charging."

"Who's Knox?"

"The owner. You'll meet him."

"You're not the owner?"

Rob looked at Tori, lifted his coffee mug, took a drink, then looked at her some more. "No," he finally said.

"How many people work here who don't get their t-shirt money back?"

Rob still held his mug near his mouth. "Lots."

Meredith showed up at ten-thirty and clocked in without looking at or speaking a word to Rob or Tori. When she walked away, Tori said, "She seems sweet."

Rob told Tori to "scrub in" and they washed their hands. They started a big batch of dough in the sixty-quart Hobart mixer. Rob measured out ice, water, oil, sugar, and yeast. After he mixed all that stuff, he had Tori dump a twenty-five-pound bag of flour in the metal bowl. Some got on the floor, but Rob kept going like it never happened.

Rob was emphatic about one thing. "Salt goes in last, and that's really important. It slows down the yeast. We've had some dumbasses who can't remember anything. They put salt in first, or they leave it out, or they forget to put in ice, all kinds of stuff. I'm not saying that's going to be you, I'm just saying, it seems simple, but nothing's ever simple around here."

They watched the hook spin frenetically around the bowl flipping and flopping the developing mound of dough. "You see how heavy that hook is?"

Tori watched the hook as it pounded the dough side to side and nodded.

"We had a guy stick his hand in there while the mixer was on."

"Are you serious?"

"He screamed like he was going to fucking die. At first, I thought he tore it off. He had to go to the emergency room. His hand was *fucked* up. He got worker's comp and everything. It's like people walk in this kitchen and their IQ drops thirty points. It's ridiculous."

"I don't think mine has dropped more than ten yet."

Rob regarded her soberly. "You remembered to wear a hat. That puts you in the ninetieth percentile right out of the gate. Most people wear the angry cub their first day."

"What's the angry cub?"

"It's an old Cubs hat that's almost brown. It was here when I started. It has so many sweat rings on it that it looks like a slice of a hundred-year-old tree. We keep it basically as like a punishment for forgetting your hat. Smells like shit. It's nasty."

The dough was cumbersome as hell. Like a mushy boulder. They cut off chunks with wood-handled chefs' knives and weighed them on an old kitchen scale. Rob showed Tori how to knead them under until they were smooth and domed on top like a mushroom cap. Those went into stackable rectangular plastic trays to proof overnight. "If you don't proof dough, it comes out tough as shit," Rob said.

By the second batch of dough Tori started feeling confident. Rob had moved on to dicing green peppers and onions. He looked at the clock and said, "God, it's past eleven. Where's Jake?"

Tori kept making dough balls while Rob typed on his cell phone. When he got done, he stuck it back in his pocket, looked at his hands, said "fuck," and went to wash them. As soon as he started drying his hands his phone chirped and he said "fuck" again and took it out of his pocket. He scowled at the screen, said "fuck" one more time, and put it back.

Tori gave him a quizzical look.

"Our day driver's in Columbus," he said. Then he shouted, "Meredith!"

Her fiery head appeared in the doorway near the front counter.

"Can you go wake up Knox? Jake's in Columbus and he's our driver."

She drew her head back and narrowed her eyes. "Ohio? What's he doing in Ohio?"

"Someone gave him a ticket to a Death Cab show."

She shook her head and walked off. Tori noticed for the first time that Rob was teary, and for a moment she thought he'd gotten emotional about the whole thing. Then she remembered he was chopping onions.

There was knocking somewhere in the building, followed by the sound of footsteps on the floor above. Voices and rumbling followed.

The two-way door between the kitchen and Porthos's small dining room soon swung open. A husky man with curly-yet-matted-looking, receding dark hair and a full beard that hung from his chin like a raggedy stalactite thundered in. He wore mesh shorts, Adidas slides with white socks, and a t-shirt that read "Mondale/Ferraro." His left arm was plain as hotel sheets and the right was covered in dark tattoos that started at his wrist and extended up and into his t-shirt sleeve.

"Who the hell still listens to Death Cab for Cutie? Who *ever* listened to Death Cab for Cutie? Jesus." He noticed Tori. "How you doing? I'm Knox. I own this place." He stuck out his inked elbow like he was making a single funky chicken wing. "Throw me a 'bow."

Tori stood there looking at his jutting arm. Not knowing what to do she raised her hand and said, "Tori."

"Come on, Tori, throw me a 'bow. Don't leave me hanging." Knox shook his elbow. Tori raised her arm and banged it against his. "There you go. Now you don't have to wash your hands again."

She looked at her elbow where he had bashed it and said, "Okay."

"You want me to tell Jake not to bother coming back?" Rob asked Knox.

"No, I want you to tell him to come back so I can punch him in the face," Knox said. He looked at Tori. "I'm not really going to punch him in the face. I'm a pacifist."

"You're not a fucking pacifist," Rob said.

"I try to be."

Rob turned to Tori but thumbed at Knox. "He head-butted a bartender at Applebee's."

"I apologized."

"In court."

Knox shook his head. "The hardest part was admitting I was at Applebee's." He took a Porthos Pizza car topper from where it was stuck to the metal back door like a squirrel on the side of a tree. "I'm going to go get hooked up. Text Tyler and see if you can get him to come in."

Meredith hollered from the front counter, "Tyler's playing paintball all day at a tournament in Corbin. He's got three games. He won't be back until eight."

Knox whipped his head toward Rob and said low, so Meredith couldn't hear, "Hey, how's Buttercup got such specific information?"

"You didn't know? Those two are," Rob paused and swirled his fingers beside his head like he was searching for the right words, "you know."

"She's dating him?"

"I don't get the feeling they're actually dating. I think it's just coitus."

Knox's brows went up. "Really? Good for Tyler. I didn't think he had it in him."

Tori said, "Or her."

Knox smiled and pointed at her. "Hellfire." He went out the back door with the car topper under his arm.

Once Knox was out back, Rob swept the onions into a clear plastic bin and headed toward the makeline. "When you get done with that last batch of dough, come on and I'll teach you how to slap a pizza."

Slapping dough was exactly what it sounded like: slapping it back and forth to stretch it out. It sounded simple enough, but Tori soon found out, if you didn't do it just right, you could slap the shit out of it and nothing happened. That's how it went for her at first.

Rob could flour dough, stretch it, slap it, give it a couple tosses, and lay it down to dock on the stainless-steel table all in about fifteen seconds. Docking prevented the dough from bubbling as it cooked. He docked it with a little metal-tipped aerator, and it sounded like someone shaking rocks in a metal bucket.

"One time a lady was in here with a baby that was asleep," Rob shouted over the sound of the dough he was docking. "She came to the counter to ask us if we could stop making that noise. I told her I was sorry, but no."

"What'd she do?"

Rob laid the finished dough on a gray/black pizza screen, scooped sauce from the sauce bucket, and spread fast and even on the dough. "She got mad and left. The worst people to deal with in food service are people who have never worked in food service. They think because they eat in restaurants they know about restaurants, but they don't know shit. Whenever anyone wants to give you advice about how to run a restaurant, you can just about guarantee they don't know what the fuck they're talking about. They're the same people who go online and trash us. Knox goes fucking crazy. We had somebody go on Google, TripAdvisor, and Yelp and flay us because they were all butthurt that their delivery took an hour and a half during the Super Bowl."

"You're busy during the Super Bowl? *No way.*"

"I know, right."

Orders stayed pretty steady through lunch. For every pizza Tori made, Rob made three. It was mostly carryouts and deliveries. Only four people came in and ate at the shop. The Porthos dining room was sketchy at best. The front was just a couple small tables, video games, and a pinball machine. The main dining room was off to the right, parallel to the kitchen. There were a handful of four tops with cheap chairs against the walls. At the back there were six tan, molded plastic booths with black vinyl cushions, most of which were ripped and repaired with black duct tape. Along the walls hung small frames with pictures of French Impressionist paintings that looked like they had been cut out of magazines. The lighting was dim, always.

The bathrooms at the back of the dining room were wallpapered with a blue toile pattern. It was peeled in places and there were a couple holes in the men's room that went clear through the drywall.

Between the bathrooms was a door that had a small red sign on it that said "Private." When Tori took a minute to go to the bathroom, she looked closely at the sign. Below it someone had written the word *dick* in tiny letters with a pencil. It looked like it had been that way a long time. It also looked like no one had ever bothered to try to erase it.

As they worked through the day, Rob gave Tori the basics of the Porthos pizza-topping philosophy. "The money's in the cheese. It's the most expensive thing we buy. Some people always give extra. Like they're ripping people off if they don't give extra. We put more cheese on our pizzas than anyone in town, but it doesn't matter, they still give extra, and it makes the pizzas not as good. Half the people who work here don't give a shit if we make a dollar or go out of business." He carried a finished pizza to the conveyor oven and put it on the belt.

Rob took the last ticket from the makeline ticket holder and moved it to the one at the other end. "Line's clear. You want a smoke?"

"I don't smoke."

"Cool," Rob said. "That makes you, like, a minority in this place." He picked at the corner of his fingernail a bit. "Listen, you think you can catch this last pizza and watch the front counter while I have one? Meredith's already on break, so it'll just be you for a couple minutes. If anything happens, you can come get me."

"I got it."

"Okay. You're supposed to wear gloves when you catch. There's a box over there. Just drop the screen under the table, we don't wash them. It's a fourteen inch, so you eight cut it. Make sure you put a pizza protector in there. Stick it in the warmer when you're done." Rob cocked his head. "You got it?"

"I can handle it."

"You sure?"

"Yeah, there's just one thing," Tori said.

"What's that?"

"Do I box it cheese side up, or cheese side down?"

Rob picked up a yellow hard pack of American Spirits from a table near the mixer and drew one out with his lips. He raised his thumb, and with the cigarette flopping as he spoke, said, "Always up," and walked away.

The pizza Tori cut was boxed and in the warmer. She stood at the counter reading a carryout menu trying to memorize as much as she could when a guy in an Ireland National team zip jacket came in. The guy's hands were clasped and he looked around funny, like he was going to beg for money or something.

Tori said, "Did you have a carryout, sir?"

"No," the guy said. Then he glanced this way and that before fixing his eyes back on Tori. "So, uh, I'm supposed to order something from Knox."

"From Knox?"

"Yeah. Is he here?"

"No, but what is it you want? Maybe I can help you out."

His eyes became slits. "Could I get, like, a slice of Spinach Special?"

Tori looked at the menu again. She didn't remember seeing that anywhere. She flipped it over about five times and squinted trying to find it. "I mean, I don't think we sell by the slice and I never saw a Spinach Special."

The guy said, "I don't think it's gonna be on there."

Rob turned back up. "Hey, Tori, you got this?"

"I don't know, actually." Tori gestured to the man at the counter. "He asked about the Spinach Special but I can't find it on the menu. Do we still have it?"

Rob looked at Tori. Then he looked at the guy. He tapped his fingers one at a time across the counter, like he was gathering his thoughts. "You know, I think Knox is the only one who knows how to make it. If you want to hang out here a few minutes, he'll be back."

The Ireland guy nodded. He rummaged in his pocket for change before going over to the Indiana Jones pinball machine. Tori was lost. "Do we even have spinach? I haven't seen any."

"Maybe Knox knows."

"He's wanting a slice. We don't sell by the slice, do we?"

"Not exactly. Let's just let Knox handle this."

Tori stood there bewildered, but Rob seemed intent on glossing over it and going about his business.

Five minutes later, Knox walked in the back and tripped on his feet coming through the door. He caught his balance and looked back at the step. "Fuck me running."

Before anything else, Rob said, "Uh, Knox. There's a guy up front asking for the special."

Knox's brows rose. He hung his hot bag and went to the lobby where he spoke to the guy in the Ireland jacket. They looked out the front window while Knox gestured and pointed what seemed to be directions somewhere. After the guy left, Knox came back to the kitchen. "I've got to run up to my apartment a minute, kids."

Before he could go, Tori asked, "Do we have a Spinach Special?"

Knox kneaded his chin through his beard and pursed his lips. "The thing is, sometimes we do. If anyone wants it, just let me know. It's like, special order. In fact, if anyone else comes in asking for it, just text me and I'll come take care of it."

Tori looked from Knox to Rob, and back again. She knew there was something she was missing, but didn't know what. Neither Rob or Knox said anything. Not knowing what else to say, Tori said, "Okay."

$\mathcal{D}$URING TORI'S second week, Knox and Rob were both still running deliveries and managing at the same time—which by law they weren't supposed to because the manager was required to be on the premises. The driver who went to Columbus never turned back up and nobody spoke of him.

All but one of Tori's shifts so far had been cook shifts. She got one short server shift because Meredith was two hours late for lunch one day. Tori hardly knew what she was doing on the floor, but Rob helped her through it and it went okay. The service expectations of Porthos's dine-in customers seemed pretty low.

Tori had started working daytime kitchen shifts by herself. Whoever was driving would typically help in the kitchen when they weren't on the road. If it got slow, Tori folded boxes, washed pans and dishes, or chatted with the delivery driver between runs. Meredith never talked to anyone if she didn't absolutely have to. There was another server named Kendra who was pleasant enough, but she was married and had two small kids at home. She seemed to be there just to get out of the house and earn a little spending money.

Tori had breezed through a day shift with Meredith on the floor while Knox was out on the road. She was at the sink scrubbing a sub pan when Rob showed up for his closing shift. Knox came in right on his heels singing "Send in the Clowns." He stopped by the back door and delivered the last line in an overwrought baritone. Porthos didn't have a dishwasher so everything was by hand in a three-compartment steel sink. A metal sprayer with a nozzle like a showerhead hung above it. Knox stopped his song and stood silently behind Tori. He was close enough that Tori could smell his radiating body odor. Rob had warned her about that the first day.

"You're a natural," Knox said to Tori's back. "You're like Bobby Fischer playing chess. Or Beth Harmon."

Tori was trying to dislodge a stubborn ribbon of caramelized cheese from a pasta dish with a stream. She held it up so Knox could see the brown bubbled crust break loose under the force of a point-blank deluge.

"Look at that," Knox said. "It's not even hard for you. Your midi-chlorians must be off the charts."

Tori never looked at him. Knox went to the line and spoke to Rob. He was so loud all the time, even when Tori couldn't understand what he was saying, she could still hear him. Eventually he shouted, "Yo, Tori!" over the sound of the sprayer. Tori put the sprayer on the hook and went to the line.

"There's a pizza in the oven bound for Idylwild subdivision and it's got your name on it. If you want to make a run, I'll go with you and make sure you've got a handle on the basic concepts of driving a car with a pizza in it, and whatnot."

Tori scratched the back of her head where she was sweating from the heat in the kitchen. "All right."

Despite the name of the school, EKU wasn't actually in Eastern Kentucky, it was in Central. It sat just across the Kentucky River from Lexington, the second largest city in the Commonwealth and home to the flagship college: University of Kentucky. Richmond was far smaller than Lexington, but a lot of it wasn't rural. The city center was surrounded by asphalt and concrete. Campus buildings, lawns, shopping centers, and a few parks and golf courses broke things up. That was Porthos's core delivery area.

Tori drove with Knox riding shotgun. He rarely stopped talking. He was like a radio host: averse to dead air. He asked questions, but it seemed like he hardly listened to the answers. He didn't dwell long before careening onward with follow-ups.

"You have a leg up since you already know your way around Richmond. That's one less thing to worry about. We've hired some freshmen who just moved here and it's sketchy. We had one kid we tried to send to a subdivision off Keeneland Drive. He wound up in Clark County. No shit. I don't know at what point I would've turned around if I was lost, but I'm pretty sure it would've been before I crossed the fucking Kentucky River. He lasted about a week." Knox looked up before adding, "If that long."

Tori shook her head. "GPS, man. It's not hard."

"You'd think that, but not for everyone. How long have you lived here?"

"Like four years. Started at EKU as a freshman and went straight through."

"What'd you study?"

"Political science."

"Rob said you're thinking about law school."

"That's the plan. I kind of wish I'd taken undergrad a little slower, so I'm giving it a minute."

"That's cool. I'm glad you landed with us. We need good people." Knox rubbed his hands together the way people do to warm them, but it seemed like just a tick. "Where you from before college?"

"Louisville."

"Louisville where?"

"You know where Windy Hills is?"

"Maybe."

"Up off the Snyder. Kind of near Valhalla."

"Nice," Knox said. He brushed each of his shoulders like he was knocking dust off them. "You're pedigreed."

"It's not like that at all. My sister and I lived with my mom. Our house was nothing fancy. My dad mostly stayed in J-Town. It's not like I had a rough childhood or anything, but it definitely wasn't plush." She pulled into the driveway and shifted to park.

Knox reached in the back seat for the hot bag and handed it forward to Tori. "You're going to do great, I just know it." He grinned like a moron.

Tori rolled her eyes at him. She did that often. He seemed to enjoy it.

Tori walked back to the car with the empty hot bag hanging from her hand. She threw it in the back seat as she got in.

"Well," Knox said, "how's your tip, T-Bone?" as Tori backed out.

"No bueno."

"Nothing." Knox shook his head. "Fuck sake. Idylwild used to be a good tipping neighborhood. It's slipped here just lately. We've had some heroin dealers move in from Detroit and that's helped kill it. The funny thing is, it's not just the dealers. The whole place is down. A lot of the college students around here'll fuck you over."

"This was like a twelve-year-old skater kid. He didn't even talk to me. After I gave him the cash he stood there with his hand out for the change."

"The silver? Little cocksucker."

"He needs that money, man. He's saving up for a new flat-brim hat."

"There's no justice in tipping. Ever." Knox opened Tori's glove box, got out her Accord owner's manual, and started thumbing through it for no apparent reason. "One thing you can try is acting like you're slow. Sometimes that works."

"What?"

"Just act stupid. Dig in your pocket for coins before you do anything else. Don't even get the cash out. Act like you can't even count. People get impatient and just say fuck it and let you keep the difference. You really have to commit to it, though."

"That really works?"

"People are hungry. They just want to eat. It doesn't always work, but it works a lot. Especially if it's just a few bucks and they're acting like they want it back. Credit cards are another story."

"I can do slow."

Knox put the manual back and started playing with the power window. He ran it down a few inches, back up, down again, and back up. He did this over and over. He continued even as he asked, "Speaking of slow. Do you ever like to slow things down?"

"How do you mean?"

He laughed. "I mean, do you smoke pot at all?"

Tori hesitated. She studied Knox out of the side of her eye. "Very rarely."

"Just not into it?"

They reached the red light at Lancaster Road and the bypass, one of the busiest in town. "I'm not saying I've never done it, but it's not really my thing. I've never even bought it."

"That's cool."

"You smoke?"

"Sure. When the mood strikes. And it strikes." Knox ran the window all the way down, stuck his head out, drew it back in, and rolled it up. "Summer's hanging in there," he said. He gazed out the front windshield a little while. Then he looked at Tori directly. "You know, the reason I asked you about pot is this: a lot of my employees like a little smoke every once in a while, and I don't want to see anyone get in trouble for doing something harmless. You know what I'm saying? So, if you ever have a need, let me know. Even if it's not for you. I look out for the people who work for me. I look out for their friends, too. You follow me?"

Tori did follow. "That's the Spinach Special, isn't it?"

Knox nodded. "That's right."

Tori drummed her fingers on the steering wheel waiting on the light to change. The rest of the ride was quiet.

*N*OBODY CAME out and told Tori she got a raise on her second paycheck. It was in a stack beside the kitchen phone. When she opened the envelope, she noticed the hourly rate was fifty cents higher than it was the first pay period. She approached Rob in the kitchen and held the check in front of his face as he worked on a hoagie on the makeline. He squinted at it, not comprehending.

"My check is too high," she said.

He side-eyed her. "Give it some water and tell it to take a nap."

Just then Knox came into the kitchen through the dining-room door. Tori turned her attention to him. "Is this right?"

"Is what right?"

She held up her check. "My hourly's fifty cents higher."

"That's what you call a raise."

"How'd I get a raise?"

"By not doing stupid shit."

"That's it?"

"That's it. If you don't want it, I can take it off there."

Tori held the check with both hands and looked at it again. "I just never got a raise without asking before."

"I don't know what to tell you. Me and Rob talked it over and we want you to stick around. Hence the raise."

"I appreciate it."

Knox put a finger to his lips. "Just don't talk about it. Nobody else got one. They didn't follow the rule."

"What rule?"

"Don't do stupid shit." Knox took the wrist of one hand in the other and raised it over his head, stretching his back. He groaned. "So, listen. We've got a situation we can play a couple ways. Kendra's texted that she's not coming in, so we need a server. One of you all's going to have to do it. That's pretty much the situation until close tonight."

Rob laid the hoagie pan on the conveyor, took his phone from his pocket, and while looking at it said, "Welp, we've got three deliveries hanging and not a single dine-in's come in yet. I'm not trying to swipe Tori's tips, so I'll take serving until lunch is over and she can run the deliveries."

Knox set his eyes on Tori. "That work for you?"

Tori gave the okay sign.

"You know, in some foreign countries, that means asshole," Knox said.

"What does?"

Rob directed his thumb at Knox. "The sound of him talking."

"Don't listen to him." He waved Rob off. "That gesture you just made. That's how you call someone an asshole in other countries. It's like giving somebody the finger."

Tori said, "Who knew? This place is educational."

Knox smirked a demented smirk, kicked Rob in his lower leg, and when he had Rob's attention, he made the international symbol for asshole, stuck his index finger in it, and poked in and out.

Rob picked up his drink cup and headed to the lobby to refill it. "You're a mental defective."

When Tori got back from her first run of deliveries, a shady looking dude in jeans with a wallet chain was hunched over the keypad at the back door messing with it. There were two locks on that door. One was manual and the other digital. When Porthos was open only the digital one stayed locked and the keypad opened it.

Tori got out of her car hastily. "Hey, what're you doing?" Wallet chain walked away without looking back. Tori shouted "Hey!" again at his back, but the guy picked up his pace and kept going. Tori watched him go, not really knowing what to do. After standing there a few seconds feeling clueless, she keyed the code herself and went in.

Knox was at the hand sink holding a new roll of brown paper towels in one hand and opening the dispenser with the other.

"Hey, Knox. Some little hoodlum was trying to key in the back door just now."

"Really. Who was it?"

"I have no idea."

Knox installed the new towels without looking at what he was doing. "You kick his ass?"

"He took off. I didn't even get a look at his face."

"Next time you catch someone doing that shit, you run him down and bring the pain." He snapped the face up on the paper towel dispenser. He slashed a finger across his throat. "No quarter."

"What happened to being a pacifist?"

"Eh. Whatever."

There was a fourteen-inch cheese pizza on the prep table with a huge hole in it. Holes like that happened when a pizza stuck to a screen. Tori pointed at it. "You care if I have some of this?"

"Nope. Help yourself."

Tori got a misshapen piece and took a bite. Still chewing, she said, "I was thinking though, do you ever change the back-door code?"

"Yeah. When we got it the code was 1234. I figured I shouldn't leave it like that, so I changed it to 3332. I figured anybody could remember that."

Knox went to the line with Tori following, still eating her pizza. The intense heat near the ovens sweltered around them, but Tori had gotten used to it. Knox looked up at a ticket, took a dough ball from a tray under the table, dropped it in the flour bin, laid it on the table, and started to stretch it.

Tori said, "That's kind of my point though. It's still 3332, and anyone who's ever worked here probably *does* remember it."

"It's only good if we're open though. It's not like someone can break in when no one's here."

"But don't you worry someone who worked here could give it to someone who doesn't and that person could walk right in? Like that guy who was just back there. What if he came in? Especially with, you know, your spinach situation." Tori put the back of her hand to her mouth like it was some big secret. "The pot."

Knox jutted his chin at the lobby as he slapped the dough. "He could walk in the front door just as easy. What's the difference?"

"I don't know, just seems—I don't know." He had Tori sort of stumped until logic took hold. "If you don't care who comes in the back door during a shift, why bother with the digital lock?"

Knox laid the dough back down and started to dock it. He shouted over the metallic racket of the docker clattering on the table, "Fucking safety."

By the end of the night, Knox was upstairs while Rob and Tori closed the restaurant. Tori had never handled the cash drawer, but Rob handed it to her and said, "Take this up, will ya? Knox wants to talk to you." She took ahold of the drawer but Rob didn't release it immediately. "You might want to knock first."

When Tori got to the door at the base of the stairs she paused there and banged on it.

"Come on up!" Knox's voice sounded far away.

As soon as Tori began to ascend the stairs, she was overwhelmed by two things: all the crap on the steps that made climbing a hazard, and the way the smells of must, stale pot smoke, and dirty clothes got stronger as she climbed. By the time she reached the top she was about choked.

When she cleared the landing, Knox was deep in his couch amongst the most extensive collection of junk Tori had ever seen. "Hey, lady. I see you come bearing the drawer. I told Rob I wanted to talk to you, but I guess he's going to make me do the count, too."

"That's what he said." Tori went to him with it in hand.

Knox groaned as he stood. He was shirtless. His chest was loose and as hairy as the rest of him, which is to say, very. Knox's stomach hung out over his shorts' waistband like an outcropping. "You don't gotta knock before you come up. It's all good up here."

"I didn't want to barge in on you."

"Nah, it's fine. I'm not worried about it."

Tori gazed at the awing disarray that surrounded them. "Why do you keep all this stuff in your apartment?"

"It's my estate. I have some valuable items, man."

Tori wandered around like she was trying to find lost keys. She picked up a VHS boxed set. "*My So-Called Life*. Why do you need this?"

"That's a watershed moment in American television."

"I've heard of it. Never saw it."

"Oh my god. How have you lived? You can borrow those if you want. In fact, you probably should. It's only the first five episodes, though."

Tori looked over the shelf-worn blue cardboard case, turning it in her hands. "I'm good." She set it aside and pointed. "Why do you have all that lumber?"

"What, the poplar?"

"No, the other big pile of wood."

There was only one pile of wood. "I bought it to make bookshelves."

"How long ago? There's like an inch of dust on it."

Knox didn't answer that one. "Have you seen my books?" He pointed in the general direction of four big cardboard boxes. "I gotta put those somewhere."

Tori walked toward the boxes. "So, what, are you going to make, a big pile of books on top of your big pile of wood?"

"Picture that wood as shelves. Glorious shelves."

Tori opened the top of one of the boxes and shifted stuff around. "You've got some good stuff in here."

"You a reader?"

"You bet your ass."

"You see anything you want in there, you can have it."

Tori looked up. "Seriously?"

"You ever know me to say anything I didn't mean?"

"Constantly."

"Shit. What you talking?" Knox uncorked a long yawn.

Tori held up a paperback copy of Ed McClanahan's novel *The Natural Man*. "Is this book about you? Is this your biography?"

"Fucking hilarious. I wish. Take it. Keep it. Cherish it."

"You sure?"

"Deadly. It's signed even. Guy lives in Lexington. He's an old hippie. I met him at a bookshop. That book's a legend."

Tori leafed through the opening pages. She held up the title page and showed Knox the signature and little line drawing the author had made.

"Awesome, right? It's yours." Knox held out his hand. "Have a seat."

There was nowhere to sit. Tori had to move a cardboard box with a Nintendo 64 and a bunch of games in it, a canvas bag, and a jacket off a wingback chair. There was another box on the floor in front of the chair, and when Tori moved it, she realized what was in it. "You going to a rave or something?"

"No. Raves are for infants."

"Then why do you have this giant box of glow sticks?"

"Oh, I traded for those."

"What'd you give for them?"

"A wagonwheel. That's a half gross of glow sticks, though. I got a good deal." Knox was digging at his belly button like something was caught in there.

Tori picked up a blue glow stick in a shiny black wrapper and looked it over. "What're you going to do with these?"

"Fuck if I know, but I have them if I need them." Knox put the thumb and finger that had been in his belly button to his nose and smelled deeply, looked at Tori, and shook his head. "What do you think so far?"

Tori raised her brows, not too sure the context. Her answer depended heavily on that. "About what?"

"About Porthos. You've been here, what, about a month? How you like it? Any complaints?"

"Not really. None I can think of." Maybe she would've liked Knox to shower more, and maybe not blurt out every last thing that popped in his head, but she couldn't say that.

"Good. Seems like you're doing a really good job. You picked up everything pretty fast."

"Thanks. I like it here. Everyone's pretty cool."

"Good. We like you, too. That's kind of the reason I brought you up." Knox slouched a little farther, drew his hands back, and laced his fingers behind his head. "The thing is, we need another shift leader. We've been down one for a long time now. Rob's getting burned out. Me or him manages any time the shop's open. We get one day off a week. He's trying to get a hops farm going but he has no time for it."

"Really?"

"Yeah. At his place out in Poosey. I'm afraid he's going to bail on me if things don't change. I think he'll be okay if I can just cut his hours. That's part of why we gave you the raise, but what we really want to do is bump you again, this time to shift leader."

"Shift leader?"

"Yeah. We can send you to the management class at the health department. After that, you could start leading your own shifts. It's basically the same as being a manager except you don't have to do the counts at end of day, and you get an extra buck an hour. What do you think?"

Tori took air in slowly through her nose. "Could I still deliver and serve some?"

"Of course. We don't need you managing full-time. Maybe, like, twenty, twenty-five hours a week. Train some people in the kitchen. That'd help us out big time."

"I might be able to do that."

"The thing is, you're the first new hire we've felt comfortable moving up in a long time. I mean, it seems like you really have your shit together."

Tori chuckled. "Not altogether."

"I mean, nobody has their shit totally together. I don't. Anyway, I can also tell you aren't going to steal. I can't always tell who will, but I can tell who won't, you know?"

Tori looked blank.

"Are you planning to steal?"

Tori couldn't tell if Knox really wanted her to respond. He didn't say anything else, so she went ahead and answered, "No."

"See. I knew it. The last reason is," Knox held up his hands, "we like you. We want you here in the Porthos nest. All snuggled down. What do you say? You ready to join the Porthos blue-ribbon management team?"

Tori held her chin in her hand and laced one finger across her lips. "Maybe." She hesitated before going on. "There's just one thing I want to ask about, first."

"What's that?"

"The whole pot thing. That stays up here, right?"

"Absolutely. I felt like you deserved to know, so I told you. I knew you'd find out either way. This is my deal, though. If anything goes wrong, it's all on me."

"So, if you get busted, what happens?"

"I kept the whole thing hidden from you guys. This apartment is a private home. It has nothing to do with Porthos or any of my employees. It's just me. That's why I route everyone out of the store. I make them all come in through the alley. Nobody but you guys come up through the store."

Tori bobbed her head slowly. "As long as that's the way it is."

"It is. I promise."

She puckered her lips. "Hmm. I guess I'm okay."

"So, are you our new shift leader?"

"Looks that way."

"Cool, cool." Knox dug into a bag of raw almonds on the couch beside him. The handful he came out with was huge. Tori was amazed when he crammed them all in his mouth at once. He chewed with determination, but before he was done chewing he started talking again, somewhat garbled. "Listen, you can do what you want. Rob'll be so glad we have another manager, he won't mind closing by himself." He reached under his coffee table and came up with a tiny iridescent blown-glass pipe. "I know you don't want to be around the whole sales part of it, but we can celebrate your promotion by smoking a welcome-to-the-management-team bowl if you want."

Tori wrinkled her nose and started to get up. "No. I'm good for tonight. Can I get a rain check?"

Knox gave a double thumbs up with both his hands raised high in the air, his pipe clasped in his right. Tori took her new book and headed back downstairs.

"Don't listen to him," Rob said. "Always knock, and maybe count to ten. Kendra won't go up there at all anymore. If you go up there without knocking, you could see anything. I don't unless it's an absolute emergency. Things you don't want to see happen up there. In fact, even if you do knock, it doesn't guarantee you won't stumble into some kind of depravity."

"Like drug activity?"

"Or worse."

Tori was mopping the area where the makeline normally sat. It was pulled out from the wall. "Like what?"

Rob hoisted a big gray garbage bag out of one of the trash cans with both hands. He dropped it on the floor with a thump that kicked up a huff of air. He tied it. "Like anything."

Tori stopped mopping and leaned on the handle. "Give me an example. Like the worst thing you saw."

"I'm not going to say it was the worst, but it was the most star-tling. One night, I was on my way up, and I could kind of hear this creaking. I didn't make anything of it, because with Knox that could be anything."

"And?"

"And I get to the top of the stairs, and his girlfriend was just riding the shit out of him. They were right there on his couch in the middle of the room."

"Holy fuck."

"For real. Holy fuck's right. So, I'm thinking I'm just going to sneak back downstairs, but she looks right at me, you know, hardly even slows down, and she goes, 'Oh hey, sorry, Rob,' and fucking waves at me."

"What'd Knox do?"

"Not a damn thing. Just laid there. They kept right on going, and I left."

Tori held up both hands beside her face and shook them. "I am *so* going to knock first."

"There's certain shit you can't unsee. That's some unseeable shit. Knox's girlfriend was beautiful, but she was kind of a bigger girl. She was covered in tattoos. And you know what Knox looks like. I'm gonna tell you, it was vivid."

"Man, people do not look good having sex. Nobody does. I don't like being in a room with a mirror in it."

Rob put his forehead in the crook of his elbow, blotting sweat. "There were also, like, these noises. Lots of noises."

"I'm never going back up."

"It was an act of love. That's what I told myself, anyway."

"Was Knox embarrassed?"

"Is Knox ever embarrassed? They were both totally unfazed. Afterward, they acted like nothing happened. Right now, I don't think you have to worry about anything like that. Knox has been in kind of a drought. I don't even know if he's gotten laid since his girlfriend moved away."

Tori resumed swabbing. "I'm not taking any chances."

"That's the wisest course." Rob slung the bag of trash over his shoulder and headed for the back door looking like the dirty, sweaty, Santa Claus of garbage.

*O*N A TUESDAY in mid-October, Tori was working as server/cook while Rob was delivery/cook. She was catching ovens. The only pizza in the pipeline was rolling out. Rob stretched a fourteen-inch dough ball absently. Tori lifted the pizza off the conveyor. Their faces wore the expressions of meaningful conversation.

"It started out great, but I wouldn't even watch it anymore after they switched over to Joe," Rob said. "I mean, how do you kill off Steve? Steve *was Blue's Clues*. The fucking dog couldn't even talk."

Tori lifted the lid on a box and slid the pizza in. She grabbed a cutter and made her cuts fast and decisively. She stuck a pizza protector in the middle to keep the lid from sagging, snatched the ticket from the holder, tucked it in the front lip of the box, and put it in the warmer because it was a carryout.

"For one thing," Tori said, "they didn't *kill* Steve. He went to college. He even came back one time for a visit. For another thing, the guy who played him was the one who didn't want to do it anymore. He quit so he could go make an album with one of the guys from Phish."

"I think it was The Flaming Lips."

"Yeah, that." Tori came back to the cut table, picked up the peel, and started spinning it like it was a tennis racquet and she was waiting to return serve. "Either way, they had no choice. They had to get a new nerd."

"You thought Steve was a nerd?"

"Are you kidding? He was a huge nerd. Joe was a nerd, too, but Steve was the nerdiest."

Rob laid down the dough, reached behind himself for a dough cutter, and pointed it at Tori. "Don't be talking shit. Steve was my friend."

"I'm not talking shit. I liked Steve. Besides that, my high-school boyfriend was in the marching band."

"So?"

"I went to college on an academic scholarship. I'm twenty-two and I still have braces. *I'm* a nerd. Joe's one of those nerds who's within the realm of actually being kind of cute, though. He's a guy you might actually hook up with. You'd just have to get him to put on something besides cargo pants and a primary color shirt. Steve, never. He's like a nerd nerd. Like a weird older neighbor. Have you seen either one of those guys lately?"

Rob shook his head. "I didn't even notice you had braces for the longest time. They're only on the bottom. You can hardly tell."

"Yeah, but still. Anyway, I saw a picture online. Joe looks like a model now and Steve looks like Moby. It's not a hard call."

Rob grimaced. "Either way, I don't need that visual."

"What visual?"

"You and *Blue's Clues* Joe hooking up."

"I don't mean like *hook up*," Tori said, banging her fists together. "I mean like, hang with. Have a conversation. Get to know. Then maybe, with time . . ." She knocked her knuckles again and laughed.

"I'm so disappointed. I can't believe you'd rather sleep with Joe than Steve."

"What can I say? I like who I like. I'll tell you who was hot though. Mr. Salt. But he was married, so, you know, off-limits."

"Mr. Salt? Come on. Would you go for someone that pasty?"

Tori pulled a face. "What do you mean?"

"You keep so tan all the time. Mr. Salt's so pale."

Tori's mouth parted. "Hold on. Do you think this comes from a tanning bed?" She waved her hand in front of her face. "Or it's like a spray tan or something?"

"It's not?"

She dropped her chin into her chest and let it hang there. "Are you serious right now? This is my skin color, knucklehead. I'm Dominican. Have you really not figured that out?"

Rob's face flushed red. He started and stopped about three times before he got out, "Oh, man. No. I didn't. I seriously thought you were just tan." He wouldn't look her in the eye. "God, I'm fucking stupid, aren't I?"

Tori waved him off. "Oh, I don't care. It's not like you're the first person to think that. I'm not *just* Dominican. My dad's white bread as hell. He's a big goon. My mom's the one who's Dominican."

"Oh."

"She was born in the DR. My abuelita and a bunch of my family are still there."

"God, I feel like a moron."

"Look, it's no big deal."

"Okay. I'm still sorry. I'd never intentionally say something crappy."

"I know you wouldn't, and it wasn't. Don't be so sensitive. You're wrong though."

"About what?"

"Tons of stuff, probably, but Mr. Salt specifically. He's married to a woman of color, so that blows the lid off your whole theory."

Rob pulled off his bandana and threw it on the floor. "Mrs. Pepper."

Tori looked at it. Then she looked at Rob again. She pointed at his bandana. "What's all this then? What's your boggle? Why'd you throw that on the nasty floor?"

"Because it's official. I'm truly a dumb person. I'm just another dumb Porthos employee."

The phone rang. Tori drew in her chin, puckered her lips, put her index finger to her cheek, and said in a high, ditzy voice, "I wonder who that could be?"

Eventually, a few deliveries came in and Rob ran them, but there wasn't a single dine-in. Tori mostly just took and made carryout orders. One of them was for two twenty-inch wagonwheels. The name on the order was "Greek." When Tori asked the guy on the phone if it was his first name or last name, he only said, "It's my name."

All the dishes were done and prep was ready for night shift. After the wagonwheels were cut and boxed, Tori couldn't think of anything else to do, so she sat in a chair in the kitchen and texted her sister. She didn't look up until the front door chimed. The guy who came to the counter wasn't all that tall, maybe just over six feet, but still, he was huge. He wore a skin-tight gray t-shirt, track pants, was comprehensively tatted, and had exceptionally fair hair, including some wicked chops.

On Tori's way to the counter she said, "You have a carryout?"

They guy nodded.

What's the name?

"Greek."

Tori took the two wagonwheels from the warmer and checked the slip to get the price. Both were specialties, so they weren't cheap. The total was over fifty dollars. When Tori set them on the counter and told him the amount the guy looked at her. "We don't pay."

"Pardon?"

He smirked.

Tori went from that smirk to the man's veined, tremendous,

inked forearms and biceps. Tori said, "Do you have a credit in the book?"

The guy shook his head. "Your boss knows."

Tori had both hands on the pizza boxes. She looked at the man. He still wore an unsettling smile and had what Tori took to be a murder of crows tattooed on his arms. She mashed her lips together, took the pizzas, and put them back in the warmer. "Let me ask him."

Tori banged on Knox's door but didn't hear any answer. Reluctantly, she went up. She found Knox on the floor in his apartment, knees under him, belly pressed against them with his arms stretched as far in front of his head as he could get them, his hands flat and his face down.

"What the hell are you doing?"

"Fucking yoga."

"Why didn't you answer when I knocked?"

"Because I was doing fucking yoga. You know you can come up."

Tori shook her head. "You familiar with someone named Greek?"

Knox didn't move. "Fuck."

"You know him?"

He groaned, "Yeah."

"Well, he ordered two specialty wagonwheels and now he doesn't want to pay for them."

Knox stayed doubled over. His breathing was loud. "Just give him what he wants and get him the fuck out of here."

"That's over fifty bucks."

"I'm aware. Just do it."

"Jesus. You owe him money or something?"

More loud breathing from Knox. He held his position. Neither of them said anything else. Eventually Tori went back downstairs to give away the pizzas.

$\mathcal{R}$OUTE 421 in Jackson County had more twists in it than six months of pro wrestling. Since Knox had been doing business with Burl, he'd come to know every one. Take any of them too fast and you could find yourself plunging down a holler praying to miss the big trees. Knox typically went a pretty good clip, but he was cautious. On his way back home, once he got down Big Hill and back into Madison County, the tighter curves were behind him, so he relaxed a bit.

Knox made a run on a Monday the second week of November. Rob watched his apartment for him, and he lit out for Burl's store. The pickup was uneventful except that sleet started falling as Knox made his way into Jackson County. A skinny boy with a lazy eye named Luther who liked to wear buffalo plaid had taken Daniel's old spot. Knox had gotten used to him and hardly thought of Daniel anymore.

Luther stood beside Knox's window holding a Chicken of the Sea box in lamplight. "I hope it don't freeze," Luther said, looking up in the near dark. "I's supposed to take a girl to Outback in Richmond tonight."

"Is it gonna get that cold?"

"They say it's going down to the twenties."

Knox held his hand out the window and felt the drops. "You might want to take a rain check, then."

Luther smiled showing long gums and little teeth. The lowers were stippled with black dots of fine cut Copenhagen. "Every time I take this girl to Outback, she gives me a hell of a shot of leg. I'm going broke on it."

"It's not worth wrecking over, is it? Couldn't you take her out around here?"

Luther shook his head and grinned again. "Where in hell can I take her out in Jackson County?"

"You wouldn't get any if you took her to Dairy Queen?"

Luther pushed out his lower lip and thought it over. "Hand job, maybe." He giggled low and guttural.

Luther loaded Knox up with three pounds and sent him on his way. He had to sell at least that much to stay ahead of the vig. Porthos's good month still hadn't come.

He coasted down Big Hill and back into Madison County tapping his brakes. He rolled past the gas and food mart at the corner of 21, which led to Berea, and stayed north on 421 headed toward the bypass in Richmond. As he passed the trailer on the left that housed the Big Hill Post Office, he lowered his visor and pulled out a little number he had tucked up there and sparked it. Sleet continued to peck the windshield, growing increasingly solid with each mile. Knox burned the joint and sang along to the radio.

The bridge over Hays Fork was in a straightaway. Knox had the tips of his fingers of his left hand poked out the cracked window releasing the last bit of that joint to the wind. He was diverted watching the little orange lightning bug bounce on the asphalt in the side-view mirror when his rear end drifted and hit the right side of the bridge. His headlights in front of him lit up the railing on the left side. He threw the steering wheel into the slide, and whether it was too hard, or it was too late, it was difficult to say, but he spun fast the other way and bashed his front end into the same side of the bridge the rear end had already hit. A blur of sparks showered his hood as his front grill ground into the concrete and metal of the bridge. The friction slowed his slide, and when the car cleared the bridge, it rolled down the ditch in front of him. Knox locked the brakes, dug into the wet grass, and the car stopped with a lurch, embedded.

After the fury of the crash, the sudden stillness was startling. Knox hurt, but couldn't tell if it was anything bad. Something ticked under the hood that sounded like an egg timer. He looked out, but there was nothing visual other than smoke, ripples in the hood, and a new crack fingering up from the bottom of the windshield.

Knox's seatbelt had cinched until he thought it might cut him in three pieces. He managed to get it unlatched. The release of pressure was instantaneous. He slumped forward into the steering wheel. It wasn't until then he realized the airbag had never deployed. His vision was foggy, and he had the sensation that even though he had undone his seat belt, it was still touching him. When he reached for it to get it off again, it wasn't there.

The driver door seemed intact. When Knox tried the handle, it stuck, but creaked open grudgingly. He spilled out the door, slumped on his side, and rolled to his back on the cold, wet loam. Being out of the car felt like having an ice pack laid on his whole battered body, and he was momentarily grateful for it. He lay there, letting the sleet patter his face repeating, "Holy shit, holy shit, holy shit."

Whatever relief he might have felt at being out of the car didn't last past him raising his head to discover his trunk had jarred open. He flipped to his belly, rose to his knees, and gingerly got to his feet. He lurched to the lighted trunk and found a red pizza-delivery bag hanging half out, and nothing else, most notably the Chicken of the Sea box was gone. Knox had lost his handle on three pounds of Burl's pot. He grabbed the trunk and slammed it down, only for it to pop open and hit him in the chin. "God-fucking-damn-it!" he bellowed. He did the same again, only harder, and this time laid on the trunk belly first as it closed, something clicked, and it latched. The downside to this was immediately apparent in that the trunk light was the best light he had.

He pushed off the trunk and stared stupidly into the dark. Aside from his headlights and red taillights, porch lights and flood lights of nearby houses were all he could see through the murky dark and trees. The storm clouds blunted whatever the moon and stars might have thrown. Nothing from the homes gave him any useful illumination.

Whatever chemicals Knox's body had released, along with those from the joint he just smoked, left him numb and slow-witted. When he finally remembered he had his phone in his pocket, it was a revelation. He pulled it out half-expecting it not to work, but the screen lit, and wasn't cracked any worse than it already had been from him dropping it a hundred times before. He tapped the flash-light app and was glad for what little light it gave.

He made his way up the ditch back to the bridge over the creek. As he reached level ground he exhaled at the sight of the box, but his throat tightened again when he saw one of the packages on the asphalt nearby. Once Knox drew closer, he found ashy green buds scattered like spilled popcorn from one of the bundles. Another package hung from the torn box, apparently undamaged. The third was still inside.

Just as he bent to pick up the battered box, headlights were on him. The approaching car decelerated but its beams were blinding. All Knox could do was stand back up and cover his eyes. Once the car was stopped, the hazard lights flashed on and the driver's door opened. A thin man in pale blue jeans with white tennis shoes, a nylon jacket, and a University of Kentucky hat with an enormous logo on it that started on the brim and ended on the crown approached. "Everything all right?"

Knox looked the man over thinking he could either cold cock him or run—your basic fight or flight urges. He quickly registered that both options were fucking insane. After probably too long of a pause he said, "I was in a wreck."

The man in the gaudy hat squinted. "Anyone hurt?"

"No. It's just me. I think I'm okay."

The man looked at what was at Knox's feet, so Knox did too. Then they met eyes. The man mashed his lips together and worked them around as if he had some water in his mouth he was thinking about squirting out between his teeth. Unless he was stupid, or very sheltered, he knew what lay there. He pointed. "Looks like a whole lot of marijuana in the road."

Knox nodded and considered what to say next. Behind him a woman's voice said, "Everybody okay out here?" A large flashlight beam filtered onto them. "My kids said they heard a car wreck." A woman in her early thirties had a coat on over pajamas, her feet in winter boots and a phone to her ear. When Knox turned back to the man, a Dodge Ram pickup truck—one of the big ones—came in behind the man's car and gradually stopped. "I've got 9-1-1 on the line," the woman said. "They want to know if anyone's hurt."

Knox's eyes went back to the woman, to the weed catastrophe, and then again to the man in the UK hat who watched expectantly. Knox pulled a long breath in through his nostrils. "I'm a little beat up, but I think I'll be all right." He looked the man hard in the eyes. "This box was in the road. I lost control trying to miss it. I think my car's totaled."

"At least you're okay," the woman said. "Thank god for that."

Knox didn't take his eyes from the man, and the man didn't take his from Knox.

The cops bought none of it. After checking to be sure Knox wasn't dying on the spot, one of them led him away to the grass near his ruined car for questioning.

He was a state trooper and a kid, really, Knox thought. Not much older than Rob, but with a short haircut, a big stiff hat, a gray uniform, and a very different conception of civic responsibility. After he had Knox away from everyone else, he commenced the browbeating. "You really think anyone is going to believe that pot isn't yours? You smell like goddamn Snoop Dogg and your car reeks like a grow room."

Blue lights and red lights flashed all around. The strobe effect combined with the crash was making Knox dizzy. The paramedics wanted to take him, but the trooper insisted since he was up and around it was okay to talk a minute. The paramedics seemed kind of pissed. Knox stared at the trooper's silver name tag with the letters etched in it trying to maintain some kind of equilibrium. "I don't know what to tell you. It's not mine." Knox swayed a little side to side, and the trooper reached out and held his arm until he steadied. "Man, I'm not feeling too good. I think I need to go to the hospital."

The trooper glanced at the paramedics standing impatiently at the roadside. He got quieter, like he was telling a secret. "Why don't you just give it up so we don't have to waste all this time? We found a roach in the road back there, and when we run the DNA on it, you and me both know what it'll show. You're getting charged with DUI either way. If you'll just tell me the truth now, I'll let you go home after the hospital." He shook his head and squeezed one eye closed like what he had to say next pained him. "You don't come clean, I'll have to take you to jail after you get released. You really want to go to jail?"

More and more, the taste of blood in Knox's mouth came through. He worked his tongue in vain trying to swallow it down. "It's gotta be like that?"

"I'm afraid so."

"Okay," Knox said, drawing nearer to the trooper. "I'm going to tell the truth."

The trooper's eyes opened wider.

"That's not my pot. It belongs to someone else." Knox held up his right palm. "Honest injun. I'd take a polygraph."

"Your DNA's on that joint and you know it."

"Do you have it?"

"Your DNA?" The trooper nodded. "Not yet, but we'll pull it at the hospital, and then we'll test it for a match at the lab."

"No," Knox said, "I mean the joint."

"You bet I do."

Knox popped his chin at the road. "Did you pick it up with gloves? Can you really test something for DNA if you don't wear sterile gloves?"

"Oh, so now you're in law enforcement?"

"No, but I read a lot."

The trooper looked at the ground where he was digging a toe into the mud. He took Knox by the arm again, this time much harder, and led him toward the paramedics. "That pot's yours. Everyone here knows it. We'll prove it one way or the other."

"Officer," Knox said, shuffling along with him, "I don't mean to sound disrespectful, but if that was true, you wouldn't be trying so hard to get me to say it."

He cut his eyes at Knox. "It's trooper. I'm not an officer, I'm a trooper." He didn't utter another word before turning Knox over to the paramedics.

The fact of the matter was, Knox was scared shitless, and the whole thing was a fucking disaster. He almost wanted to laugh at the young cop. He was the least of Knox's troubles. He didn't scare him, and neither did the judge he would face over the DUI. Nor that all he had was liability insurance on the old Volvo. The only thing that frightened Knox at that moment was the three pounds of lost pot and who it belonged to.

*A*FTER PONDERING fifty different ways to get his ass out of the bear trap, Knox was about ready to chew his foot off and run. The problem was, he was given to believe Burl and Greek could not only track him down, but they'd trample through his family and friends to do it. As badly as he wanted to believe they weren't capable of everything Burl liked to suggest, he'd seen Burl command the McKee Police Department and the Jackson County Sheriff's Office, and he claimed to have any number of state troopers in his pocket. Knox had also crossed paths with dozens of Burl's roughneck minions and seen the wide reach of his empire in Jackson County. He knew what happened to Daniel, and Burl had left little room for doubt that he was behind it. Knox didn't want to put that on anyone else, himself included.

After Knox wrecked his car and had to abandon three pounds of Burl's property, it was pretty hard for him to see any way out of the chasm into which he'd fallen. He never seriously considered telling Burl about what happened, or calling the lawyer, because both seemed like surefire doom. His first inclination was to cover it up if he could. The only way to do that was to get Burl his money. There

151

was very little in Knox's favor, but he had time. Because the loss occurred just after a pickup, he had a full month to dig himself out.

Try as he might, the young state trooper couldn't prove Knox possessed any pot. Maybe if they did a CSI investigation or something like that, but even Knox knew they wouldn't fool with it. All they did was confiscate the pot, and after he got out of the hospital, they threw him in jail overnight. The judge let him eat the DUI at his arraignment, and that was it. Time served, a big fine he couldn't afford, some worthless classes, and ninety days without a license. He had six months to pay the fine, so he ignored that for the time being.

The immediate problem was the license suspension. Knox had to be careful. You see, there was a big difference between being *ordered* not to drive, and actually being *incapable* of driving. Knox still had a car—as fucked up as it was, it was still operable—and he still knew how to drive it. So all he was facing was ninety days he wasn't *supposed* to drive, and he could work around that.

Knox knew three ways to make money: pizza, poker, pot. One and two were played out, but what if there was a way to rekindle the third? He couldn't sell Burl's pot. It was gone and he couldn't go back for more, but that didn't mean he couldn't sell *someone's* pot.

He made some inquiries. He asked a customer, who knew a guy, who was friends with a guy, who put him in touch with another guy who lived on Centre Parkway in Lexington. Through veiled texts he was able to establish that he could get a pound for eighteen hundred dollars that he could have gotten from Burl for twelve hundred, and he didn't hesitate. With his *Prisoner of Azkaban* gone, Knox only had to pawn his laptop, his TV, his Blu-ray player, two guitars, a French horn, and a bike. He also sold every scrap of gold and silver he owned, along with most of his comic books and a few unopened action figures. Even after all that, he still had to raid Porthos's operating account.

The grass outside the orange brick duplex on Centre Parkway was khaki, dormant. A brush pile lay in the front yard with only a few dried leaves left hanging on it that resembled the mission figs Knox's mother ate so she could shit properly. He drove slowly, careful to use his turn signal on account of his unlicensed status. He had to swerve around a handful of furnace air filters scattered in the street that nobody had run over just yet. The parking spaces were clearly denoted by the cluster of oil stains at the center of each. The only car in front of either unit was a yellow one of those Scions that looked like a toaster. This one had a nonmatching gray hatch and was missing the red cover over one of the taillights. Knox's car made a nice match, with one side smashed, the hood rippled, the windshield cracked, and the trunk bungee-corded shut. Knox stepped out and crunched on the remains of a green lighter that had already been smashed into approximately eighty-five tiny pieces. Unit A was on the left: Knox's new supplier. His place wasn't as impressive as Burl's.

Knox debated leaving the money in the car until he saw the lay of the land, but in that neighborhood, it seemed safer to keep it on him. He stuffed the bulging envelope of mixed bills in the front pocket of his coat and went to the dirty white door. He knocked twice and waited. A pudgy girl in pink sweatpants and a Tates Creek High School t-shirt with a sloppy blonde bun on top of her head answered the door. "Can I help you?"

"I'm Knox. I'm supposed to meet someone here." She fell back and opened the door all the way. He stepped in and immediately smelled what could best be described as a vomity smell. It was a clusterfuck inside, kind of like the clusterfuck from which Knox sold his goods. He thought, At least my place smells better.

The girl walked away texting. With her back to him, she said, "Stephen will be right over," as she went into a bedroom and closed the door.

Knox stood there a good five minutes waiting, and a couple minutes in, he noticed he had gotten used to the vomit smell, which was kind of nice. He heard the door at the unit next door open and slam shut. Seconds later, a kid with a round face and a well-kept afro who looked to be in his early twenties came in.

"Knox?" he said.

"That's me. You Stephen?" Knox put his hand out to shake, but the kid didn't take it.

"Uh-huh."

"Nice to meet you, chief."

The kid stood with his hands in the pockets of his dark blue jeans and looked at Knox.

"So," Knox said, "we going to do some business today?"

"Afraid not."

"What?"

The kid raised his voice, as if Knox hadn't heard him the first time. "Afraid not, *chief.*"

"I heard what you said. I'm just wondering why not. I thought we understood each other. I came all the way over here."

"We did understand each other, but things change."

Knox rattled his head side to side, as if it was malfunctioning. "What changed? Your last text was two hours ago."

"Maybe you should ask Burl that question?"

Knox gnarled his lips and eyes, like a four-year-old about to launch into a tantrum. "Fuck my fucking asshole."

Stephen drew his hands from his pockets. "What's that?"

Knox raised both his. "Nothing." He hinged his head back and gazed at the daisy pattern on the ceiling. "Nothing." He brought it back level and turned to go.

"Burl said to tell you to get up with him," Stephen said as he went out. "You have a great day," he added.

Knox hadn't made it a mile down the road before his phone rang, and he had a pretty good idea who it was. Burl was one of the few people in Knox's life besides his parents who didn't like to communicate by text. Burl preferred cryptic phone calls. Knox stared down at the name on the screen, which was "Susan," just in case the police ever did any looking. He had an urge to hit the decline tab so badly he could hardly stand it, but he took a deep breath and accepted the call. "This is Knox."

"Where you at, son?"

"Lexington."

"Oh yeah. What was you doing up there?"

"This and that."

"How'd it go for you?"

"Not too good."

"I reckon not. Why don't you come see me. Let's have us a nice porch rock."

"When?"

"Why hell, since you was out and about, you might as well swing on by."

Knox grimaced and said "fuck" under his breath.

"What's that now?"

"I said okay."

"You goddamn right." The line cut off and Burl was gone.

$\mathcal{W}$HEN YOU drive over two hours on a suspended license in a wrecked car through three counties to your possible death, a hell of a lot goes through your mind. Knox drove it pretty slow. Part of that was on account of being careful because he had a suspended license. The fact he thought he might get murdered when he got to Burl's farm played a pretty big part in it, too.

Knox called his parents as he travelled south on I-75. His dad answered with the TV loud in the background. "Hold on," he said. "I'll turn this down and put you on speaker phone so your mother can hear."

There was a lot of clapping and people talking and electronic beeping on Knox's parents' end of the line. They were watching a game show. Thank god. After a little rumbling between them about where was the remote, and Knox's mom retorting she didn't have it, and his dad saying well someone had it, the volume finally went down, and his dad said, "Okay."

Knox's mom, sounding distant, said, "Hi, Knox."

"Hi, Mom. What're you guys doing?"

"Not much," his dad said. "Waiting for the Cats game tonight.

They're playing some who-done-its from Montana, but it'll be good to get a look at them."

They carried on all the way from southern Fayette County to the off-ramp in Berea, and mostly Knox just listened to their voices. The Cats looked pretty good, his dad said, but the guards couldn't shoot it, and the big men were soft, so it could be a rough year even though they were ranked preseason number one. Knox's aunt was in the hospital in Ashland, and they thought they should go visit her since her husband had died and her only kid moved to Georgia. The Buick was acting funny, but Knox's dad sanded the plugs and it cleared it right up.

"Well, all we've been doing's talking. What's going on in your world?" Knox's dad asked.

He thought, I need twenty thousand dollars neither of us have so I don't get fucking killed, but said, "Not much."

"How's the pizza business? Is it picking up at all?" his mom said.

"A little bit," he lied to her.

"Well, that's good," she said. "Hopefully the holidays will be busy."

Knox neared his exit. "Maybe. I sure hope so. I guess I should get off here."

"Okay, hon," his mom said.

"Good to hear your voice," his dad said.

"Yours, too," Knox said. "I love you guys."

"Love you, Knox," they both said, out of unison.

Knox used his forearm to wipe his eyes after they hung up. He didn't want to be alone, but that was all he could take of his parents without coming apart. When he thought of who else's voice he wanted to hear before he died, there was only one other person. Darla was never far from Knox's mind.

He brought up the contact and a tiny image of Darla's face lit the shattered screen. His thumb hovered over the call button before he tapped it. He laid the phone flat in his left palm and leaned his head into it. It rang once, twice, a third time. Knox had braced for the call to go to voicemail when an almost imperceptible click happened.

Darla answered, sounding winded. "Hey, Knox."

"Hey. How are you?"

"I'm good. I can't talk long though. I'm trying to pack."

"Where you going?"

"The tattoo expo in New Orleans. I'm scheduled to do a seminar in the morning and if I don't get my shit together I'm going to miss my flight."

"I can let you go if you need to."

"I kind of do. Is there something you needed or you just calling to talk?"

Knox reached a traffic light by the turn that took you to the old Fireball gas station. He closed his eyes briefly. "I was just calling to talk. I don't want to hold you up."

"Could I give you a call when I get back?"

When Knox looked, the light was green, and he started moving again. "Yeah. Maybe."

"I'm sorry. This is the worst possible moment but I answered anyway. I hope that counts for something."

"It's fine. Safe travels."

"Yeah. Okay, bud. I'll call you when I get back."

"Wish me safe travels, too."

"What?"

"Just wish me safe travels. I need it."

"Okay. Safe travels, I guess. Is something going on?"

"No. Just. No. Everything's good. I just hadn't talked to you in a while."

"We'll talk when I get back, Knox. That's a fucking promise."

"That's what you think."

"Bye, Knox. I got to go."

"Bye, Darla." He hung on the line thinking maybe she would say something else, but she didn't. The line was cold. It felt lousy, her having to go, but he was grateful she had answered at all. He took the phone from his ear and tossed it spinning into the passenger seat beside him, where it bounced and landed on the floor in a pile of drink cups and food wrappers.

Knox turned on the radio. Most of the stations that came in in Berea and points south were shitty, but he was able to catch the NPR station from UK for a little bit. The deejay was droll but played good music. It didn't exactly distract him, but it almost did.

When Knox passed the Frosty-Ette in Sandgap, he wished it was summer. He wished it was warm enough to stop and get a big chocolate shake. He wished he could order from the older lady who wore a white hat who was always so nice to him, and who called him *honey* but it sounded like *hawney*. He wished he could sit at the picnic table and drink it, and maybe that little yellow dog they called Missy would pad up for a pat on the head, and then he'd let her lick the sweat off his calves like she always wanted to. He wished he could do all that and go on home. He at least wished he knew he'd get the chance to do all that again someday.

*T*HE HANGING baskets were gone from Burl's front porch. Three bales of hay, a fodder shock tied with a big orange ribbon, a passel of multicolored mums, and pumpkins surrounded the black lamppost out front. The old gravel crunch didn't summon Burl's dogs right off, but after Knox stopped and got out, they spilled from the front door and lit for him, their tails flying. If he didn't know them and didn't understand their body language, maybe he would've gotten back in his car, but instead he put his hands out to catch them as best he could and pet their necks. Their ecstasy to see him was a sharp contrast to his misery being there. Burl and Greek had slipped out the door behind the dogs.

Burl shouted from the porch, "Quit fooling with them dogs and get your fool ass up here."

Knox did as he was told but the dogs followed so close at his heels that they bumped him continuously, knocking him off-kilter. Burl was in a rocking chair to the left by the time Knox came up. Greek stood sentry by the front door. On this trip, Burl didn't offer to shake hands.

"Get them goddamn clothes off."

"It's not forty degrees. You know I wouldn't wear any wire."

"I don't know what I know. I knowed you got all your product from me until today."

Knox stepped closer. "About that. I never—"

That was all he got out before he flew backward with Greek's hand cinched around his neck. He struggled a moment until Greek had him pinned to the porch and drove his knee into Knox's chest and leaned over him with his hands now controlling both of Knox's wrists. Waylon and Johnny went wild barking, lunging around them.

Knox shouted, "What the fuck, dude!" and tried to pull his hands free, but might as well have been cuffed.

Burl said, "Shh," long and loud. "Hush, boy. Just shut the fuck up. For one thing, we seen you in short pants when they was snow on the ground, and you're in short pants right now, and for another, I don't give a rat's tiny ass if you're cold. When Greek turns loose of you, you're going to lose them goddamn clothes. You got it?"

Knox didn't answer.

Burl stepped a boot right in front of his face and raised the pant leg, exposing his brown leather holster and the butt of his revolver. "You got it?" He repeated, louder.

It was hard for him to say anything because his chest was so compressed, but Knox managed to squeeze out, "Got it."

Greek lifted his knee off first. Once he was nearly standing, he let Knox's wrists go. Knox had a hard time deciding which he wanted to rub more, his chest, his wrists, or his throat, because they all smarted like hell. He stood up kneading them all in succession.

As soon as Knox was on his feet, Burl said, "Don't make me wait no longer."

Knox took off his coat and shirt and kicked off his slides. Last he dropped his shorts and underwear in one movement, letting Burl get his second long look at his dick, close enough to see the lint. The only thing Knox still wore was a pair of white socks. Greek picked up his clothes and rifled them as Knox glared at him out of the corner of his eye. When Greek found the envelope Knox had to pay Stephen, he tossed it to Burl, who caught it, and immediately began leafing through.

"Burl that's—" Knox started, but Burl put his finger to his lips, shushing him.

Greek dropped all Knox's clothes on the porch beside him. "He's all right."

Knox bent to get them.

Burl thrust his hand out. "Leave them clothes be. You just wait until I tell you."

Knox crossed his arms tight and huffed. He squeezed his knees together, trying to keep his legs warm. Burl counted the money silently to himself, but his lips moved. "I brought you a payment," Knox said, his voice scratchy from having his esophagus collapsed by Greek.

"Did you now?" said Burl, still counting. "How much?"

"Should be eighteen hundred."

"Well, huh. Ain't that a coincidence. Ain't that what you was aiming to pay my business associate, Stephen, when you ain't paid me nothing on your last three pounds? When you're already sixteen in the goddamn hole? Getting ready to be more after I pop your vig for nonpayment."

"Something happened, Burl. A fucking act of God. I wasn't trying to screw you over, I swear. I was desperate. I was trying to get you paid."

Burl looked up. "That so?"

"It's true. After I got that last batch, I wrecked on my way home. Take a look at my car." Knox pointed at the gnarly heap in the driveway. "It busted my fucking trunk open and the weed flew out everywhere. I couldn't do anything before the cops got there, and I remembered what you said, that I should ditch everything if the police ever showed up, so I said I didn't know where it came from."

"They bought that?"

"Well hell no. But they couldn't prove any different. I took a DUI and I've been scrambling ever since. You can check my record. It's all on there."

"Why's this the first we're hearing about it?"

"Because I was fucking scared, man. I owe you so much already. I was afraid."

"Of what?"

"You going to make me say it? Of you, man." Knox pulled his thumb at Greek. "Of him. Of whoever. I already couldn't pay you back, now I'm down another three pounds? I couldn't see any way out. I was scrambling."

Burl pointed at him with the stack of money. "You know what your problem is, Knox?"

"I could guess."

"I never seen anything like you. You're smart, you just ain't no good at thinking." Burl tapped his finger to his temple one time. "I never seen no one make worse decisions."

Knox bobbed his shoulders. A cold wind whipped the trees at the perimeter of Burl's property. It took hold of everything and set Knox shivering. His penis's slow crawl inward sped up.

"Who was it got you for DUI?"

"Some little shit. I don't remember his name. Maybe Carver."

"What department?"

"State police."

"A trooper? And you didn't do nothing about it? It ever occur to you that was something we ought to know about? It ever occur to you that they might be looking closer now that they run across you and three pounds of product in the same place?"

Knox studied his own feet. His nipples were hard as Corn Nuts. "I thought you had connections with the state police."

Burl popped up and came six inches from Knox's face. "And how in fuck am I supposed to use them connections if I don't know what you've got into? Police attention is like a fucking virus. You got to contain that shit before it spreads. Goddamn it, son. I knew you was short sense, but I thought you at least had some."

"I did, too."

"Well," Burl said, and pointed abruptly over Knox's left shoulder, "you ain't."

Knox wheeled to see Greek lunging toward him with a gun handle gripped in his fist. The lights went bright. Then they went out.

KNOX'S HEAD ached. His face hurt. He was cold as hell and wind ran over him like icy water. The four-seat RZR's engine grumbled as it traveled across rough ground. Knox's chin sagged to his chest and the seat belt dug into his bare, raw skin when the RZR bobbled over bumps. His back felt frozen to the cold vinyl seat. Knox was in, he was out. It was better when he was out. Inside his mouth was ragged and rich with iron. He came around a little when the engine got killed and the motion stopped. He felt someone's hands on him unbelting him before he was flung face-first into deep mud. He raised his head just enough to turn it so he could breathe. He kept his eyes closed tight, fighting the ache. His naked ass jutted up a little and he shivered like a scared rabbit. He could hear something moving nearby. It was punctuated by feet sucking in and out of the saturated ground and the sound of a dozen grumbling voices.

Burl's talking came through in snippets. Knox hardly comprehended. He found himself wishing that whatever they did, he only hoped they'd go on and get it over with and put him out of his misery before he came around. He was terrified of dying, but he wanted it.

Big hands fell on Knox's shoulders. Greek's hands. He pulled

Knox to his teetering feet. His knees gave, but Greek didn't let him fall. His hands dug hard into Knox's armpits. Knox's socked feet squished in the thick mud.

"This ain't time for no nap, Fort Knox," Burl said. "It's bath time, not naptime."

Knox tried to open his eyes, tried to look at Burl, whose voice came from right in front of him. Mud covered his face, including his eyes, and the left one sung out in pain where he'd been hit with the gun butt. Knox couldn't force the lid open. He could smell Burl's cigarette smoke, but all he could make out of him was a blur of dark moving colors, nothing else.

"All right, Greek. Give this fool a bath. He's a damned mess."

One of Greek's hands went from under Knox's arm to the hair at the back of his head, grabbing it in his fist. Knox squealed.

"Shut up, Knox. Don't embarrass yourself," Burl said.

In one motion, Greek plunged Knox face-first into water, frigid, up to his waist. He flailed and kicked, but Greek's grip never faltered. A panic unlike anything Knox had ever felt coursed through him as Greek pressed his nose into a metal bottom without flinching while Knox's midsection dug into a hard metal side. Knox hadn't gathered any air before going in, and already his lungs were screaming. He managed a last wild flurry with his arms and legs that budged Greek maybe a half inch. Then he went still.

As fast as he went in, Greek tore Knox's head back out. Knox gasped so hard he felt like he got stabbed in the chest. As he groped for a second breath, Burl said, "Look there, he ain't clean yet." Greek jammed Knox's head back under, and it was crueler than the first, Knox drawing hard for air as he went in and getting a gulp of water instead. He spasmed and writhed, clutching the sides of the metal tub, tearing back his nails. The overwhelming cold of the water left him with hardly any external feeling, but inside he was in fucking agony. He wasn't thinking clearly enough to understand that he was in his death throes, but that's what they were. His struggling had no more effect on Greek than a chicken's wiggling does before its neck's wrung. Then Knox was done. The fight was lost, and he had no more. In the split second he relented, went slack, and began to suck in even more icy liquid, Greek jerked him out again.

He scarcely drew in air before he was back in again. And out, and in again. Each time Knox felt at the edge of death, the outer edge of pain and misery, he came out and went back in, until finally, when Knox was absolutely desperate to die, Greek stopped.

Knox coughed uncontrollably, unrelentingly, vomiting water from deep inside, retching blood. Greek released his grip on his hair and wrapped an arm across Knox's chest, holding him up as he rocked and staggered. Knox had the insane sensation of being a little child, when his mother lifted him from the bath naked and before she wrapped him in a towel. Knox continued his contortions and heaving for some time. Nothing was said until he finally stilled. Once he did, bleating cut through the quiet. It was the only thing Knox heard.

Burl's voice sounded. "All right, Greek. Now that he's good and clean, let's feed this dumb motherfucker to the goats."

Knox managed to get an eye half-open, and there they were. Staring, milling, curious. A pack of big, scraggly, black and white, horned goats better than ten deep watched intently. Waiting.

"Go on, then. Them goats is hungry."

Greek took a step toward the goats and Knox lost it again. He shrieked almost without sound and threw every limb, every finger, every toe, into a frenzy. He wrenched his face at Greek's arm trying like hell to bite him, and he gouged him with his fingernails. Knox's head rocked to the side when Greek's fist slammed into his ear, and Knox stopped moving at once. For the first time, Greek spoke, pissed. "Cut that shit out!" Knox's mind was a fuzz of static again.

Burl howled. Knox had heard him laugh, but never so hard. "Goddamn, son. You really are a fucking idiot. Goats won't eat nobody. It's hogs'll eat you. A goat might eat your clothes, but you ain't got none on. For Christ sake."

Greek turned Knox to face Burl, who stood beside the corrugated metal trough where he had just been. Burl shook his head and was still chuckling quietly to himself.

Knox managed to sputter, "Just fucking kill me. What're you waiting for? Just do it."

"Oh, hell, Fort Knox. You trying to sell me some Nike shoes?"

"Just kill me."

"You ain't selling shoes?" Burl popped his chin at Greek. "All right then. If this boy wants killed, I reckon we ought to oblige him."

Greek released Knox before kicking him between the shoulder blades so hard he left his feet. One of Knox's socks stayed down in the mud. He landed on his knees with his forearms flat in the mushy ground. He had no will to do anything, and when the muzzle of Greek's gun pressed to his occipital bone, he stilled and submitted to what was coming.

Greek waited, saying nothing. Another twist of the knife. After a passage of time Knox couldn't guess at, Burl finally spoke up. "Naw, we ain't going to kill you today, Fort Knox. What good would that do? How would I get paid?"

Knox made no reply.

"I will tell you, I'm tired of fooling with you, and I don't trust you to do right no more. So, here's what I'm going to do. I'm going to give you a month to make some real progress. One more month to start getting your ass square with me, and I ain't going to help you out no more. I don't care what you got to do, but you're going to pay me. Surely to God they's somebody who cares enough about you to get me paid."

"There's nobody," Knox croaked out.

"Come on now, Knox. You got you a big family. We know every goddamn one of them. It's like my boys who owe child support.

They don't pay a lick until they go to jail, but then, by god, they momma's can't stand to see them in jail, and here the money comes. What you're looking at is worse than any jail, son."

Knox lowered his head farther and closed his one working eye.

"You may be thinking you have other options. Maybe you go to the police, or run off, or some such as that. You know what'll come should you pull any shit like that? Bad things'll start happening, but they ain't going to start with you. No sir. They'll end with you. So remember, when you go talk to your kin, you ain't just helping your own self."

"Nobody has that kind of money."

"You'd be surprised. Not only that, you got you a leg up. You paid that eighteen hundred today. That's the best you done in a long time. We'll be checking in with you to see if we need to have us another business meeting like the one we had here today. You want to have another business meeting?"

Knox stayed still. "No."

"Chin up, honey. You been born again. Things is looking up. We just need to make sure you don't forget. Greek, give him something to remember it."

The gun went from the back of Knox's head to the side of it so fast Knox didn't register. The explosion of the gun firing was followed instantaneously by unyielding ringing and a sulphurous stink. The pain in his ear was so acute it took a beat before Knox realized his face was on actual fire.

$\mathcal{T}$HE LITERALLY searing pain from the powder burns on the side of Knox's face were enough to force his right eye nearly closed from wincing, but he fought to keep it open as the left eye was already swelled shut altogether. Had those been his only injuries, they would've been debilitating. He also couldn't hear anything aside from the ceaseless ringing in his ears.

Greek had deposited Knox and his clothes beside his car and left him. Knox lay unmoving for a length of time before he finally summoned the will to get in and drive.

He tracked the road ahead through the one rheumy eye. He was in such a variety of pain during the drive home he could barely function. He literally begged his car heater to warm up, hoping it might stop his trembling. His feet and hands felt like they would shatter if touched with any force. His slides were lost to Burl's fiefdom, and he had pulled off the remaining muddy sock so that he drove with naked feet. As Knox went past the Frosty-Ette again, he couldn't comprehend what the desire for a chocolate shake might even feel like.

Blood leaked from both his nostrils, and no matter how hard Knox squeezed, it wouldn't stop. He twisted drive-through napkins he had in his glove box and shoved one up each side, which seemed to do the trick. Breathing through his mouth was his only option. The inside of it was mostly numb, but he could feel his tongue sag into the space where one of his lower molars had been earlier. He pulled over to throw up out the window three times, splashing it down the side of his car, beyond caring. By the third, there was nothing left, so he retched a bit before carrying on. Each time, he had to replace the napkins in his nose.

Even as damaged as Knox was, he felt like a man whose death sentence had been stayed. Dread and doom would roll in ever heavier, but at that moment, even though Knox had been laboring under his debt to Burl for over a year, and it had more than tripled, he still had the insane hope he could somehow meet Burl's terms.

Knox managed to get to his apartment, where he took Hydrocodone he had stashed, and slept until it wore off. He stayed holed up in his apartment recovering, waiting for his hearing to return. The only one he saw was Rob. Rob begged to take him to the hospital, but Knox wouldn't budge. Rob brought him food and whatever else he needed, which included weed. Knox felt a bit like Howard Hughes, only instead of a swanky top floor penthouse over a casino, he was in a second-floor apartment over a rundown pizza shop, beaten to the brink.

Once Knox fully understood his position, one word entered his mind and stuck: inexorable. Knox was down to a single business: pizza. There was no way he would try to go around Burl to sell pot again. He wondered if Burl was right, too. Maybe that trooper was looking at him, lying in wait. At that point, all he would have found was Knox's meager personal stash, but he still didn't welcome a visit.

Rob and Tori had to run every aspect of the day-to-day Porthos operation. It was all they could do to get the doors open. Knox made Rob promise not to tell Tori what really happened. They concocted a wild tale about Knox wrecking a moped. Rob was irritated he had to lie to her, but Knox knew he would keep his word. If she left, and it was just Rob again, Knox was pretty sure Porthos would end.

Knox's sight and most of his hearing came back after a week, but the tinnitus persisted. He finally left his apartment to work part of a Friday kitchen shift, and the cat was out of the bag about his face. That one shift spurred Knox back into his routine. In fact, he was now free to work more hours at Porthos than before because he couldn't deal anymore.

Knox's phone still blew up and people came to his door all hours, but they all wound up disappointed. He sent so many *out of biz* reply texts to pot requests that he could type it without thinking. He dug in and worked extra hours to drop payroll because he had stripped the Porthos bank account bare. There were a number of nights Knox cut the closers and closed the whole shop himself, because why not? He didn't have anything else to do.

Knox had had to make some hard choices to get the eighteen hundred to buy that pound from Stephen, but he still had more to sacrifice. After picking out a handful he wasn't willing to part with, he loaded up his boxes of books and took them to Lexington. There was nothing nearly as valuable as *The Prisoner of Azkaban* in those boxes, but he had some good stuff. He managed to marshal a few hundred dollars from used bookstores. He took that money to Grub's Gun Shop and bought a used Glock that the manager insisted was his best option. As much as he hated guns, Knox hated feeling helpless even more. He thought about what Rickie Vasquez said in the "Guns and Gossip" episode of *My So-Called Life*: "Maybe some people who have guns are, like, victims too? And they're, like, forced to carry?" That was exactly how he felt. The Glock changed things. Failing protection, it gave him a way out if he wanted it.

He kept coming back to the idea of selling Porthos. Lane Spicer, a lawyer in Richmond, had tried to buy Porthos before. Knox kicked himself for not taking the offer when it was made, but at the time he still thought he could bring Porthos back. It seemed ludicrous now, but he hadn't wanted to sell low. Lane had a plan to buy the business from Knox and the building from the owner. Knox had always wanted to buy the building, too, but had never had the money. In spite of all the signs telling him otherwise, he had always believed he eventually would.

He approached Lane one last time after his business meeting with Burl, his goats, and Greek's gun. He wanted to wait until his face was more presentable, but ultimately, he just had to go. He had tried getting an appointment to discuss it, but Lane's secretary kept saying, "Are you looking to hire a lawyer, sir?"

Finally, Knox said, "Yeah. It's about my DUI. I think I need a lawyer." Thirty seconds later, he had an appointment.

Lane's secretary gave Knox a client-intake form the instant he walked in the smoke-smelling lobby. After he filled it out and gave it back, he said, "How are you this morning?" trying to make nice.

She grumbled, "Fine. Have a seat." The concentration of lines radiating from the pucker around her lips was incredible. Her vocal chords sounded as if they had been barbecued over the course of years by roughly nine million cigarettes.

Knox found a *People* magazine and sat down on a leather nailhead couch to read it. Alyssa Milano was on the cover with a Christmas tree behind her and a toddler in her lap. Knox had a soft spot for her. She was a year older than him, but she had held up much better. He had bought her exercise video on VHS tape when he was fourteen years old strictly so he could watch her work out in the comfort of his bedroom. You had to do shit like that before the internet. The video was called *Teen Steam*. Knox had spent countless hours watching Alyssa do lunges and deep knee bends. She felt like an old girlfriend.

Lane left Knox sitting ten minutes. He finally came in the lobby with the clipboard in hand. "Hey, Knox. You get yourself in a scrape?"

Knox stood up shaking his head, acting dejected. "Yep. DUI."

"Is that what happened to your face?"

"Uh, yeah."

"Wow." Lane cocked his head and trained his eyes, taking in the damage. "Come on back. Let's talk about this thing."

Knox guessed Lane was somewhere in his late fifties, though he wasn't too good at guessing such things, and the fact Lane was pretty much bald didn't help. He was not an attractive man to begin with, and his lack of hair drew attention to his worst feature—his face—and made you more aware he was ugly. He was a loyal Porthos customer though, and that counted for something. He also let the homely old lady work at his front desk, so he didn't discriminate against his own kind, and Knox respected that.

Lane's conference room smelled of old books, and somehow, money. Once the door was closed, Lane said, "For starters, when's your court date?"

"I already pled guilty."

Lane frowned. "I'm not sure what I can do for you then."

"The thing is, the DUI has put me in a position where I need to sell Porthos. I came here to discuss that."

"Okay," Lane said, and paused, seeming to consider. "Why didn't you just say that when you called instead of this stuff about a DUI?"

"Because that old bridge troll up front wouldn't give me an appointment until I said I had a DUI, and I'm selling because of that."

"Hey, that's my sister."

Shit. Bad genes. Knox kicked himself for not guessing. "Sorry. I just don't think she likes me."

"She's kind of a hard ass, but most of my clients need it. She's looking out for me. Let's just move on."

"So, here's the deal. You offered me fifty thousand for Porthos—however long ago that was—but at the time I didn't want to sell."

Lane raised his hand. "Sorry, Knox, but if you're trying to sell me Porthos again, I've told you, I'm not in the market anymore."

"Hear me out, though. You wanted to do craft beer and pizza, man. That's only getting bigger, and nobody's really hit that market in Richmond yet. The timing's perfect."

"That may be true, but my situation's changed. The money I had earmarked for that is elsewhere, and my niece who I planned to have run it moved to Oregon. She was the key to the whole deal. That's what I tried to explain to you the last time."

Knox tried to picture Lane's niece, wondering if she was the secretary's daughter. He pictured a girl smoking and making pizzas at the same time. "But I could stay on and run it for you. You wouldn't need her."

"You know I like you, Knox, but I don't think that would work. I've seen it too many times. Porthos is your baby. You wouldn't be able to run it for someone else. Those arrangements never work. Not well, anyway."

It made Knox crazy because he knew Lane was right. Knox needed the money, but he couldn't run the business for someone else. He'd be in hell. "Listen. I'm willing to go down on price. I'd take forty. I just really need to sell it."

"I appreciate that, Knox. And I appreciate your situation, but it's not in the cards for me, really at any price."

Knox fiddled with the zipper at the bottom of his coat. "Seriously?"

"Seriously."

Knox looked at a framed picture of a courtroom scene on the wall behind Lane where some old-timey guy in an old-timey suit stood in front of a jury of old-timey people while other old-timey lawyers and an old-timey judge looked on. "You know anyone else who might be interested?"

"Not right offhand. I'll keep my ears open." Lane tapped the clipboard on the surface of his conference table a couple times. "You know, the fact that you've been selling marijuana out of your shop may not help you here."

Knox's eyes darted to Lane's. "You know about that?"

"A lot of people know about it, Knox. Spinach Special, right?"

"Damn. I thought I kept it underground."

"You can't keep that kind of thing underground. Word of mouth. Where do you think your customers come from? You think they just guess?"

"I don't know." Knox tapped his foot, stalling, trying to figure out another angle. Lane was the only way out he'd come up with. The only realistic one, anyway, besides getting a Glock. Before giving up, he had to try one last time. "Is there no way you'd even consider buying it? You know, if I gave you a really good deal?"

Lane put his hand on his weak chin and breathed deep. Knox's hopes rose. It really looked like he was considering. "I'm afraid that window has closed. I'm sorry. I don't see it anymore. Not under any circumstances."

Knox said, "Fuck," not very loud.

"Sorry."

Knox shrugged. "Let me ask you one more question."

"Shoot."

"You care if I take that *People* with Alyssa Milano on the cover?"

Lane stood up and patted Knox's shoulder in a way he guessed he did to a lot of people he was done talking to. "It's all yours."

*K*NOX'S SITUATION with Burl and Greek was pretty much a life-and-death scenario, and Rob knew it, but he stuck by him. The problem was, Knox was afraid if Rob stuck too close, he'd end up going down with him. They agreed to do everything they could to keep Porthos afloat until they could find a way to both bail out safely.

Since Knox's computer was gone, they had transferred all the books to Rob's laptop. They were up in Knox's apartment working on payroll when Knox told Rob he'd gone at Lane Spicer one last time and whiffed. That was when Rob suggested they try putting Porthos on Craigslist. "There are all kinds of businesses for sale on there."

"Do any of them actually sell?"

"How the fuck should I know, but they're on there."

Knox blew air out, rattling his lips, making a fart noise. "Worth a shot I guess."

"Lane wanted it at one time. Maybe someone else is out there. We're going to need to take some pictures and whatnot. Make it look good. How much you want to ask for it?"

Knox didn't hesitate. "Fifty thousand."

Rob tossed his hands. "Are you fucking kidding me? You need

twenty grand and you want to ask fifty? We're talking about your life here."

"You know how hard I worked to build this place? I'll be out of a job. They'll be getting the equipment and everything."

"Knox, man, used restaurant equipment isn't worth shit. You know that."

"It's worth something."

"Maybe the ovens, but that's about it."

"So, I'm supposed to give this fucking place away? Everything I worked for the last fifteen years you want me to give away?"

"Who said give it away? Not me. I didn't tell you to give anything away, I just said you shouldn't ask fifty grand. This is a fucking fire sale and you want to walk away with money in your pocket?"

"Okay, forty."

"You told me these guys'll kill you and you want to go for a premium? You don't even own the building and it doesn't make a profit. The buyer would have to get a lease. How do you figure it's worth that much money?"

Knox grabbed his beard at the base of his chin and stroked it like Jim "The Anvil" Neidhart did when he was in the Hart Foundation tag team. "Thirty-five."

"Fine. Thirty-fucking-five."

The first day Rob posted the ad to Craigslist, Knox texted him just about hourly for updates. His responses kept coming back, *Nothing so far*. Knox slowed down as the week wore on. He came down that Friday just before a shift change to relieve Rob. The kitchen was deserted except for the two of them. Knox sidled up. "So, nothing on the Craigslist ad at all?"

"One guy asked if you'd be interested in selling to him on a promissory note and he could pay you out of all the money he's going to make. He also wanted to know if you'd cosign with him for a second loan."

"Well, that's fucking worthless. It's not even worth talking about."

"You asked."

"That it?"

"Not exactly, but you won't like it."

"I never hear anything I like anyway."

"A company in Nicholasville that refurbishes pizza ovens wants to know if you want to sell ours. Sight unseen they offered six thousand for the stack as long as they both work when they get here."

"And we're out of business."

"Yep."

"That doesn't do us any fucking good."

"Nope." Rob picked up the dough docker and flipped it end over end a couple times. "Unless, you know, you only sold them one."

"Say what?"

"Unstack them. Sell the top oven and we can still use the bottom."

"And what happens if we get hit with a rush?"

"I don't know. We fucking deal with it. It's not like we're getting hit with too many rushes these days. We could get by on one oven."

"No way, chief."

"Just a thought. All I'm doing's trying to keep you out of the fucking hangman's noose. Literally."

"I know, and I appreciate that. You know I do, but I can't do it."

Rob stared at Knox. The corner of Rob's mouth compressed inward. He stuck out his elbow. "Throw me a 'bow, man."

Knox stuck his out. They bashed them.

"I don't want to see anything happen to you, Knox. Do you understand that? This isn't just about you, you know. People care about you, man, and it would hurt all of us if this went bad." Rob slowed down on the last sentence. "So stop being an asshole, and let me call those guys."

$\mathcal{I}$N THE MONTHS Tori worked at Porthos, she saw some weird shit. At some point, it became almost impossible for her to be surprised by anything. One morning, when she got there, the pizza warmer was full of Knox's socks, shorts, boxers, and t-shirts. It turned out Knox's dryer wasn't working, so he put his stuff in there overnight. It was all superhot, super wrinkled, but not dry.

Another day, Tori was on her way in and did a double take at the front window. Someone had painstakingly scraped off some of the lettering, changing the store name from: "PORTHOS PIZZA" to "PO T   PIZZA."

One night shift, when she showed up to work, Rob was in the lobby getting cussed out by a kid who looked like he was twelve. On the way out the door the kid shouted, "Fuck you, you fucking loser!" and threw straws and napkins all over the floor.

Rob rushed outside after him and yelled "Fuck you too, Bieber!" at the kid as he took off. Rob came in and picked up the trash from the floor and threw it away, then went back to the line like it was just another day.

Tori followed him. "What the hell was that?"

"That little kid was trying to buy weed."

Tori laughed. "You should've just given him Knox's number and let him handle it."

Rob pulled a ticket from the printer, hung it on the line, and went for a dough ball under the counter. "No, because Knox probably would've sold to him." He dropped the dough in the flour. "And then we'd all be fucked."

Just recently, Knox had gotten into a moped accident, and didn't work for like a week. When he finally turned back up, his face was beat up, cut up, and for some reason, burned. Once he came back to work, he didn't talk about it. The only thing that changed was he actually started working more.

In spite of all that stuff, what weirded Tori out the most was the Friday in early December when she came in for an opening shift and found the top oven gone. For an idiotic moment, she thought someone had stolen it. Since that was basically insane, she looked the situation over a little longer and realized the kitchen was in perfect order except for the missing oven. Why would someone break in and take nothing but one pizza oven? They wouldn't. She stood there slack-jawed for five minutes trying to piece it together until she gave up, turned on the vent, and fired up the remaining oven.

A weekend cook had recently walked out on his shift, so Tori was supposed to train two new ones. When Rob told Tori he hired two people to replace one, Tori asked why.

"Because I know what I'm doing," Rob said. "Don't even give them shirts. Think of new cooks like hatchling turtles on the beach trying to find the ocean. They aren't all going to make it. If either one of them gets to the water, I'll give them shirts."

It was Tori's first time training a cook, and thinking about everything she was supposed to show them had her preoccupied. A lot of restaurants had employee handbooks and training manuals and that sort of stuff. Porthos was not one of those restaurants. At Porthos, it was all see, then do. Free form. That might have accounted for why new employees had such a high failure rate. A half-dozen part-time cooks had already come and gone since Tori started.

Tori's driver, server, and trainees were all due in at eleven. She heard someone peck on the front door at quarter till. A girl in a shiny heavy coat with dozens of tiny braids extending out from under a knit hat was huddled outside blowing into her hands. Tori opened the door to her. "You here to train?"

"Supposed to," she said.

Tori moved out of her way as she introduced herself. The girl's name was Bria.

"You're prompt," Tori said as she led her to a booth to fill out her new hire paperwork.

"Always."

"I like that hat."

Bria pointed at Tori's. "I like yours, too."

After Bria was done with her paperwork, the two made small talk while Tori finished her opening stuff. Everything she did, Bria offered to help. She didn't volunteer much about herself, but when Tori asked her she said she was a freshman at EKU studying computer science and that she was from Hopkinsville.

Kendra turned up, and so did the driver, but by ten after, the second trainee still wasn't there. "Looks like it's just going to be you and me today, Bria. You want to get started?"

Stretching dough was the primary skill every cook had to have, so Tori started there. If you couldn't stretch, you were useless at Porthos. About thirty minutes in Bria pretty much had the slap down pat. That was when a guy turned up at the counter. Tori assumed it was someone placing an order.

Kendra came into the kitchen. "That's the other new cook."

"Where's he been?"

"I don't know but I'm going with *not a bath tub*." Kendra pinched her nose.

Tori said, "Just keep slapping," to Bria, and went to the counter.

The guy standing there scratched at his neck like a bug bit it. "Hey there. You're kind of late." There was a smell about him that hit Tori's nose. Like a dog's ears when they go bad.

"I know," the guy said. "I got held up." The spot where he had been scratching was bright red, angry. His eyes had some of the same red.

"You got held up? You mean like robbed?"

He sniffed, then rubbed his nose with the back of his wrist. "No. You know. I had some household issues." There was something tattooed in dark cursive sticking out of the top of his collar. "I'm here now."

"Where's your hat?"

He touched the top of his head. "Oh. Shit. Yeah, I forgot."

Tori coughed. The guy's eyebrows rose. "Look," Tori said, "I don't think this is going to work out."

"For real? How come?"

"Because you're a half hour late and it's your first day."

"I know, and I'm really sorry about that. Why don't you give me a chance though, sweetie? I'm a real hard worker." The guy dabbed his nose again.

"I don't think so, darling."

He gave Tori a hard look. "Why not?"

"Honestly, because I don't really think you care all that much." Tori pointed her thumb over her shoulder. "And we've got work to do."

"That's not fair."

"Really? I think it's totally fair."

He stood there looking at Tori and started scratching again. He bobbed his head a couple times before he walked out muttering under his breath. The only word Tori could make out was *cunt* because he said it louder than anything else.

Kendra approached from behind. "What was that about?"

"Dude was pilled out."

"You *think*? When he said he was here to train, I was like, For what?"

Tori rolled her eyes. "Rob hired him."

"I swear to god, I think he was pranking you."

"Maybe he is pranking me. This day is all an elaborate prank. Maybe that's why we only have one oven."

Tori went back to Bria still standing at the makeline slapping dough like a champ. "You got this."

Bria laid her dough on a screen like Tori had showed her, checking to see if she had it big enough. "It's not hard."

Tori got her phone out and sent Rob a text. *One of the turtles showed up a half hour late pilled out of his mind nice hire!*

Rob wrote back, *Haha how's the other one?*

Swimming in the ocean where's the top oven?

We downsized

Tori typed back, *Bananas*, put her phone back in her back pocket, and headed for the sink to wash her hands so she and Bria could start saucing.

*T*ORI HAD agreed to work a split shift since they were short, so she left in the middle of the day and Knox took over, including training Bria. Tori wasn't real sure what store policy was, but she figured it was only fair to warn Bria about Knox's intermittent stank. Wouldn't you know it though, he seemed to be freshly showered.

Tori came back that night for a serving shift while Rob ran deliveries. At close, everyone was cut except Tori and Rob, while Knox was upstairs counting the drawer. Rob had shut down the one remaining oven and had pulled out all the tables and the makeline and started cleaning the kitchen while Tori swept the floor and wiped down the booths in the dining room. It was maybe twenty minutes after eleven.

There was a loud banging at the front door. Tori shouted, "I got it," in the general direction of the kitchen and headed toward the lobby.

A little old dude in Western clothing who looked like he had a pint of pomade in his hair was hammering on the doorframe. He saw Tori coming but didn't stop banging. "Go get Knox. Tell him Burl's here."

She shouted over the noise, "I might do it if you'll quit banging on the door like that."

"Get Knox." He banged even harder now, belligerently.

"Keep it up and I call the cops." She took her phone from her back pocket and showed it to him.

The Dapper Dan man stopped hitting the door all at once, the corner of his eye twitched, and his chest puffed up. Before Tori could do anything else, he turned on his heel and stalked off.

Tori was standing there watching him disappear when Rob turned up in the lobby holding a wet rag. "What the hell was that racket?"

Tori turned her eyes to him. "I don't even know. Some mean little cowboy named Burl was pounding the door demanding to see Knox. I told him I'd call the cops if he didn't stop and he took off. It was so bizarre."

"Oh Jesus."

"What?"

"That's not good." Rob moved fast toward the back of the store, headed for Knox's door. "That's not good at all."

Tori followed him. "What's going on right now?"

Rob threw open the door and yelled up the stairs, "Yo! Knox!"

Knox's bleary voice came back, "What up, chief?"

"Dude, get the fuck down here. Burl was just at the front door."

Knox turned up at the top of the stairs looking foggy. "Burl's here?"

"He was."

"What'd he want?"

"To see your big ass."

"Aw fuck," Knox said.

Tori was startled by a man's voice in the dining room. "You roust him?"

She spun to find little Burl behind her. Rob flinched back about a foot and threw his hand over his heart. "Holy shit. How the hell'd you get in here?"

"It ain't like you got to know the damn da Vinci code to get in your back door. Only two numbers on the keypad is wore. Ain't too hard to guess. I got them same keypads. Difference being, we change our codes because we aren't fucking incompetent."

Rob stared at him, his hand still on his chest.

"You act like you seen a ghost. I ain't no ghost, but I'll haunt you."

Knox, his hand out, passed by Tori and Rob like they weren't there. "Hey, Burl."

The little guy took it. "Greek said you all was real inhospitable to him last time he was here, too. You might want to train your people to treat folks decent if you aim to keep your doors open."

"Sorry about that. We have to be careful. We get some weird characters around here."

"You don't fucking say."

Knox turned to Tori and Rob with one hand on his forehead. "I'm sorry, guys. Burl's a friend of mine. I should've told you he might stop by. This is my fault."

Neither Tori or Rob said anything. Knox took his hand away from his forehead. The cut across his nose was improving and the skin under his eye was now faint lemon/lime where it had been deep maroon, but the burns on the side of his face were slow to heal. Seemed like they might never.

"Me and Burl are going to go up. You all lock the place and go on, I'll finish closing." Knox's hand dropped to his side. Tori noticed it was jittery.

Rob looked hard at him. "You sure?"

"Yeah. Absolutely. You all go on. I got it." Knox headed for the stairs and waved Burl up behind him. Knox looked back a last time and said, "Go," his eyes wide.

At the foot of the stairs Burl said, "Christ, Knox. You having you a goddamn yard sale in your stairwell?" He pulled the door closed and locked it.

Once it was closed, Tori said, "You want to tell me what the hell just happened?"

"I don't know if I can."

"Who was that little asshole?"

"You don't want to know. Forget you ever saw him. Forget you heard his name. Just go home."

"After that mess, I'm going to Paddy Wagon for a beer. My friends are there. You should come with. That shit requires a beer. Also, I've got questions. Lots and lots of questions."

Rob was still staring at Knox's door. Tori noticed he had the adrenaline shakes, too. He said, "I'll try to get by later. I need to stay here for a little bit."

Tori put her hand on Rob's upper arm and squeezed it. "You going to be all right?"

"Yeah," he said and glanced at Tori's hand, then her face. "Yeah. I'll catch up. I promise. I need to talk to you about the pizza show, anyway."

"Don't make yourself a liar and not come." She let go of his arm and headed up front to clock out. She could tell Rob wasn't going to leave, but she was just as sure she shouldn't stay.

*K*NOX WASN'T so much surprised Burl had keyed in the back door at Porthos as he was he'd shown up at all. That was what made it so fucking scary. While Burl made his way up the stairs giving Knox shit about his messy apartment, all Knox could think about was getting Rob and Tori out before anything happened, and after that, making it to the couch so he could get a hand on the Glock down between the cushions.

Knox fell into the old couch while Burl looked around and rummaged. "Damn, Knox. You're like one of them hoarders, ain't you?" Burl whistled. "All this shit and ain't none of it looks like it's worth fifty cents. Not to me anyway. You got more than a yard sale in here, you got a whole fucking flea market." Burl picked up Wooly Willy: one of those cards with a bald dude's face under plastic where you take metal filings and give him hair, or a beard, or a mustache, by arranging the filings with the little magnetic wand. He shook his head and tossed it back down.

"I have something for you, Burl." Knox settled in at the nerve center of his apartment. He kept everything crucial within arm's reach of the couch: phone, bowl, weed, bottle opener, etc. His TV remote had been replaced by the gun.

Burl put a finger to his lips. "Shh. First I want you to get your phone out and turn it off. I want to see you do it."

Knox did as he was told, holding it up and letting Burl watch him slide it off. Then he repeated himself. "I have something for you, Burl."

"Do you now? For your sake, I hope to God it's a big stack of fucking greenbacks."

"I did the best I could."

"This ought to be a sight. Your best so far ain't amounted to a roll of pins."

The wooden coffee table had a drawer in it. Knox opened it, took out a bank envelope, and laid it on top of the pile of magazines and whatnot that lived on the table's surface.

"What's that?" Burl said, pointing at the envelope.

"Some of your money."

"Well, no shit. How much?"

Fuck. Knox wasn't sure. He'd been dipping into it. "It's like, twenty-two hundred, give or take."

Burl's head tilted and his eyes narrowed. "Are you shitting me? You just laid out an envelope of fucking cash and you don't know how much is in it? What the fuck is wrong with you? Don't you do nothing that ain't half-assed?"

Knox sat there trying to think of something he was truly good at, or at the very least threw himself into all the way. He squinted an eye, thinking. He counted them out one at a time on his fingers. "Poker, pizza, and fornication."

Burl creased his nose and picked up the envelope. "I'll give you the first two. You're a hell of a card player, and you make a damn fine pizza. I'll have to take you at your word on the last." He smacked the money in the palm of his hand. "I'll count this down back home, but even if it's what you say it is, it ain't enough. I gave you a month to make real progress. This ain't real progress."

Knox leaned back on the couch, trying to disguise his right hand finding the grip of the Glock. "That's my oven, man. I sold one of my ovens to get that. That's the pizza shop equivalent of selling a kidney."

"Now, you see, that's your goddamn problem right there. You ain't never gonna get me paid in drips and drops. You ain't doing nothing but bailing water out of a boat."

"It's all I can do."

"No, it ain't all you can do. It's all you *will* do, but it ain't all you *can* do. I don't know how else to get through your fucking head how serious this has got, Knox. You know I hardly do nothing in Richmond. I'm here because I don't want to see this thing go where it's headed. Only way to stop it's to find your way to my doorstep with what all you owe me. Don't do that, and I'll have no choice but to put the dogs on you, and whoever else I got to put them on."

"Burl, you have to understand—"

"I don't got to understand shit. You got to understand. You think we was playing? We wasn't. I think we made that pretty fucking obvious. You got one way out of this, so don't think too damn hard, because all you'll do is hurt yourself. Get to getting and quit fucking around selling goddamn ovens and piddly shit. You been to the bank?"

"My credit's shit. Beyond bad, and I don't own anything they'll loan against."

"Your parents got a house, don't they? They could get the money."

Knox squeezed the butt of the Glock, thinking how easy it'd be to yank it out and empty it into Burl. To cut off the head and see if the snake died with it. He was a small target, but surely to God Knox could hit him with the margin of a full clip. To do that, he had to be willing to kill a man, and withstand everything that went with it. He was by no means sure he could. Knox was sure Burl could, and he was doubly sure Greek could, and he was sure all the mutts that hung at their heels could, too.

Knox closed his eyes hard for a beat, pained. "I don't understand it, Burl. With everything you have going on, why are you so focused on me? I'm just a small fish. The littlest."

"Son, I'm focused on every fucking fish. Big fish, little fish, they're all the fucking same to me. I eat them all. What I want to know is why you're wasting time worrying about what size fish you are when you should be out getting my money. That's your mistake."

"How much more time do I have? I can't just snap my fingers."

"I don't look to fool with you past Christmas. Shit. Me personally, I don't look to fool with you past tonight. You hold up your end, we're square. You don't, you won't see me again, and things'll take their natural course." Burl tapped the side of his face with four fingers, then pointed at the right side of Knox's face that still bore Greek's burns. "How would that be a few inches to the left? Because that's what's coming."

Burl came closer. He stood with his knees against the coffee table and his hands on his hips with his elbows jutting out. "Sometimes, Knox, they's things I don't want to do, but I do them anyway. I do them because I have to. Don't make me do something else I don't want to do." He leaned in close. He smelled like talcum powder. "Get me my fucking money." He held there a moment. Then he stood up straight. "I'll let myself out."

Once he was back down the stairs and gone, Knox pulled out the Glock and pointed it where Burl had been standing. He imagined Burl's little chest bursting with each shot, his pearl snapped shirt turning to shreds. Knox held the gun suspended in air for a good thirty seconds before he let it drop. He put it back where he had it wedged. He got up and slowly made his way downstairs to finish closing Porthos for the night.

In the darkness of the dining room, Rob popped up from one of the booths where he had been hidden. "Are you all right, Knox?"

"I'm fine."

"What the hell happened?"

"He came to tell me to hurry up. I gave him the money I had, but he wasn't satisfied."

"The oven money? All of it?"

Knox approached the booth where Rob was upright on his knees. "Most of it. I already spent some."

"What the fuck do we do now?"

"You get out of here, and I finish closing."

"What if he comes back?"

"He's not coming back. Not tonight, anyway."

"I'll help you close."

Knox held up a hand. "No. I want to do it myself."

"It'll take forever."

"Good. We'll get lunch tomorrow. Now get out of here."

Rob pushed himself out of the booth and onto his feet. "I feel like I should stick around. I just do."

"I know. But you shouldn't. You're a good man, Rob. I love you, buddy." Knox hugged him.

Rob slapped his back. "I love you, too, Knox." Once they had turned each other loose, Rob headed for the kitchen to clock out.

Knox found the broom where Tori left it and started to sweep. He sang the song "Martha" in full voice.

ON SATURDAY, the day after Burl keyed into Porthos, Rob and Knox trudged up the hill together to eat lunch at Babylon Café on Main Street. Whenever they ate together, it was at one of the handful of ethnic restaurants in Richmond, all of which were owned by immigrants. One week it was Indian, then Thai, then sushi, then Mexican, and so on. At each, they were recognized as "the Porthos guys," and the owners recounted their own last pizza orders with heavy accents.

They sat hunched close together in a corner of the side dining room speaking in hushed voices and eating shawarma. "Why didn't you just shoot the son of bitch?" Rob said. "That would've ended it right there."

"It's not as easy as you think. Let's say I did it, and I killed him. What then? What am I supposed to do? I've still got to deal with the police. I've still got to deal with his people. I do that, I probably end up dead anyway. Or in jail."

"How the fuck are they going to put you in jail? No way. You were in your own fucking apartment."

"It's more than that with Burl. He's got cops. He's got thugs crawling all over the place. He's the real fucking deal. I felt like I needed a gun, but the truth is, I'd probably stick it in my mouth before I shot anybody else." Knox pointed his first two fingers and put them behind his front teeth.

"Fuck that."

"I'm just being realistic."

Rob blinked a few times before wiping his mouth with his napkin. "Dude, don't. Don't make that an option. If you make that an option, you can. If it's not an option, you can't."

"It's always an option. For anyone. That's just life."

"Bullshit," Rob said, and gave Knox a lethargic middle finger. "You're just scared. You're afraid of something you think's worse. When people kill themselves because their lives are miserable, because they don't feel like they have anything to live for, I guess I can kind of understand that, but that's not you."

"You mean to tell me my life's not miserable. I've got a guy threatening to kill me—and he literally will kill me. He's threatening my family. They beat the shit out of me, nearly fucking drowned me, blew out my goddamn eardrum, and burned my face." Knox pointed at the remnants of the blisters. "I'm about to lose a business I spent fifteen years building—my whole livelihood—but you're telling me my life's not miserable. How do you figure?"

"Because everything that's wrong with you's about money. You're not fucking sick, you're not fucking depressed. I mean, okay, you're depressed, but not, like, clinically. You're depressed because of the situation. And that's totally different."

"Yeah. I'm pretty sure that still counts."

"Whatever. If your debt was paid tomorrow, and you didn't have Porthos, and you healed up, you'd be okay. You and me, we could grow some fucking hops, and maybe we have to get jobs on the side, but that's a pretty good life. Like you wouldn't be okay with that."

Knox slouched and chuffed out all his wind, like he was deflating. "Does it really matter? Because I owe the money, and I don't have any way to get it. I don't have anything I can do. I've done everything I can think of. Burl wants me to get my parents to borrow against their house. I'm not doing it. They barely get by as it is. I usually have to give *them* money. Their house is all they have. They have shit-else."

"I know it sucks, but maybe you have to do it. You don't think your parents would do whatever they had to do to save you? What kind of retirement you think they're going to have if you end up dead? Think about it. It'd ruin their lives."

"There's no way I'm letting my parents pay Burl."

"Maybe you just have to do what you have to do. Be pragmatic, man. If you were sick, and there was a medicine that would cure you, and it cost twenty grand, you don't think they'd do whatever they had to do? The difference here is, you don't want Burl to get it."

Knox raised his hand and put one finger to his lips, shushing Rob as a couple walked past looking for somewhere to sit. Once they were out of earshot, he said, "That's all true. So what?"

"You're willing to lose your life, and ruin the rest of your parents' lives, all to keep from paying this guy?"

"I can't do it. It's not right."

"Of course it's not right. He's a *fucking* criminal. You did business with a criminal. Shit ceases being right after that."

Knox sighed with force. "You're fucking up my shawarma. I just want to enjoy my shawarma."

"You're fucking up my goddamn shawarma, too, because I just want you to not be dead. You're such a dickhead."

"If something happens to me, you're going to feel bad about calling me a dickhead."

"No, I won't. I'll feel bad if you're dead, but if it's because you're a dickhead, I'll be glad I told you. I'll be glad I did everything I could."

Knox's eyes sunk down and to the left. "How the fuck did I get here, Rob?"

Rob face shrugged. "I don't know. Shit got hard, you got desperate, you made a bad choice."

"Several. I made several bad choices."

"I was being kind. They're done, though. You can't change them. What you can do is quit making bad choices now. You can quit worrying about what's fair, and you can start thinking about doing whatever you have to do to get yourself out of this. I'm working on a loan for the hops farm. If I can get it, maybe I can use it to buy you out. How long do we have?"

"No." Knox banged his shawarma hand on the table, smashing it between his fingers so that some of the guts oozed out.

"Maybe it won't be your choice."

"Goddamn it. If you do that, I really will blow my brains out. I swear."

Rob shook his head. "No, you won't."

"I used to feel like I was young and successful. Now I'm an old failure." Knox was getting a little teary. "I'm a fucking idiot."

Rob said, "Sometimes," then took a long drink from his can of Dr. Brown's Butterscotch Soda. After he set the can down, they both ate in silence. Rob finished his shawarma and wiped his mouth. He took another drink of soda. "So, where'd you get this gun anyway?"

"Grub's. The place that runs all those ads. It's like the biggest in Kentucky."

"They know you never owned a gun before?"

"I told the guy who sold it to me."

"And he still sold you a fucking Glock? Jesus. I don't think that's a beginner's gun, Knox."

"The guy was a manager. I figured he knew what he was doing. He said it was the best gun for personal protection. Said it was the fastest to pull and shoot."

"And that's a good thing? Have you ever even fired a gun before?"

"I shot a twenty-two with my cousins when I was kid. It was a rifle though. Grub's has an indoor range. The manager took me in there so I could shoot it a couple times. I pretty much got the hang of it. It went off one time I didn't expect, and he took it and adjusted it. He said something about the firing pin being messed up, but he fixed it. Anyway, he said it was fine after that and he knocked fifty bucks off."

"You bought a defective gun because he knocked fifty bucks off? Knox, man, I know you're in some shit, but damn."

"I was on a budget. I don't want the fucking thing. It goes against everything I'm about, but I couldn't sit in my apartment waiting anymore. It was fucking killing me. I wasn't sleeping."

"This is just the most buttfucked thing I've ever seen. How'd it get this far?"

Knox put his hand over his face. "Hell, I don't know, but I'm trying to hold it together. I'm trying to keep you all as safe as I can. The thing that scared me the most last night was that you and Tori were in the shop. I'm so scared something's going to happen to one of you all. I'm thinking about just pulling the plug on Porthos, and saying fuck it, but if I do, I'm afraid Burl will come calling that much quicker. I'm so lost, man, I just keep going. I don't know what else to do."

"I don't know what to tell you. Maybe we should all bail out. I know you're worried about Burl, but what difference would it make to him if we closed?"

"I don't know. He just makes me nervous. Whatever I do, I'm pretty sure I've got some time before he makes another move. That's the way it sounded. Let's just get through this weekend. Then, we'll sit down and figure it out. If I pull everything out of the Porthos account, and I don't pay the rent, and I don't pay the utilities, that would get me like three or four grand right there. I don't know. I'm thinking about doing it."

"We'll just have to talk after." Rob licked his lips, then wiped the moisture on the back of his wrist.

Knox stared off into the corner, but he wasn't really looking at anything. He was somewhere further off than that. "You know what

I miss? I miss the smell of the green soap. Darla's studio smelled like it all the time. I can still smell it in my mind."

"I know you miss her."

Knox kneaded his forehead. "Why did I lose her, Rob?"

"You didn't lose her, man. Things just don't work out sometimes."

"No. I lost her."

"Okay. Fine. You lost her."

Knox was still. "Why? Why did I do that?"

"Because you lost your damn mind, I guess."

"Is that it?"

"All I can figure."

"I can't really argue with it. I don't have any basis."

Rob pinched the side of his pop can lightly, indenting it, then let the dents pop back out. "Man, I can't keep track of all your dejection. It's too much. Are you really going to skip the pizza show?"

"There's no reason for me to go."

"You still want me to take Tori?"

"Yeah, that's the plan."

"I thought you might want to go up there and try to make some money playing poker." Rob rubbed his thumb against the pads of his fingers, signifying cash.

"I can't make enough. I probably couldn't make enough in a year. Besides, I'm too fucking desperate. It's no good to play when you're desperate. You do desperate shit. Desperate money can't win, and scared money can't win either. It's better if I just stay out of there altogether so I don't do anything else stupid."

"I guess. You know better than I do."

"You and Tori earned it. No big deal for me to go open to close on Sunday, anyway. Bria can handle the kitchen. We can hash things out more when you get back."

The wife of the couple who owned Babylon came through carrying green baskets with gyros in them for another table, a white squeeze bottle of tzatziki under her arm. Rob pushed his chair back and looked around the room. "You ready to get a move on?"

Knox stayed still. "Not really."

Rob stood. "Stay here then, but I'm going to get down to Porthos to give Tori a hand." He patted Knox's broad back as he walked past carrying his basket to the trash can.

*S*UNDAY MORNING, Tori parked by the dumpster behind Porthos. Rob's truck wasn't there yet, and it was December cold, so she sat in her Accord listening to the radio staring at the places where dirty rivulets had run down the dumpster and dried, leaving behind filth trails.

Rob had offered to drive to Belterra. When Tori said she'd pitch in for gas he waved her off. "You can just buy me dinner once we get up there."

"I thought everything was free?"

"Yep."

"So how am I going to buy you dinner?"

"I don't know."

They were supposed to meet at nine. It was a few minutes after. Nobody else would be showing up to work for at least another hour. The only cars in the back lot were the ones that belonged to the tenants who lived in nearby apartments, and Knox's wrecked Volvo. When Tori had asked Knox why his insurance wouldn't fix the damage, he just said, "Does a bear shit in the lumberyard?" and left it at that.

True to form, Rob slow-rolled into the back lot in his brown pickup, unlike virtually every other Porthos employee, who all pulled in unreasonably fast with their car radios unreasonably loud. As Tori stepped out of her car and got her overnight bag and a chunky brown purse, Rob parked to her left and reached across and cranked down his passenger window. He had a short cigarette in his hand resting on the wheel. "Morning. You ready to go?"

She stood at the window peering in, trying to figure out how to broach it. Ultimately, she just had to say it. "I appreciate you driving, but I don't know if I can handle the smoke."

Rob looked at the stub, took a short drag, then lowered his window and flicked it out. "Say no more."

Tori winced. "Do you mind?"

"Not at all. Bad habit anyway."

They crept up I-75 north in the right-hand lane with Rob turned in his seat talking, chewing a stick of gum, and drinking coffee simultaneously, only his left wrist on the wheel. It was almost like he was driving with his peripheral vision. Most of the time, when he took a drink, he swerved either off the side of the highway onto the rumble strips or into the next lane. Tori tensed as they careened side to side. When a car laid on its horn as they drifted into the center lane, Rob corrected, chomped his gum, and said, "Good god, relax why don't you."

For the first time, they recounted the back-door break-in in detail. "That guy was so little, but somehow he was still scary. You could just feel it. He comes off as—I don't know—dangerous."

"That's because he is," Rob said. "I had never laid eyes on the man, but I know all about him. Knox was pretty shaken up. He usually stays in Jackson County. It's like his stronghold or something. Supposedly he's got everyone down there bought off. He came to Porthos because Knox has fucked up big."

"Knox fucked up? *No way*," Tori said.

"Knox is terrified of him. You know he bought a Glock?"

Tori whipped her chin Rob's way and drew it in. "He what?"

"He bought a Glock." Rob held up his hand with two fingers pointed and his thumb drawn back.

Tori shifted in her seat, slumping with her head against the side window. "He's going to shoot his own dick off with that thing. You hide and watch."

"I worry about worse than that. If Burl sends that Greek motherfucker after him, that could end bad a hundred different ways."

"Hold on." Tori threw up her hands. "So Greek works for Burl?"

"Oh yeah. He was the only one of those guys I had ever seen before."

"That's the same guy who came in and made me give him pizzas. Knox told me to let him have whatever he wanted. No wonder. Dude was scary as hell. He had the dead eyes."

"Yeah, no shit. He's done the same thing to me. I don't care if Knox has a gun. He'll just make that guy mad. He's in so far over his head. I'm not just saying this to be dramatic. Knox could seriously get himself killed."

"What makes you think they'd stop at Knox?" Tori said. "What about collateral damage?" Tori's eyes trained in on a collection of burn holes in the driver-side dash. "I was already pretty much freaking out, but if this Burl dude's some kind of kingpin, he won't care. He won't leave anyone behind he thinks he has to worry about."

"That's the thing," Rob said. "Knox is more afraid of that than anything. He wants to act like he isn't worried about himself, just us, but I know he's scared. I'm not supposed to say anything, but he's thinking about shutting the whole thing down. Getting everybody out of Porthos. That way, if Burl does make some move, nobody gets in the way."

"Man," Tori said, "is this real life?"

"I'm afraid so. And one thing that's scaring me the most, like, is scaring me right now, is that Knox is talking about killing himself."

"Do you really think he would?"

"I want to believe he wouldn't. That there's no way. But if I really believe that, then why am I so scared?"

For the first time in forty miles, Rob turned back to the road and put both hands on the wheel. He reached for his cigarette pack, but after he picked it up, he glanced at Tori and laid it back down. Tori went slowly into her bag and came up with a tube of Chapstick and put some on. As she did, her imagination ran wild. As wild as it ran, she was only being realistic.

*T*HEY WAITED in a long line to check in with the Mangia! staff. Most of the people had on sweatshirts, jackets, t-shirts, polos, hats, and whatever, with pizza-shop logos on them. The Porthos pair was incognito.

A tiny woman in a Mangia! shirt came at them smiling, "Hey, Rob. How's the Porthos gang? Where's Knox?"

"He didn't tell you? He couldn't make it this year. I hope it's okay, but he sent Tori in his place. She's our new assistant GM." Rob cut his eyes at Tori for a millisecond.

"Yeah. Absolutely." The lady shook Tori's hand. "I'm Candice. It's so nice to meet you." Candice was all smiles, all energy. "I only had badges made for the guys, but if you give me a minute, I can get one made for you." She took a little notepad from her purse. "What's your last name, dear?"

Tori didn't look away, she didn't blink. "Amos."

Candice cocked her head. "Really?"

"Yeah, why not?"

Candice pursed her lips before she said, "Okay, why not?" and wandered off to get their badges.

"It's so hilarious," Rob said. "When she has to come to Porthos, she's so lethargic and pissed off. We're like her worst account. With her bosses all around, it's like she loves us."

"Eh. She won't have Porthos to kick around much longer. Go with it."

"Good point."

By the time they got to the head of the line, Candice was behind two cloth-draped check-in tables at another table rifling through a big cardboard box full of manila envelopes. A woman with a check-list about a dozen pages long asked for a store name. When she found Porthos, she marked it out with a yellow highlighter, twisted in her chair, and said, "Porthos."

Candice waved her hand. "I've got that one." She came around from the opposite side of the tables carrying two lanyards with red, white and blue straps that said Mangia! on them, and a big envelope. She motioned for Tori and Rob to follow her to the area beside the check-in line.

Once they were clear of the tables she gestured them in closer. "There's only one thing I need to clear with you guys. I can only give you one room, but it has two queen beds. We're really tight this year. Is that going to be okay?"

Tori didn't hesitate. "It's fine."

Rob looked at her, then at Candice again. "I guess it's okay."

Outside the exhibit hall, there were booths displaying point-of-sale systems that made Porthos's system look like a slide rule, stacked ovens, makelines, frozen-yogurt machines, and on and on. Sales representatives hovered at each booth smiling, pointing, whoring. In the exhibit hall it was all food. Food and food and food. Not health food. The other kind. Pizza, subs, sausage, macaroni and cheese, deep-fried shit of every shape and description, including chicken wings, boneless chicken wings, chicken strips, chicken nuggets, chicken fingers, chicken breasts, chicken planks, chicken patties, French fries, curly fries, sweet-potato fries, tater tots, corn dogs, peppers, pickles, cheesecake bites, bananas-foster bites, brownie bites, etc. You name it, somebody in there had battered or breaded it and dropped it in a fryer. Just like outside, there were eager sales representatives at every booth in the exhibit hall.

"What are we supposed to do?" Tori asked.

"You pretend you're interested in buying this shit, and you eat it," Rob said.

"That's it?"

"That's it."

Eating started out fun. The food wasn't all good, but most of it was. When you don't care how many calories, or how much fat, sodium, or sugar you put in stuff, you can make it delicious. Tori stopped at nearly every table they passed and got something, which she soon realized wasn't a sound strategy. Rob was more selective. According to a map of the room, there were more than sixty food exhibitors. Tori slowed down by about the tenth table. She hit the wall around the fifteenth. Nausea set in. She drank from tiny free bottles of water trying to dilute the swamp of saturated and unsaturated fats, starch, and artificial flavors roiling in her belly, but it didn't make much difference.

She held her stomach. "I'm not gonna make it. I think I'm done. I'm definitely going to have to take a run in the morning."

"Rookie," Rob said. "We haven't even had dessert yet."

Tori's eyes expanded. "I might be able to do dessert, but just a little. Do they have cannoli?"

"Somewhere."

"I think cannoli and a cup of coffee are just what I need to get straightened out. Then I need to go lay down."

"That's fine with me. I want to spend some quality time with a cigarette."

Tori shook her head. "You should quit."

"I plan to." Rob extracted his cigarettes from his pocket. "But not today."

$\mathcal{R}$OB WENT for a smoke while Tori went to the room by herself. She hung a dress in the closet, turned on the TV, pulled back the covers on one of the beds, and lay down. Within minutes she was asleep in her clothes.

When she woke, she had no idea the time, but it was dark outside. She looked at her phone and it was nearly seven. Her food coma had been major.

The TV was turned off, but the sink was running. It cut off and Rob came out of the bathroom. "Hey, how you feeling?"

She propped on an elbow. "Better. Less disgusting."

Rob sat on the other bed across from her. "So, what do you want to do now?"

"What are my options?"

"Gamble or go to dinner."

"I don't have any money. Did you bring money?"

"Not enough to gamble."

"Dinner it is, then."

"It's kind of fancy. There's a band and everything. That's why they call it the pizza prom. It's a trip."

Tori sat up all the way. "Wait. Are you asking me to go to prom?"

"Well." Rob's face colored a shade. "I mean, it's not really like prom."

Tori put her hand on Rob's knee and fixed her eyes on his. "The correct answer is yes."

He caught his lower lip in his teeth. "Then, yes."

"I accept." She squeezed his knee, and stood up. "Let me wash my face and change. If I'm going to prom, I'm putting on my dress."

The dinner was a buffet served in the casino's biggest ballroom. A cover band was hard at work on stage. The singer sounded pretty good. Not as good as he thought, but good. He was highly animated. There was no question he thought he was a star.

Rob's expression while the band played was like the one people get when a little kid tells them a story they don't believe. He sat with a beer and a half-eaten plate of buffet food before him that had never been cleared. The table was near the back, far from the band. It sat eight people, but topped out at five all night. As the night had worn on, the other three people either moved closer to the band, or went on. It was just Tori and Rob now. She had on a casual striped dress with Mary Jane heels and held a waning gin and tonic in her hand. The middle of the table was a garden of empty bottles and rocks glasses.

"I can't stay there forever no matter what happens," Rob said. He pulled from a bottle of Corona with a frayed lime sliding up and down the neck. "Knox knows that. He's been supposed to replace me for a couple years, but it never happens. He had it in his head that there would be this perfect moment for me to leave, and we'd both know when it got here, but it's never going to come. Now we might both have to go at an imperfect moment."

"You ever think maybe he didn't want that moment to come for you?" Tori said.

"I know he didn't."

"He's codependent. Your loyalty's admirable, but I think it enables him."

Rob spun the bottom of his bottle in circles on the table. "It's not easy. He's done a lot for me. Now that we're near the end, I think I have a responsibility to fight to get him through it, even if he doesn't like it. Knox and I have been through a lot of shit together. He's basically been my best friend from the time I started working for him. At the lowest point in my life, he was all I had. You don't forget that shit. You know how they say some people will give you the shirt off their back? He gave me his fucking shirt."

"So, what're you going to do?" Tori asked. "You think you can really save him?"

"I have to try."

Tori shook her head and took a sip from her drink. "Did you know that a lot of people who try to save someone from drowning end up drowning themselves? It's because the drowning person takes them under."

"This isn't about water, it's about money," Rob said. "He's never told me exactly how much, or how it happened, but Knox got into Burl for a lot of money. Something like twenty grand. We had a bad equipment catastrophe and Knox borrowed from him. That's where it started. He tried to keep the loan a secret, but then he got fucked up and told me. He never gave me all the details, but just enough. I know it's gotten worse. Since they tuned him up, he's started talking to me about it even when he's sober. You know those burns on his face? That was a fucking gunshot. They fired it off right next to his ear."

That pushed Tori back in her seat. "You fricking liars. You guys told me it was a moped. That story always seemed like bullshit to me. I knew there was no way."

"I know. I'm sorry. Knox made me swear I wouldn't tell you. He also swore Burl would never come to Porthos. You see how that worked out. I promise I won't lie to you about anything like that again. I never should've in the first place."

"My god. That's like, *trauma*. He's disfigured. That'll never heal right. They did that on purpose."

"Yeah. It was a warning. Like I said, it's all about money. If Knox could pay it, he'd be fine. But Porthos doesn't make money. It used to, but not anymore. It's pretty much breakeven at this point, and that's on a good day."

"So how do you come up with the money?"

"That's the problem. I don't know. He won't go to his family. He refuses. I don't think they have it anyway. Everything I have, I've put into trying to get my hops farm going. I'm trying to get a loan from MACED, the economic development people, and I think I can. It'll ruin me, but if I have to, I'll use it for Knox."

Tori shoved Rob's shoulder, hard. "You can't do that. No way."

"There's nothing else." Rob rubbed his shoulder and kept his eyes on Tori. "Except Porthos."

"You said it doesn't make money."

"It doesn't. Knox would have to sell it. He had a chance before and didn't take it. That was a couple years ago. He thought he could turn it around. It got worse. Now he says the guy isn't interested anymore. He went at him again in the last few weeks and he said no, but Knox isn't exactly the best salesman."

"Who was it?"

"Lane Spicer."

"The lawyer?"

"Yep. He wanted to keep the whole Porthos thing, but turn the dining room into a craft-beer bar. Put in a big draft system, all that. He was even looking into buying the building."

Tori sat up straighter. "That's not a bad idea. There's nothing like that in Richmond. It'd kill."

"I thought so, too. Lane's got some niece who worked in pizza.

She ran a Wick's in Louisville. He was going to have her run it, but now she's out, and he doesn't want to do it anymore."

"Damn. That would've been perfect. There's a bunch of places like that in Louisville. They do a ton of business."

Rob rolled his bottle back and forth between his palms. "It still could be perfect."

"What do you mean?"

"If I could get Lane back interested, maybe I could get Knox out of this thing. We tried hard to find someone else but there's no one. Lane's the only one who ever showed any interest."

"How are you going to get his niece? You even know who she is?"

"I have no idea. I don't plan on getting his niece, we just need to give him someone to *be* his niece."

"What are you talking about?"

"Us, man. You and me. We can be his niece. If we agree to stick around and get it off the ground, maybe he'd still do it."

Tori frowned. "I think you just need to get away from it. We both do."

"I agree," Rob said, "but I also owe Knox a shirt. I can't let anything happen to him. The biggest thing would be to convince Lane he could trust us. That we could be as good as his niece. If I could pull it off, would you be willing to stick around with me? At least for a little while?"

Tori watched the people waiting at the bar, laughing, slapping each other on the back. A man at a table near them was leaned back in his chair with his legs out and his mouth wide open, looking like he'd been shot and left, but just asleep. Older couples were on the dance floor dancing with varying levels of grace. "If it would save Knox's life, I'd do it. But not if it risks mine."

"What if it doesn't risk yours at all."

Tori cocked her head. "Then I would."

Rob nodded. "I knew it. Knox is right about you."

Tori ran her palm up her forehead and over her hair. "How so."

Rob looked at her and smiled. "He says you're a good egg."

"Eggs get broken."

"Don't be so literal."

The two fell quiet and sat listening to the guy sing "Night Moves" passably. From there the band moved into another well-worn radio tune. Eventually, Rob broke the quiet.

"Listen. From what Knox told me, I don't think there's anything to worry about immediately. If we can just get Porthos shut down, it'll be okay. After that, I'm going to try to get him this money."

"Why do you think there's no danger now? Burl was literally just there."

"Exactly. And he gave Knox some time. What he wants is to get paid. He won't do anything else right away. He'll wait to see if his prodding worked." Rob held his beer bottle up to the light. Still a sip left. "I'm not saying you shouldn't start looking for another job, I'm just hoping you'll hang in a few more days before you bail. Give us a chance."

"A few more days is probably it for me. If I was smart, it'd be no more days."

Rob yawned, covering his mouth when it got big. "Shew. I'm about to give out."

The cover band had scarcely played the opening notes of "Billie Jean" when Tori downed her drink, crunched on one of the ice cubes, and stood up. "Oh no. Don't even. You're asking a lot from me." She put her hand out for Rob's. "You brought me to this prom and we're going to dance at least one song, by god."

Rob sat serenely, still holding his beer, looking up at Tori. He drained the end of it, the lime rattling at the base of the neck, took her hand, and let her pull him up. Tori skipped her way to the dance floor and started dancing before she even got to it. Rob trailed behind. When he first reached her, he stood watching. She shoved him in the shoulder, and said, "Come on." When she did, he laughed. Then he laid down some moves.

Tori had kept Rob on the dance floor for a couple songs, but when the band struck up "Into the Mystic," he looked uncertain. She smiled. "Well, what do you think?"

"Up to you."

"Okay then." She draped her arms over his shoulders. "Let's do it."

Rob seemed a little hesitant to put his hands on Tori's hips, but once they settled there, he leveled out. She didn't exactly tower over him, but her heels added to the height difference. They moved around the dance floor among more than a dozen other couples, circling like a rowboat with one oar.

When the song ended, Tori detached from Rob, and said, "Okay, I'm good. We can stay or we can go."

He wiped sweat from his brow with the back of his hand. "I'm about killed if you're ready."

"When do they announce the king and queen?"

"I don't believe they do. That's one of the shortcomings of pizza prom."

"Well, they should. I think you and me won the thing."

The walk back to their room was long. Tori's nap, combined with a good number of gin and tonics and dancing, had left her feeling energetic. Rob had drunk more than a half-dozen beers. He was more subdued. Amiable still, but subdued. Typical Rob.

He paused by the hotel-lobby door to go have a smoke. Tori said okay, she'd go up, and headed for the elevators by herself. She was still waiting for one to come when Rob turned up at the elevator bank.

"I decided I don't need it," he said.

Tori started to say something. Then she thought better of it.

Back in their room, they took turns getting ready for bed in the bathroom. Rob let Tori have it first, and it took her a bit to get washed up and into her long, red pajamas. By the time Rob was done in the bathroom, she was in her bed, under the covers, propped up on pillows, reading a book. He was in plaid flannel sleep pants and a black band t-shirt with a bird on it.

Tori looked at him over her book. "Is my reading going to keep you up? I can turn off the light if you want."

"Nah." Rob scratched his head. "I should be fine. I'm pretty tired."

He got in bed and rolled over in the heavy hotel blankets facing the wall away from Tori. She went on with her reading, but she was fidgety, and honestly, a bit drunk. After a few minutes she said, "You sure the light's okay? I'm not keeping you up, am I?"

"I promise you're not." Rob didn't move. "I'm worn out, but I'm good."

Tori was having a hard time focusing on her book even though it was right in front of her. She laid it down and looked in the direction of where Rob lay. "I had fun tonight. Did you?"

He rolled over and looked at her. "As a matter of fact, I did."

"Cool." Tori patted her hands one on top of the other. "Thanks for dancing with me. I hope it was all right."

"It was good. I hadn't danced in forever."

"Okay. I just wanted to say that. Now I'm going to let you sleep." She looked at him a moment before she said, "Good night."

"Good night." Rob rolled back over.

Tori laid with her book on her, not reading it, gazing at the ceiling for a couple minutes. Rob lay still in the next bed, facing away. She turned and watched him lying there. Then she got up, padded to his bed, and nudged him in the back.

Rob rolled over again. "Yes?" He smiled at her.

"I'm cold. Can I get in with you?"

"Sure. If you want to."

Rob raised the covers and Tori slid in beside him, her body close to his. Their noses inches apart. "That's better," she said.

"You know, no matter how much I wanted to, I was never going to put a move on you," Rob said.

"Isn't that typical," she said. "Make me do all the work." Then Tori kissed him one time, quick and clean on the lips before she regarded him again.

Rob took hold of her hands deep under the covers. "There's something I wanted to tell you."

"What's that?"

He held her gaze. "I just want you to know, I'm a nerd, too. Total."

A wide smile broke across Tori's face, from her mouth, to her eyes, to her ears, and she laughed. "Duh." She kissed him again, and this time didn't stop. Her braces dug into her lower lip creating pleasant discomfort. Their bodies pressed together in earnest now, and their hands unclasped and began to move.

$\mathcal{K}$**NOX HAD** been up and down all night, but he woke up for good on Monday morning wondering how many more shifts he had left at Porthos. He could probably count them on one hand. He usually placed Mangia! orders on Mondays for Tuesday delivery. If he and Rob followed through with what they were thinking, the next couple days at Porthos would be the last. Knox would skip the Mangia! order, and that would be that.

Knox hadn't slept a full night in weeks. He read and reread the few books he had left, dozed for an hour here and there, but mostly was awake fending off anxiety and emptiness. Ernest Hemingway wrote of the difficulties of lonely people at night. Because of that Knox had always assumed it was nighttime when Hemingway put the gun to his head. Then he stumbled on an article and was surprised to find out it was in the morning. All Knox could figure was, the morning didn't bring the relief he was hoping for.

The day before, he had been feeling tired at midday, so he went upstairs to rest between deliveries. He left Bria and Kendra in the shop. He managed to doze a couple hours. When he came back down, an EKU professor was sitting at one of the tables on her laptop. She was a regular. He waved going by, but she never looked up. She might as well have been in her own living room.

Kendra and Bria had gotten the old artificial Christmas tree from the storage room, put it up in the front lobby, and were hanging ornaments.

"Quiet, huh?" Knox said.

Kendra stood up from a box holding a snow-globe ornament. "Yeah. We felt like decorating."

Bria gazed at the tree. "You have the coolest ornaments, Knox. They all have cities on them. Every single one."

"That used to be my thing. I bought ornaments everywhere I went for a long time." Looking at the tree, he thought about how long it had been since he'd gotten a new ornament. "At one time we counted, and I had ornaments from twenty-three states and five countries."

Bria grinned. "I love it."

"We're pretty much out of ornaments," Kendra said. "Once we get the star on, we're done."

"I thought we decided to do the angel," Bria said.

"Did we?"

"I don't know, but I like her. It's whatever." Bria eyed Knox. "Why do you have both, anyway?"

"We used to do two trees. I'd get a real one for the shop and put the fake one up in my apartment."

Kendra had the angel in her hands now. She smoothed the angel's flowing fabric skirt. "Which topper went where?"

"We switched it up. I don't know. I don't even remember the last time we had a tree."

Kendra let Bria put the angel on, and they all stood there a moment admiring the tree before Knox went into the kitchen.

In spite of everything else weighing on him in the morning, Knox was feeling bad about how hard Kendra and Bria had worked on the tree, and how few people would get to see it. Since he was awake for good, he brewed a pot of coffee and waited for Rob to get back from Belterra so the two of them could decide what to do about Porthos. He had kind of expected to hear from him overnight, but nothing came across. Since Porthos was closed that day regardless, and he wasn't sure he was placing a Mangia! order, he didn't have anything to do. Looking around his apartment, he had one of the rare moments where he registered the clutter. He never cleaned it up, but sometimes he organized it.

Even though he had sold off a lot of his things, his place was still overrun. As he rearranged the morass, he came across something that had no resale value, but was invaluable to him. He eyeballed his *My So-Called Life* tapes and wondered whether he was ready to watch them. It didn't really matter. His VCR was broken—a copy of *Blade Runner* was stuck in it—and he had pawned his TV.

Darla had called him back after she returned from the New Orleans expo. Knox was so damaged at the time—couldn't hear, could hardly talk right—that he didn't answer.

Knox checked the time on his phone. It had gotten late enough that he thought Darla would be up. He navigated the shattered screen to her number.

Darla answered, "Where you been, bud?"

"Right where you left me."

"There's a fucking shocker. How come you never called me back?"

Knox reclined on his couch. With one hand he held his phone. With the other he fingered the burns on the side of his face. "I'm sorry. Shit's been a little crazy around here."

"Crazy how? Is everything okay?"

Knox hesitated. For just a second, he was tempted to let it out, but he bit his lip and got over it. "All's well. Business as usual." Then he turned it. "What's going on in Texas?"

"Where should I start?"

The answer to his question was "a lot." In Austin, a great tattoo artist, which Darla unquestionably was, didn't stay a secret. She had gone into an established studio and raised her own profile and the studio's in the bargain. As a result, people were waiting weeks to book with her, musicians playing in Austin sought her out while they were in town, she was in demand for appearances, and all the goals she couldn't reach in Richmond were suddenly falling.

It was clearer than ever that leaving Knox for Austin had caused Darla's ship to rise. He betrayed nothing, but while the call salved the sore spot caused by her absence, it cut him even deeper in ten other places. He couldn't share in her success, and the reason for that was his slew of mistakes. Everything that had happened she saw coming. He had always thought he and Darla fell in together because they were equals. Now he knew it wasn't true. She was smarter than him. Their situations reflected that reality.

The conversation stayed tilted toward Darla's life because Knox wasn't interested in discussing his own. Before they got off the line, she asked him, "So, when are you coming down?" Before Knox could answer, she said, "I know, I know. You can't do it."

"I fucking wish."

"I'll give you one thing. You're consistent."

"Sorry to disappoint."

"How can I be disappointed when I already know what's coming?"

Knox was still lying down. His eyes were closed. "I'm sorry I fucked everything up. I'm sorry you had to leave because of me."

"I know you feel bad," Darla said, "but in the end, I left for me."

There wasn't much more to say after that, but they both did say a little more.

After talking to Darla, Knox didn't feel like cleaning up anymore, so he read. After one o'clock, someone finally banged on the door leading up from the pizza shop. Knox hollered, "Come on up!" The stairs creaked. Rob turned up at the top with Tori a step behind.

"Hey, guys. How was it?"

Tori and Rob looked at each other. Rob said, "It was good."

"Yeah," Tori said, "it was a good time."

Both then went quiet. Something was up. Knox knew it. What he knew, he wasn't sure, but he knew something.

Rob knocked a bunch of stuff off the wingback chair and let Tori have it. He tilted dirty clothes off a gold café chair, set it beside her, and sat down, too.

"I want to hear all about the pizza show. Give me the dish, y'all."

Rob was usually real dry, but typically easygoing. Knox noticed right away that today he was stern. "We can talk about that later. Right now, we need to figure out what we're going to do about the shop."

Knox motioned at Tori. "I don't think we want to get Tori involved in all that, do we?"

Tori leaned forward. "I'm already involved, Knox. If you recall, your pot guy broke in while I was here."

"I told her everything," Rob said.

"Everything?"

"Everything I know. Since she's right in the middle of it, she should have a say in what we do. It's probably going to be just the three of us until Porthos closes. We're all you've got."

"What about everyone else? I can't put them out of work."

"Bullshit. You're not hurting anyone letting them go. You're hurting them keeping them here. They need to get away from this place for their own safety. I've been on the phone all morning. I can get everyone on at Paddy Wagon or Gillum's. They're just waiting to hear back."

"And I'm willing to stay until you guys can get it shut down," Tori said.

"I'm glad you guys have this all figured out," Knox said. "It doesn't sound like you even need me, which is weird, seeing as I own the place."

Rob clapped his hands in front of his face like he was trying to get a dog's attention. "Wake up, Knox. No offense, but your decisions are what got us here. Those guys already fucked you up. Now you're risking getting everybody else hurt. I love you, man. You know I do. But it's time to let somebody else do the driving for awhile. You keep wrecking."

Knox shook his head but didn't say anything.

Rob patted Tori on the upper arm with the back of his hand. "Me and Tori are going to go back at Lane Spicer one more time and see what happens."

"He'll say no."

"Probably, but maybe not. We have a little different proposal. We got an appointment with him Wednesday morning. We told his secretary we got busted shoplifting. We're putting a plan together."

"I'm going too," Knox said.

"No, you're not." Rob was unwavering. "If you go again it's just more of the same. We need to start fresh. We need to pitch it as something different. You just need to concentrate on keeping this place running so we can tell him it's still open when we try to sell it. If it's closed, it has less value."

"If I don't place a Mangia! order we probably can't stay open much longer anyway."

"If Lane buys it, we tell him we need to shut down to reformat. If he doesn't buy it, we shut down anyway and start working on plan B."

"What's plan B?" Knox asked.

"We'll figure that out if plan A doesn't work." Rob had never showed Knox so little deference. He spoke with absolute purpose. As he stared at Knox, his hand drifted absently to Tori's knee. Tori put her hand on his and discreetly moved it off.

Knox crossed his arms. His eyes darted between Tori and Rob, then stayed on her. "Tori, I want to ask you a question. Forget Rob's sitting here."

She sat more upright. "Okay."

"What do you think of all this? What should we do?"

"We've gone over this backward and forward, and I'm with Rob. You can't ask people to keep coming to work if you know it's dangerous. You especially can't ask them to keep coming if *they* don't know. That's not okay at all."

"Do you really think Porthos is dangerous?"

"Are you being serious?" She pointed at him. "Look at your face, Knox. Think about that little asshole breaking in here. That's insane. I should've left as soon as I found out you sold pot, honestly, but you guys were cool and I liked working here. I used bad judgment. I'm only agreeing to stay a couple more days because I don't think anything else is going to happen right away, but I should probably just leave now."

Knox slumped back on his couch and let his head loll back. "I'm sorry."

"If you really are sorry, let us do this. Let us get everybody out of here and shut the place down. That's how you start to fix it. After that, we can work on you."

Knox's head was still tilted back. He took a series of deep breaths. Then he brought his head forward and exhaled hard one last time. He got up and looked down on Rob and Tori still resolutely sitting in their chairs. He made his way around the coffee table and drew close, leaned over, and got one arm around each of them and hugged. "God bless you kids. I'll do whatever you want."

*I*T SNOWED off and on all day Tuesday. It didn't stick. Knox worked the kitchen from open until close. Rob handled deliveries and Tori did everything else. They got hit with a rush of deliveries at the end of the night. Kids studying for exams realizing they were hungry. At quarter till, Knox took the phones off the hook. He had his head in his hand. "I'm getting a fucking migraine."

A couple minutes later, he started getting texts from people he dealt weed to who wanted pizza and couldn't get through on the landline. "Goddamn. If people bought this much pizza before now, we wouldn't be closing." He turned off his cell, put the shop phones back on the hook, and said, "Let them ring. I need to go lay down. Can you all close up? I can't take it."

Tori and Rob said they would. She locked the front door and turned off the open sign. She and Rob split up the remaining runs. The snow fired back up just as they left with the last deliveries of the night, and maybe ever. She didn't even bother with a car topper. Her run was quiet, the pizza buyer a small student in a dorm room who looked like he was probably good with computers. He had on a *Deadpool* t-shirt with him riding a T-rex.

Rob's truck was already there when Tori got back to Porthos, and his topper was off. She came in shaking snow out of her hair. She turned the Allen wrench in the manual lock behind her, making the keypad useless. She had gotten more diligent about that since Burl had keyed his way in.

Rob was out in the lobby sweeping. She pulled off her sweatshirt and started scrubbing the pans piled up on the dirty end of the three-compartment sink. The phones rang insistently until she didn't register it anymore. She was spraying a pasta dish when the front door chimed, breaking up the monotony of the ringing. Rob must've been going out to get the cigarette butt hut. She forgot to bring it in when she locked up earlier.

A moment later, it chimed again. Tori put down a dish and picked up a towel to dry her hands as she made her way to the lobby. When she rounded the front counter, she said, "Hey Rob—" then stopped dead. There was no mistaking Greek, who was just inside the door holding Rob by a fistful of his hoodie sleeve.

Tori had her phone in hand without thinking about it. Greek's mouth moved but Tori couldn't make out what he was saying. As she drew nearer, she said, "Get out or I'm calling the cops."

Rob held up a hand, and said softly, "Don't."

Not until Tori was within a few feet did she hear Greek's voice. "Neither of y'all's going to get hurt, but I need to talk to Knox." One of his hands rested on the black butt of a gun that stuck out from a holster under his jacket. His expression was icy.

"I told you, Knox isn't here," Rob said.

Greek made a face like he smelled something bad. "Don't do that. I know he's here."

Rob got out, "I swear—"

Greek clenched his jaw and drew back the hand that was on the gun like he might hit him. "Rob, you're not helping him. He's up there." Rob's head flinched when Greek said his name. "He's got a problem that's not me. You ain't leaving until I talk to him. That includes you, Tori. If anyone would answer a phone in this fucking place, I wouldn't be here. I've been calling for an hour."

It took Tori a moment to find her voice as the fact Greek knew both their names sunk in. She managed to get out a question. "Can't we just tell him whatever it is?"

Greek's chin shifted, and his light blue eyes held Tori's. His lips barely moved. "No. I need to talk to him." His fingers closed around the grip of the gun, and he raised it half an inch. "Now lay that fucking phone down or Rob here'll see some damage."

Tori slid the phone across a puckered veneer tabletop to her right. She caught sight of Indiana Jones on the pinball machine, his whip raised, looking brave. Tori didn't feel brave.

Greek shook Rob. "Where's your cell phone?"

Rob had his hands open, palms down. His right eye blinked and blinked like there was something in it. "I left it in the kitchen."

"You sure?"

Rob gave a small nod and mouthed, "Yes."

Greek wrinkled his brow and cocked his head. "What's that?"

Rob cleared his throat. "It's in the kitchen, by the printer. I don't have it."

Greek stared at Rob another moment before he moved him by his sleeve toward the door. "Lock it."

Rob did as he was told. Greek pulled him back. "Y'all be all right if you do two things: be quiet and do what I tell you. After I'm gone, I wasn't here. At all. Now, we're going to walk one, two, three, in a line to Knox's door, and go on up. Y'all do just what I say, there's no problem. None at all. Anyone does the triflingest thing different, that's a problem. Understand that?"

Nobody spoke. Small nods.

"Tori, you're leading the way." He turned Rob's sleeve loose. "Rob, fall in behind her." They didn't move. Rob's eye was twitching and his chin waggled side to side, like he'd been startled by a loud noise.

"Go on, then." Greek's voice never rose above quiet. "Don't make this difficult. I'll win that. I'll win either way, but y'all don't have to lose unless you choose to."

Tori took a few tentative steps. Rob fell in line. He followed so close behind he had his hand on her lower back. She was glad for his touch. Her legs were unsteady with adrenaline the entire way from the front of the shop to Knox's stairs. Rob stepped on the backs of her heels when she reached the closed door. After their footsteps stopped, all she could hear was Rob's labored breathing.

Tori turned the knob. Greek prodded them onto the first few steps before he said, "Stop here." The air changed from the restaurant: the stairs smelled of damp and dust and fresh pot smoke. Still at the bottom, standing in the open doorway, Greek called out, "Knox, I'm down here with your people. We're coming up."

Tori couldn't see him, but there was fumbling and rumbling and things hitting the ground upstairs. Then Knox's voice came back from right around the top of the steps. "Leave them alone, Greek. I've got a gun." He was shrill, like a little kid getting bullied on the playground. No sooner had Knox said it than Tori twisted back to see Greek sidestep out of the doorway, draw his huge black pistol, and point it up the stairwell past her and Rob's heads.

Tori and Rob dropped to the stairs at once. He had his hand on Tori's shin. He said, "Fuck." Then he said "Fuck" again, a little louder.

Greek hollered, "That's a mistake, Knox. A bad one. Drop that gun and show me your hands."

"Not until you let them go, you asshole. You're not going to hurt them."

"I'm here to help you, Knox. Drop that gun and let me do it. If anyone gets hurt here, it'll be because of you."

"You think I'm fucking stupid?"

It felt like a long time before Greek answered. "Yes, but that's got nothing to do with this. Now, for once, be smart, and drop your gun. Show me your hands."

Knox didn't give. "You can go eat a dick. Not until you let them leave. Let them leave and I'll give you my gun."

Greek huffed before responding. "Knox, shut up. That's not going to happen, so just shut up about it. I'm here with a message. Y'all don't answer phones, so I didn't have a choice. I'll go on as soon as we talk. I'm not here to hurt anyone, but no one's leaving until I do what I was sent to do."

"Okay," Knox shouted, "we're talking, so tell me the fucking message already."

The once tan carpet on Knox's stairs was more dark gray stains than not, and with Tori's nose down close, it smelled like a dirty kitchen sponge. She stared at the colorful art on a Star Wars comic book that lay on one of the steps. The bottom half of the cover had been torn off. Han, Lando, and Leia were all missing their legs.

When she looked back down at the base of the stairs, one of Greek's eyes peered up the sight of his pistol. He cleared his throat before speaking. "State police have a search warrant, Knox. They're planning to execute it tonight. You've got about an hour. We don't know what you're holding." As his head slid a little to the right, a wider slice of his face came into view. "That includes money. If you have any product at all, and you have money, they'll seize it. All of it. You'll never see that money again."

Knox's voice came back. "State police?"

Rob piped up. "That's what he said, now put that fucking gun away, Knox, before someone gets shot!" Under his breath he tacked on, "Goddamn it."

After Rob said that, things were quiet. Everyone waited for whatever Knox would do next, praying it wouldn't be stupid. Nobody was prepared for what came. A crack tore through the building and reverberated in the fixtures. Tori and Rob both flinched, hard. It was a gunshot, followed by a thud. There was no mistaking it. The end of Knox's tattooed arm flopped out into the landing at the top of the stairs, limp.

"Christ god, he's fucking killed himself!" Rob charged over Tori like he forgot or didn't care Greek was there. As Rob leapt past, all the shit Knox had piled on the stairwell tumbled down. A landslide of crap collected against Tori.

Rob made a bawling sort of noise, and there were words, but none that could be made out. Tori lay there, chest down, not moving, not wanting to move. She felt a hand on her calf. Greek loomed behind her with his pistol, big as a monkey wrench, trained on the back of her head. "Go on up," he said.

Tori pushed herself up with both hands. When she did, the rubble that had collected against her skittered on down. She trudged grimly to the top, and nearly doubled over as she reached the landing, anticipating finding Knox with half his head gone.

Blood formed a dark cloud in the carpet at the top of stairs, but Knox's head wasn't touched. His face looked whitewashed to gray. He lay sprawled, motionless, the bottom of his right leg ruined, shiny and slicked in his own dark fluid. The blood squirted hard from a crater in his calf, then stopped, then squirted again, then again. Knox's gun rested near his right hand, at the edge of the growing pool coursing from him.

Rob knelt beside him, his hand against the wound trying to stop the bursts, like a kid in the bath hopelessly trying to keep the water from coming out of the spout. "Fuck, fuck!" he shouted. "Call 911."

Greek's voice rumbled close to Tori's ear. "He ain't got time for 911. If you wait on that, he's dead. He hit an artery. That's why it's doing like that. I might can save him, but y'all got to move."

Tori said. "What're you gonna do?"

"If I have to explain it, he dies. He's in shock already. He won't last."

"Fucking do it," Rob said.

Greek grabbed Rob by the arm and pulled him off Knox. He reached at Rob's front collar and yanked him close like he was a puppy, helpless on a leash. "Give me your shirt." He didn't wait for Rob to respond: he ripped it over his head one-handed. "I need a stick or something."

There was still shit all over the place in Knox's apartment. Tori scanned the room but couldn't see anything like what Greek wanted. She started rummaging around and finally found them: devil sticks. She grabbed them and took them to Greek.

Greek still held his handgun in one hand and had the wadded shirt and velcroed bundle of three sticks in the other. He pointed at Knox with the sticks and at the same time Tori and Rob with the pistol. "Y'all get against the wall. Understand, either of you move, or run off, y'all are dead. All y'all." It was then that Tori noticed the flying objects he had tattooed on his arm weren't crows at all, they were bats.

Rob and Tori moved away toward the wall. Rob was bloodied from his chest to his shoes. Tori grabbed his slicked hands as they looked on. Greek drove one of his knees into the back of Knox's knee, and the other into his hamstring. He wrapped the shirt under and around Knox's lower thigh, above the knee, and knotted it. He then took the three sticks and laid them on top of the first knot, then knotted around them again. He twisted the sticks in the knot like he was spinning a valve closed. When he did, the rhythmic squirts from Knox's calf trickled down.

He motioned with his head at Rob to come close. "Okay. Put your knees where mine are, and keep this twisted just like this. No tighter."

Rob stared at Greek with his mouth open, still not moving. He squinted, like he was working something out. "Why are you helping him?"

Wrinkles stacked on Greek's nose. "Dead men don't pay. Now get over here." Greek looked up at Tori. "I'm going to leave out the front door. You're going with me. You can call 911 after I'm gone. Make sure you tell them he's losing blood. Tell them he hit an artery." When Tori didn't respond Greek became cross. "Do you understand that?"

"I got it. I can do it."

Greek scrutinized Rob and seemed satisfied. He took a deep breath and pursed his lips, like he was deliberating. He reached down one foot at a time and took off his bloodied athletic shoes and stepped clear of the mess. He held them both dangling from his hand.

Then he went in his jacket, to his obsidian gun again. As big as it was, it was in proportion to him. He raised it slowly and gestured Tori closer with it before he pointed it at the back of Rob's head. He locked eyes with Tori. "I've killed a lot of things in my life, and a lot of what I killed were people. You all are no different to me than any one of them." His sour breath washed over her face. "Y'all understand, everyone in this room is dead should you so much as mention me. We find out that shit." He dropped his thumb on the hammer and cocked it with a metallic click. "Always do."

Tori nodded. Greek eyeballed her hard before he uncocked his weapon and shoved it back into the holster, took her by the sleeve with his free hand, and led her toward the stairs. As they reached the top, she dug in. "Wait."

He jerked her arm. "What are you doing?"

"Why don't you just go out the alley? It's right there." She pointed at the alleyway door.

"Fucking Christ. Burl said there was only one way up."

Greek pushed Tori toward the door and made her open it for him. He took one last look back, then he was lost to the darkness outside.

$\mathcal{M}$INUTES AFTER Tori dialed 911, sirens howled. They drew closer and closer until the lights began reflecting off everything outside and the world was all red strobes. Tori waited on the line with the operator until the first paramedic appeared at the front door to Porthos. She had told the woman on the phone everything Greek said to say, and she repeated it as the paramedics came in. She led them through the restaurant and up the stairs to Knox not knowing if they would find him alive.

Once the paramedics were up in the apartment, they moved Rob back. They replaced Rob's shirt around Knox's leg with a strap that seemed to do the same thing, but better. Knox's face rocked side to side, but it was lifeless, his expression blank. Richmond police officers came in right on the heels of the paramedics. Tori and Rob were asked hurried questions, mostly about how long it had been, when Knox lost consciousness, that sort of stuff. A paramedic gave Knox something by IV, but it wasn't blood, it was clear.

Rob asked again and again if Knox would be okay, but got no firm answer, only, "We're doing everything we can."

They strapped Knox to a metal stretcher with handles down the sides and had him out of there. The urgency of their work seemed to indicate how seriously Knox was hurt. When Tori and Rob went to follow the paramedics down the stairs, one of the officers in a dark-blue uniform with yellow patches said, "You all need to stay right here for now."

Tori held onto Rob. Both his legs and arms were painted in blood. Tori's body was numb and her head full of static that let up only when someone spoke.

They stared at the place where they found Knox. The deep-burgundy stain seemed to spread ever larger, and at the edges were countless bloody footprints. All around was Knox's proliferation of junk. A thick officer with a graying mustache took a few photos before the other officer, young and wiry, put on a pair of gloves, picked up the bloody Glock with a little stick, and showed it to his partner. "Glock," he said. "No wonder." He dropped it down into a clear plastic bag and sealed it. He found the shell casing and did the same. He looked at his partner. "You see anything else here worth bagging?"

The larger officer stroked his chin with a hand that held a pen. "I don't know just yet. There's a small amount of marijuana we probably ought to take. Let's see what these guys have to say." He turned to where Tori and Rob stood near Knox's alleyway door. "Just what went on here tonight? We know that fellow got shot, but what was he doing before that? Were either of you all up here when it happened?"

Tori said, "We were both downstairs. We heard the gun go off and came up."

"Was it just the two of you?"

Without hesitation, she said, "Yes."

"Who tourniqueted his leg?"

Tori poked her knuckles into Rob's side, and he said, "I did."

"If he makes it, you probably saved his life. Nice piece of work. You in scouting?"

"I guess," Rob said.

The officer didn't seem to make anything of it. "Do either of you all know what he would have been doing with that gun?"

Rob had looked back on the bloody spot on the carpet. "I don't know why he had it out. He just got it."

"You know if he had much experience with guns?"

Rob shook his head. "He didn't have any."

The littler officer who had bagged the gun edged in. "Then he never should've had a Glock. There's cops that train on Glocks who have accidental discharges. A Glock's a great gun, but it's the last thing you want if you don't know what you're doing."

The bigger fellow with the mustache said, "You have any idea where he got it?"

"It came from Grub's," Rob said.

The two officers looked at each other. The big one said, "Well, whoever sold it to him's an idiot." He sighed. "We're sorry about your friend. I sure hope he pulls through. From what I'm seeing here, it looks like a pretty textbook accidental discharge." He looked at the other guy. "Wouldn't you say?"

The wiry one nodded.

"We'll keep looking into this. I need to get both your names. If we thought anything was out of the way, we'd have separated you and taken you in, but based on what I'm seeing, I'm not inclined to do that. The angle of the shot and everything tells me this was self-inflicted. There's no point in testing for residue. It's all over you all anyway. I hate to treat you all like suspects when we don't suspect anything. Especially since you tried to save his life."

Tori put her arm across Rob's back, "We just want to get to the hospital if we can."

Big mustache said, "I think we're going to let you all go on." The officers milled around a little bit longer, collected Knox's stash. Eventually they led Tori and Rob down the stairs to the shop. At the bottom, a young state trooper was in the dining room looking up the stairs. He had white papers rolled up in his hand. He asked the Richmond officers, "What in the hell happened here?"

"Self-inflicted gunshot."

"Fatal?"

"Don't know yet. Leg shot. Transported to UK."

The trooper didn't say anything else before heading up the stairs. Tori and Rob, huddled close together, followed the Richmond officers. Rob got his phone and Tori her sweatshirt and they headed out the front door. As they left, Tori heard the younger officer mention to the older one that he wanted to go to IHOP. The older one said that sounded good.

*A*s **THEY** got in Rob's truck in the Porthos lot, he wondered aloud what it would have been like if he wasn't white. "If Gabe was here instead of me, and there was a gun, is it that easy?"

"I don't know," Tori said, "maybe not."

They huddled close together as Rob cranked the engine. The windows were lightly frosted, but he backed up and drove off anyway with his face close to the glass so he could see out.

They went all the way out to Rob's place in Poosey and cleaned up. Both had Knox's blood on their clothes. Rob loaned Tori a shirt and a pair of gray sweats with a drawstring waistband. She didn't care what she looked like.

Rob smoked a cigarette outside before they left. "I'm working on it," he told Tori, "but right now, I need this."

They headed back out. Once they were on I-75, Rob started to fret because he didn't have Knox's parents' number. Knox's last name was Thompson, but Rob didn't know his parents' first names, so trying to look up their number online was worthless. "He's named after his grandfather, that's all I know."

It was past midnight and there wasn't much traffic in Lexington. The hardest part of getting to Knox at University of Kentucky

Hospital was finding the parking. The information desk where they entered the hospital directed them to a different one that seemed to be the headquarters for emergency surgery. The good news in that was Knox had survived the ambulance ride. Even so, they were still on edge. No one at the hospital was making any promises. In fact, they wouldn't tell much at all.

"Ma'am," Rob said to a stocky woman behind the desk. "I don't have a number for Mr. Thompson's parents. They should know he's here."

"We're working with the police in Richmond on that. It's a priority for us, too."

"You know, if you could reach them, they'd just be terrified," Tori said to Rob. "It's not like they could see him. Maybe it's better if they don't know anything until morning." Rob was unconvinced, but without Knox's phone there wasn't anything he could do.

The woman directed them to a waiting area near the operating room. It was scattered with gray fabric furniture. Rob and Tori were the only ones in there besides an older lady with a toddler sleeping on her chest. The lone TV had CNN on. A small plane had crashed into a neighborhood, taking out a house. Tori marked the passage of time by how many times she saw the tail of that plane sticking out of the living room. They showed interviews with the police, and with the homeowners and their lawyer, but Tori couldn't hear any of it because the set was on mute.

Rob carried on about reaching Knox's mom and dad until he fell asleep with Tori's head on his chest. He had an arm wrapped around her shoulder. She alternated watching the news and watching the woman with the toddler until weight pressed her eyelids.

Tori awoke to Rob standing over her, jostling her arm, holding a cup of coffee with a black plastic lid. "Knox is out of surgery." Fifteen feet away stood an older couple both wearing plaid shirts. Knox's parents.

Tori stretched and worked at her eyes with her palms. "He made it?"

"So far." Rob held out the coffee to Tori. He smelled like a cigarette.

"Can we see him?"

"It looks like that's about all we can do. He's in post-op recovery, whatever that means. We're only allowed to look at him."

Tori followed Rob and Knox's mom and dad to a desk where a lean woman with dark skin and short hair sat in royal-blue scrubs. She led them to a room where Knox lay behind a window with oxygen in his nose and a white sheet over his body. His left foot pointed up under the sheet. Where his right foot should have been, there was a depression.

"Did he lose his foot?" Rob asked.

The woman nodded almost imperceptibly. "He's lucky he got here when he did. I really can't say any more than that. The surgeon will be along to talk to him once he's awake. She'll tell him the details and he can share them with you."

Knox's mom sobbed while her husband rubbed her back. He swirled in circles one way. Then he'd swirl back in the other direction. She blew her nose into an already soggy tissue. He eventually led her away by the arm.

The woman from the hospital stood there a little longer, then, without a word, she went back to her station and left the two from Porthos looking over Knox. The oxygen line in his nose seemed so strange to Tori. Knox's dark beard and hair were both a mess, no different than always. His face was motionless, but the color had begun to return, and it was serene. It seemed to Tori then, that if Knox had made it that far, it was a good sign.

Rob had his palm flat to the glass, his nose was inches from it. "This is crazy. Knox lost his fucking leg. He could've died. I shouldn't even care about it right now, but I keep thinking someone needs to go open the shop. It's over. Porthos is over. I don't even give a shit. I don't know what the hell we're going to do. After this clusterfuck, selling's probably a fantasy. Probably was all along. If Lane Spicer wanted it, he'd have bought it already. Nothing about last night makes it more attractive."

"I don't know." Tori tapped her middle knuckle against the window. "I think you're wrong about that."

Rob's eyes darted her way. "Knox shot his goddamn leg off in there. We might as well board up the motherfucker."

"No. Don't lose hope. I've got something in mind."

*T*HREE DAYS after Knox's surgery, Tori and Rob rode back to the hospital. Rob had talked to him on the phone, but it was the first either got to see him awake after the shooting.

Knox's mom was there when they arrived. He had been moved to a regular room. The gunshot had severed Knox's posterior tibial artery and shattered his tibia. He lost his right leg from the knee down. He was heavily medicated for pain, but he grinned blearily when they came in.

Tori went straight to him and hugged him around the neck. As she withdrew, she said, "Hey, you smell good."

"Yeah," Knox said, his voice breathier than usual, "one of the nurses just gave me a sponge bath. You should see her."

Tori's eyes rolled back. "Don't even."

"What? She's good at giving sponge baths. That's all I meant."

"Uh-huh," Tori said.

Knox reached out his hand and Rob took it. "My brother," Knox said.

"How you doing, quick draw?"

Knox wheezed. "Great." He pointed at his absent foot, causing his IV to swing. "I lost twenty pounds."

Knox's mother, who was hunched and stern-faced, said, "He thinks it's funny that he's been disfigured."

"Ma," Knox strained out, "would you rather I cry?"

She stood up. "Yes." She left the room.

"I'm her baby boy. She loves me."

"Is she not just glad you're alive. I sure as hell am," Rob said. "You did everything you possibly could to get yourself killed."

Knox threw up his arms and the IV line clattered against the bed. "I never get anything. There I was, lying in wait, gun in hand. It was all going to be so heroic. You saw how that came out."

"You did a bang-up job," Tori said.

Knox got winded from the effort of talking so much, but he couldn't help himself. He gathered and kept going in a low voice. "I still can't believe Greek saved my life. I was so sure he was going to kill me."

"Maybe he didn't want you jumping line," Rob said.

Just then there was a light knock on the doorframe. Lane Spicer stood in the doorway in a gray suit with an ugly head. Tori had never seen him outside Porthos. He picked up a pizza once a week. Rob had gotten him to come to the hospital.

"May I come in?" Lane said. He went to Knox and shook his hand. He made his lawyerly talk, asking how he was feeling, telling him he was in good hands.

Finally, he said to Rob, "You called me. You said Knox needs some legal help while he's laid up. What can I do here?"

Tori tapped him on the arm to get his attention. "Mr. Spicer, I'm Tori Branch." They shook hands. "I have a proposal for you. You need to buy Porthos."

"This again?" Lane's eyeballs ascended. "I don't mean to sound rude, but Knox and I have been over this several, several times. I'm not interested. Did you bring me here for that? I'm glad to see Knox, but if that's what you're hoping for, I'm afraid you're going to be disappointed."

"Hear me out first. There's more to it." Tori spun her closed right fist in the middle of her left palm. "Did you know Knox shot himself with a Glock?"

Lane's fingers were twined. He raised his thumbs, signaling agreement.

"The thing is, Glocks are super dangerous, right. The cops who came to Knox's apartment said so. They said even policemen screw up and fire them without meaning to. Knox had no clue what he was doing. That Glock was like a time bomb in his hands." Tori threw her hands open, demonstrating an explosion. "If you look online, you'll see there've been a bunch of lawsuits about Glocks going off."

"And how many were successful?" Lane swiveled his head. "I'm not going after Glock. You're talking about a product-liability case against a huge foreign corporation. That would cost a fortune. I'm not interested in anything like that."

"I'm not talking about suing Glock, Mr. Spicer. I'm talking about suing Grub's. The gun shop. That's where he bought it. Knox asked the manager what to buy and he sold him this defective Glock. Knox told the guy he never owned a handgun before. He never even fired one. Apparently the one they sold him misfired at the range. They tried to fix it, but they obviously didn't. It's crazy."

Lane looked at Knox. "Is that true?"

"Yeah." Knox said.

Lane's eyes brightened. Tori went on. "Grub's has to have a ton of insurance. You know they do. Knox lost half his leg. This guy at Grub's sold him the single stupidest thing he could have sold him— and he even marked it down because it was defective. There's no way they should have let Knox have that gun, let alone pushed it on him. Like I said, this guy was the manager. It wasn't some peon. That should matter."

Lane asked Knox, "Do you remember the name of the man who sold you the gun?"

"Gordon something. I had to fill out all these papers. He signed them. I know it was Gordon."

Lane's fingers went to his upper lip and rubbed up and down. "They have to keep your application. We can get it." The lawyer wheels had begun their turning.

"Mr. Spicer," Tori said, "Grub's is huge."

Lane's hand was still under his nose. "I'm aware. I'm also aware of the reputation of Glocks."

"There's money there."

Lane looked at Knox, then Rob, then Tori. His eyelids fluttered. "There very well may be, and Grub's couldn't take me federal. It's a case I could consider. I'd have to prepare a fee agreement." Lane had this faraway look now. Tori could tell he was doing math.

Rob broke in. "Before he could sign anything like that, Knox would need twenty thousand dollars."

Lane snapped out of his calculations and made a face like Rob had called his mother a whore. "I can't pay him for his case. That's first-day ethics. I don't want to be anywhere near the suggestion."

"It wouldn't be for the case," Tori said, "it would be for Porthos."

Knox blurted, "I want thirty."

Rob cut his eyes at the hospital bed. "Fuck off, Knox." He looked back at Lane. "You buy out Porthos, and I bet you Knox would feel pretty comfortable hiring you as the lawyer for his case. What's the most you can take? You know, percentage-wise?"

"It's like forty," Tori said.

Lane nodded. "Forty percent is the customary ceiling."

Rob gazed up, ciphering. "So, if Knox got a hundred thousand, you'd get forty grand. You doubled your money and you got a pizza shop."

Tori homed her eyes square on Lane Spicer's. "An insurance company would pay at least a hundred thousand for a lost leg. Probably a lot more than that."

"I'll tell you what . . ." Lane said. He pondered. "If I made a consumer-protection claim, I might be able to get this thing in Madison County instead of Fayette. Maybe. I'd have no trouble getting past summary judgment."

"Before Knox does anything," Tori said, "what about Porthos?"

"I really don't want it."

Rob motioned between himself and Tori. "We could run it for you. At least for a while."

"I don't know. I'd have to think about it. I could always try to resell it. At twenty, it's a lot more palatable, that's for sure." His face went very still. "You all would have to understand, and I'm saying it here to all of you, if I did agree to buy Porthos, it wouldn't have anything to do with this lawsuit. We all understand that, right?"

"Of course not," Tori said. "It's two different things. We all know that."

Lane Spicer didn't give a damn about Porthos. Didn't need it, didn't want it, but he saw money in Knox's leg that would make him do it anyway. The same thing Tori saw in that lawyer's face after the plane crash: dollar bills y'all. She looked at Rob and grinned just a little as Lane Spicer rationalized making a sham business deal to get a lawsuit.

Lane said he would have to think about it, and he shook all the hands again, and spoke to Knox like he was a foreign dignitary before he left. Rob had his doubts, and Knox was a pure fatalist, but standing there in the hospital room, Tori felt like she had closed the deal.

*T*ORI AND ROB rode to Jackson County the day before Christmas Eve. Rob drove. Tori was shotgun. A green bank bag with a zipper lay in the console between them. He insisted he was going alone, but she wouldn't let him. Just in case things went south, they left notes saying where they were going and who they were going to see.

Twinkling lights washed out in daylight, store-bought festive displays made of plastic, and the occasional inflatable Christmas character lined the way to the arcade in McKee. Rob seemed to know his way. It was the first time Tori had ever crossed the Jackson County line. A lot was shabby, but a lot was pretty, too. In places, it was both. Some of the curves were so tight, Rob dropped his speed down to around thirty. Tori looked up those hillsides at the tangles of bare trees, the thin branches like pen scratches on a paper background that was the sky.

They got stuck behind a gravel truck. Stenciled on the back it said, "Not Responsible for Flying Debris. Stay Back 200 Feet."

"So, it's our fault if they throw shit out of their fucking truck?" Rob said. "How do you like that? They decided that's on us." Rob always got worked up about stuff like that. A business he thought was stepping on people.

Parking was easy. There weren't too many cars in downtown McKee that day. As far as Christmas shopping, there didn't seem to be much of anywhere to go outside of a Dollar General and a Rite Aid. The thin commercial carpeting in the stairwell had a path of dirt up the center, and the walls looked and smelled like they had been water and smoke damaged and never repaired. The room at the top of the stairs was about the same.

Little Burl sat at a green felt-topped table lined with neat collections of papers, envelopes, notepads, pens, and various other items of record keeping. He said, "What do you know. You done found us."

"It wasn't hard," Rob said.

Greek stood behind Burl looking like one of those statues they put up outside casinos, trying hard to be majestic, but being real tacky nonetheless. He didn't say a thing, or acknowledge anything was up, really.

Burl's eyes seemed drawn to the bank bag in Rob's hand. "What's that I see you packing, son? Looks promising. Maybe you wasn't blowing smoke."

"Nope." Rob tossed the bag on the table in front of Burl.

Burl unzipped the bank bag and smiled a bit. He cleared the space in front of him before he drew out the money and counted it. He laid the hundred-dollar bills down in diagonals, each one peeking out from under the next, in groups of ten. Once those were done, he counted them up to be twenty groups. "I gotta find me an ink pen," he said. He took a pad of paper and worked a few figures. He took sixteen hundred from what lay in front of him and went into a gray metal cash box for a little more. He held the bills out.

"What's that?" Rob said.

"Old Fort Knox didn't owe me quite twenty. He's got him a little change coming back. Sixteen hundred twenty-eight."

Rob stared at Burl. Tori winced, and braced herself for Rob to say something wiseass, but all he said was, "Seriously?"

"I don't joke about money, son. Wouldn't never."

Rob took the change. "So that's it? Y'all are square then, right?"

Burl stood with his hands in the pockets of his deep-blue jeans, his thumbs sticking out. "We are, but that don't go for Greek. Ain't Knox got his bill yet? Greek don't do nursing for free." He looked at Greek and grinned. Greek never moved. "I's just fucking with you. Unless one of you all is looking to take up Knox's proprietorship, I'd say that wraps things up."

Rob said, "No," and Tori shook her head emphatically in the negative as well.

"You tell old Knox merry Christmas for me then. Ain't no hard feelings. I'm glad this didn't go no further." Rob and Tori started to go but paused when Burl cleared his throat, beckoning their attention. "Listen here. One more thing. We have us a good card game here every Saturday night. Either y'all feels like trying your luck, you're welcome to come out."

They got the hell out of there and on the road back to Madison County.

On the ride home, Rob asked Tori if they could stop off in Berea on the way. He wanted to go to Morgan's Discount, where they sold Coach purses with minor defects for cheap. "I get one for my mom for Christmas every year. She loves them. I'll get you one too if you want."

Once they reached Berea proper they drove past College Square and Boone Tavern. Rob pointed. "You know what's right on the other side of that block?"

"What's that?"

"Papaleno's."

"Yeah?"

"So, after we're done at Morgan's, you want to get lunch?" He patted the bank bag on the console. "It's on Knox."

"You really want pizza?"

"They have other stuff. If you don't want it, we could go to Mexican Hardee's. It's pretty good, too."

"What's Mexican Hardee's?"

"It's an old Hardee's they turned into a Mexican restaurant. Some of the door handles and stuff still say Hardee's. We could watch some soccer highlights. They're always on."

Tori smiled. "Papaleno's is fine with me if you want it."

Rob winked as he clicked his cheek and took Tori's hand. They drove on down Chestnut Street by the big red brick Berea College buildings. There weren't as many crunchy girls out walking around campus as normal. Berea was usually overrun with them. It was two days to Christmas. Most had gone home. Wherever that was.

*P*EOPLE TALK about how badly they want a home-cooked meal. You'll notice they say *meal*. That's because one is enough. After two weeks of his mom's green beans, broccoli casserole, corn, sauerkraut, mashed potatoes, soup beans, salmon patties, meatloaf, pork chops, and deviled eggs on repeat, Knox was about to lose it. His parents ate that stuff for dinner every night and had the leftovers for lunch the next day. He had been convalescing at his parents' since the week before Christmas. Whatever they ate, he ate too. Being as it was New Year's Day, Knox's mom was fixing corned beef, cabbage, and black-eyed peas.

Knox's doctor told him not to drive, his license was still suspended, his insurance was lapsed, and he didn't have his car. That put him at his parents' mercy. The only time he got any company was when his physical therapist came for a home visit. He would have killed for a pizza, even a shitty chain pizza, but he had called every shop in Frankfort and his parents' house was too far out to get delivery. Pizza wasn't even what he really craved. He was jonesing for a burrito.

Rob knew Knox's plight. Knox had been complaining to him since the day he got moved there from UK Hospital. Rob had texted him early that morning to say a care package was on its way. It was an hour drive from Richmond. When Knox pressed for details Rob wouldn't give any.

All Knox's parents ever seemed to do was watch partisan news and game shows—interrupted occasionally by Kentucky ball games—so he spent most of his time alone in his childhood bedroom: a sad place to be when you're forty-two years old. He didn't have much of a choice. Almost all of his Porthos money went to Burl, and the fifteen hundred dollars he had left he was saving. If he was ever going to see any money from Grub's, it was a long way off.

The house stunk of the food cooking that Knox feared he'd be eating for the next three days. He was so desperate for entertainment, he had started one of his mom's John Grisham books.

Whether it was the doorbell, or the landline phone, it always took Knox's parents an unreasonable amount of time to answer. New Year's Day was no different. The TV in the living room blared, but he could still hear the doorbell followed by a couple short knocks. The news volume went down a little bit, but nothing happened. Knox's stump wasn't healed enough for a prosthetic, so he could only get around on crutches. Whoever it was rang the bell again. Knox braced to get up himself, but the front door hinges squealed and his dad's voice offered a distant greeting. Two sets of footsteps creaked their way down the hall toward his room and there was no suspense about it. Rob had finally arrived.

Knox's dad pushed his door open. "You've got company, Knox." He padded back the way he came, and Knox sat up, lowered his book to his lap, and craned to get a look at Rob. Tori materialized in the doorway with a cardboard box in hand. She drawled, "Lieutenant Dan, ice cream."

"No *way*. T-Bone, you dog."

"Believe it, bitch. I brought you a delivery."

"No you did *not*. You brought my care package?"

"Yep." She set the box at the foot of Knox's bed and lifted out a brown paper bag he recognized immediately.

"Chipotle. My god."

"Carnitas burrito. Double meat."

"How'd you know?"

Tori handed it over. "Rob gave me some pretty specific instructions."

"Robbie and Tori, taking care of their one-legged friend." Knox took the burrito from the bag, pressed his nose to the foil wrapper, and inhaled. "My god. I *so* need this." He unpeeled a few inches and started to eat.

"There's more." Tori went back in the box and produced a wobbly stack of books. "We bought you some new books. There's a bunch of DVDs in here, too."

Knox flung the Grisham book over his shoulder, and it hit the wall. "God, I love you all."

Tori's eyes brightened. "Hold on now. You haven't even seen the show stopper."

"There's more?"

"I had Rob get it from your apartment. Your landlord let him in. I hope your parents have a VCR."

"Oh my god. Of course they have a VCR. They're old as shit."

"Then maybe," Tori reached in the box and pulled it out fast, "you'll appreciate this." She held up his *My So-Called Life* box set like it was Simba just born.

Knox fell back and let his hands hang off the sides of the bed, his burrito still gripped in his right.

"And that's just the first runner-up. I got Miss Colorado right here." Tori glanced at the door behind her before she produced it. A sandwich bag dangled from her hand with what looked to be a full ounce of glorious green bud with gold trim. "Space Queen."

Knox popped back up. "Holy shit. How'd you get Space Queen?"

Tori waggled her eyebrows. "Rob had a buddy ship it from Denver." She rummaged in the box a bit before she produced Knox's go-to bowl and an orange lighter. "You're lucky he loves you. He went all out."

"Oh my god, dude. You want to smoke this with me?" Knox pointed his thumb. "We just have to open the window."

"No. I've got to get going."

"You came all this way and you're going to run off?"

"It was on my way. I'm going to Louisville to see my family."

"Seriously?"

"Afraid so."

"Where's Rob?"

"Working. They've got him managing every other shift at Gillum's. He promised he'd come see you as soon as he can. They're working him a ton, though."

Knox grabbed either side of his head. "Dude, he has got to come see me. I've got one leg, I've eaten nothing but country food for weeks, and before you came in I was reading John fucking Grisham. In another week I'll be wearing Sansabelt slacks and doing crosswords."

"He's coming. I promise. He felt bad he couldn't today." Tori still held the cardboard box. It was a cheese box from Porthos. "What do you want me to do with this?"

"Just leave it. My mom's cat'll get in it. He'll fucking love it."

Tori set it on the floor. "I gotta go, boss. My mom and sister are waiting for me. We've got mani/pedi appointments. I'm cutting it close already."

"On New Year's Day?"

"They're open."

"You seriously have to go already?"

"I'm afraid so, buddy."

"Are you at least going to hug my dumpy ass?"

"Awww." Tori moved to his bedside. "Of course I am." He leaned forward and she hugged him around his neck. "Keep your chins up, Knox."

"You're fucking awesome."

She withdrew and receded toward the door. "You are, too. We miss you." Tori gave a little nod on her way out, and started to close the door behind her.

Knox hollered, "Hey!" at her back.

Tori stopped, doorknob in hand, and looked back. "What up?"

"Come back with Rob and make it soon."

"We will. I promise."

"Who's your pal, T-Bone?"

Tori pulled the door closed and went on.

Knox shouted, "I am! I'm your pal!"

Knox could hear his dad say something to Tori as she went, and the front door opened and closed again. Knox looked over the pile of books in the bed with him. Then he found his box set and just held it. "We're all gonna be okay."

He laid his burrito down on the nightstand and picked up the little baggie of magic flora. He opened it wide, put his nose down in it, and pulled deep. As enchanting as the burrito was to whiff, Space Queen bested it.

He sat up and let his two legs—such as they were—hang off the side of the bed. He dropped his windfall weed, lighter, and bowl into the nightstand drawer before gathering his crutches. He was dying to smoke it, and even if his parents smelled it, what would they do about it? He'd make some libertarian medicinal argument to throw them off and it would blow over.

First, he needed to do something he'd been uneasy about since he'd woken up in the hospital. He wiggled around until he found his phone under him in the bed. Tinny ringing went on for thirty seconds after he dialed. Darla didn't answer. Her voicemail asked that he leave a message.

"Okay, so, I don't know your address. If you want me to, like, come down there, I'll need it." He thought about it for a second before he went on. "You wanted me to change. Well, I did. I'm coming as soon as I can so give me a call back." He considered what else to say before tacking on, "Happy new year." After hanging up he watched his phone for a minute, hoping it would ring right away, but it didn't.

He set down the phone and gathered himself there on the edge of the bed. Half his leg was gone, he'd almost died, he'd lost his pizza shop, and he was literally living in an old folks' home, because that's what his parents were. Even so, in some ways, he was more hopeful than he'd been in years.

Knox was primed to smoke his first bowl since the accident. There was just one thing he had to get situated first. One thing that would make him perfectly content for the rest of the day. He raised up with his crutch handles in his hands and got aligned. He put his weight to the crutches, but stayed balanced against the bed. He let his left foot—his lone foot—swing forward, and he was off.

He didn't have Darla, or Rob, or Tori, or half his leg, but he did have Angela Chase, Jordan Catalano, Rickie Vasquez, Rayanne Graff, and Brian Krakow. And he had a fat sack of designer bud. What else he didn't have was everything that had dogged him so long, and that was worth something. He crutched his way down the Berber-carpeted hall into the heavy scent of boiled cabbage, the shrill exhortations of bought-off newspeople, and the new year.

Knox's dad was on the couch scowling at whatever he heard on television. He was in his comfort zone. His mom was in the kitchen lifting a metal lid from a pot and stirring. She was in her zone, too. Once he found that goddamn VCR, Knox would finally be in his.

Acknowledgements

MY FIRST THANK YOU is of course to Valetta, Barrett, and Grady, who are the reason I do anything. They have encouraged, endured, and fed my writing habit. I also owe unending thanks to my parents, Arthur and Joyce Browne, who supported their challenging third child, as did the first two, Shannon and April. To all my nieces and nephews, who inspire me so. Also, thank you to Larry and Thelma and the rest of the Hardwick clan, who welcomed me over twenty years ago, and who made me a part of an Eastern Kentucky family. Thank you as well to all the Dunhams regardless of last name, and all the rest of the Brownes, whatever you call yourselves.

I've been blessed with a multitude of great writing teachers, foremost among them my mentor and friend George Singleton. There is also another handful who helped me specifically with this book: Benjamin Percy's advice was the most transformative, Mark Powell led me to fine-tune it, and Amy Greene was there when it was conceived. Other teachers who were particularly influential are Darnell Arnoult, Silas House, Michael Knight, Pamela Duncan, Paul Loukides, and Charles Dodd White. I owe each of you a debt.

The list of other friends who helped me is also long and I fear I am forgetting people. Each of the Hell of our Own Writers have propped me up, but particularly Carrie Mullins, Bobby

Amburgey, and Robert Gipe, who helped mold this project. My honorary life coach, Denton Loving, has been unwavering in his support and giving with his time. Elizabeth Glass has been incredibly generous, having read more of my writing than anyone. David Joy and Leah Hampton helped usher this book to print and made it better. Others who read this—or some of the quite rough work that led to it—and helped me improve are Susan Ishmael, Rebecca Elswick, Celeste McMaster, Matthew Ratcliff, Tom Somerville, Emily Abrutyn, Aden Amburgey, and Hannah West. Don McNay also offered me endless encouragement, and I will always appreciate that.

West Virginia University Press has been wonderful. Abby Freeland picked this project up, and it has benefitted from her hand from the day she touched it. Rachel King edited it, and she made it better still. Sara Georgi was indispensable down the home stretch. Also, my peer reviewers, Jesse Donaldson and Sheldon Lee Compton, both influenced the final draft tremendously, and I can't thank them enough.

The Appalachian Writers' Workshop at the Hindman Settlement School gave me a writing home when I didn't feel like I had one, and for that I credit Mike and Frieda Mullins, Jeanne Marie Hibbard, and Brent Hutchinson. They also gave me a cat. The staff and my fellow students at the Tin House Summer Workshop were exceptional and influential. The English departments at Albion College and Michigan State University provided me a great start. Although I have never attended Eastern Kentucky University, the writing department there has treated me like its own, most especially Bob Johnson and Hal Blythe. The faculty of the University of Kentucky College of Law also benefitted my writing in the oddest ways. I should also mention the Mountain Heritage Literary Festival and the Western Carolina Spring Literary Festival, both of which have supported me.

Others who made it possible for me to get this done each in

their own way are Susan Rosebrough and Mike Messmore, two teachers from Brighton High School who believed in me, and Buddy Moorehouse from the Brighton Argus, who mentored me when I was a kid.

My partners, Rodney and Kimberly Davis and Felecia Johnson, and my paralegal/assistant, Heather-Anne Simpson, without whose support this book wouldn't exist.

Jake Reed and Jason Slone each provided tremendous insight regarding law-enforcement procedure and firearms.

Rob Gilkey from Big Fish Tattoo in Richmond is an exceptional artist, and his knowledge of that field was indispensable.

To Lee Keylock, Lisa Consiglio, and Colum McCann of Narrative 4. Your work inspires me. Thank you for letting me help a little with something so big.

Charles Martin. None of the characters in this book are you, but without you there would be none of the characters. I hope you are at peace, my friend.

My Aunt Roselyn, who would pull me close and say, "We all have our favorites." I miss you right now. I know you would have been so excited about me publishing a book.

To all our customers at Apollo Pizza and our other places, thank you for supporting us, for supporting local. And thank you for digging our food. And hey, thank you for reading the book and all this stuff. I appreciate you, too.